Praise for the Black Sheep Knitting Mystery Series

"The fast-paced plot ~~will~~
pages."

"Congenial characters ~~. . .~~
—Kirkus Reviews

"Maggie and her group are as efficient with their investigation as they are with their knitting needles."

—*Library Journal*

"Small-town crafty ambience . . . This enjoyable tale is similar in style to the work of both Sally Goldenbaum and Cricket McRae."

—*Booklist*

"An engaging story full of tight knit friendships and a needling mystery."

—*Fresh Fiction*

"A slew of interesting characters."

—

"Enthusiastic, engrossing, and exciting."

—*The My*

"An intriguing mystery with a few surprising twist~~s~~

—*Romance R*

"Delightful. Enchanting. Humorous. Impressive. ~~W~~
are just a few adjectives to describe Anne Canade~~o~~
cent cozy."

—*Book Cave*

**Also in the Black Sheep Knitting Mystery Series
by Anne Canadeo**

Meet the Black Sheep Knitters

Maggie Messina, owner of the Black Sheep Knitting Shop, is a retired high school art teacher who runs her little slice of knitters' paradise with the kind of vibrant energy that leaves her friends dazzled! From novice to pro, knitters come to Maggie as much for her up-to-the-minute offerings like organic wool as for her encouragement and friendship. And Maggie's got a deft touch when it comes to unraveling mysteries, too.

Lucy Binger left Boston when her marriage ended, and found herself shifting gears to run her graphic design business from the coastal cottage she inherited. After big-city living, she now finds contentment on a front porch in tiny Plum Harbor, knitting with her closest friends.

Dana Haeger is a psychologist with a busy local practice. A stylishly polished professional with a quick wit, she slips out to Maggie's shop whenever her schedule allows—after all, knitting is the best form of therapy!

Suzanne Cavanaugh is a typical working supermom—a realtor with a million demands on her time, from coaching soccer to showing houses to attending the PTA. But she carves out a little "me" time with the Black Sheep Knitters.

Phoebe Meyers, a college student complete with magenta highlights and nose stud, lives in the apartment above Maggie's shop. She's Maggie's indispensable helper (when she's not in class)—and part of the new generation of young knitters.

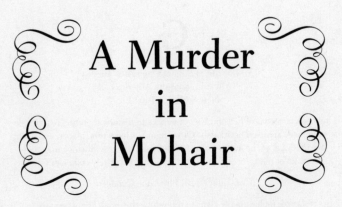

A Murder in Mohair

A Black Sheep Knitting Mystery

Anne Canadeo

Gallery Books

New York   London   Toronto   Sydney   New Delhi

To my husband, Spencer—with love

G

Gallery Books
An Imprint of Simon & Schuster, Inc.
1230 Avenue of the Americas
New York, NY 10020

First Gallery Books trade paperback edition December 2015

GALLERY BOOKS and colophon are registered trademarks of Simon & Schuster, Inc.

For information about special discounts for bulk purchases, please contact Simon & Schuster Special Sales at 1-866-506-1949 or business@simonandschuster.com.

The Simon & Schuster Speakers Bureau can bring authors to your live event. For more information or to book an event, contact the Simon & Schuster Speakers Bureau at 1-866-248-3049 or visit our website at www.simonspeakers.com.

Cover illustration by Mary Ann Lasher

Manufactured in the United States of America

1   3   5   7   9   10   8   6   4   2

Library of Congress Cataloging-in-Publication Data

Canadeo, Anne
A murder in Mohair / Anne Canadeo. —First Gallery Books trade paperback edition.
pages ; cm
I. Title.
PS3553.A489115M87 2015
813'.54—dc23
2015015091

ISBN 978-1-4767-6750-5
ISBN 978-1-4767-6752-9 (ebook)

You can fool all the people some of the time, and some of the people all the time, but you cannot fool all the people all the time.

—ABRAHAM LINCOLN (ATTRIBUTED)

No good deed goes unpunished.

—OSCAR WILDE

Chapter One

a bike ride from Lucy's cottage into the village of Plum Harbor was downhill going, uphill going back. As gravity kicked in and the long slope of Main Street grew even steeper, Lucy tried to remember that this was "the fun part."

She zipped by a row of shops, most still shut tight on the drowsy, summer morning. Then gripped the hand brakes and forced the old gears to downshift, barely slowing her descent.

The fun part, Lucy . . . the *really* fun part?

A car door swung open in her path and she swiveled around it just in time. The flustered driver shouted at her, but she didn't dare turn to face him.

Just as suddenly, the Black Sheep Knitting Shop came into view. Grateful for the sight, Lucy focused on the narrow drive.

Aiming the bike like a flying missile, brakes squeezed even tighter, she bounced over the gravel and finally skidded to a stop.

The shop was an oasis for knitters anytime of the year, but especially for reckless bike riders on this hot summer morning.

The Victorian house, turned into a retail space, had been neglected when Lucy's friend Maggie found it years ago. But as usual, Maggie's artistic eye had spotted the possibilities. She left her position as an art teacher at Plum Harbor High School to follow her bliss and turn her passion for needlework into a full-time career. Maggie had recently lost her husband and needed a complete change to pull her from a well of grief.

Using her retirement nest egg, she bought the building and set up her business on the first floor, a knitting shop as cozy and inviting as her living room. The apartment above was soon rented to her assistant, Phoebe Meyers, a part-time college student and sort of surrogate daughter for Maggie, whose own daughter, Julie, was away at college most of the year.

The shop looked especially pretty in the summer, Lucy thought. The building had been carefully renovated and painted in vintage colors, adorned with shutters, and a bright front door. Window boxes, which hung from the porch railing, overflowed with blooming flowers and trailing vines, while even more summer flowers lined the picket fence and brick path. Maggie's love for gardening—and cooking—followed a close second to knitting. Wicker chairs and tables, set out on the shady, wraparound porch, invited stitching and socializing, al fresco.

Lucy spotted Maggie there with Edie Steiber, who ran the Schooner Diner across the street. In the midst of an intense conversation, it seemed. Lucy set the bike against the fence and pulled off her helmet, wondering if they'd even noticed her.

But Maggie must have. She stood and met her gaze as Lucy walked up the path; she looked serious, Lucy thought. Something in her expression definitely seemed off.

"You saw my narrow miss with that car door, and you want to tell me I'm a terrible bike rider, right?"

"I didn't, luckily. Or I would. I guess you didn't notice the police cars up the street, in front of the movie theater?"

Lucy had not, intent as she was on landing in one piece. She glanced up Main Street to find two blue and white cruisers, along with a police SUV, parked in front of the Harbor Cinema. The lights on top of the vehicles still swirled, just beneath the old-fashioned marquee. An ambulance was parked there, too, though the two uniformed attendants stood talking with a police officer. Not in any rush to take anyone anywhere.

"What happened? Was there an accident?"

Before Maggie could answer, Edie called from the porch. "I'll say. Jimmy Hubbard, the fellow who owns the theater? He's stone cold dead. Someone found him just a little while ago."

"How awful. What happened? Did he have a heart attack or something?"

"We don't know much." Maggie started back to the porch and Lucy followed. "From what Edie heard, it sounds like there was a robbery. It must have taken place late last night."

"A high school kid who works in the theater at the candy counter found him." Edie stared up at Lucy from her wicker chair. She looked pale and winded, as if she'd just run across the street to tell Maggie the news. "The boy saw Jimmy alive and well around eleven, when he left work. He has keys to the theater and came in early this morning to clean up. First thing he notices is the light by the back door busted up. He says it was working fine when he left the night before. Then he opened the door and found Jimmy lying there. The bank deposit bag right next to him on the floor. Empty, of course.

And the boy said . . . Well, there was a lot of blood," she added in a shakier tone.

Usually a very stalwart soul, Edie had faced many challenges in her seventy-some years—and lived by the code "what doesn't kill you makes you stronger." But she seemed uncommonly stunned and rattled. Then again, the unofficial mayor of Plum Harbor wasn't getting any younger, Lucy reflected.

"How did you hear this? Did you talk to him?"

"I'll say. The poor kid was terrified. He ran in the Schooner this morning, white as a sheet. I could hardly understand what he was saying. Heck of a thing for a boy that age to find a dead body. I sat him down and called nine-one-one. Then I called his folks." She pressed her hand to her ample chest. "Set off my palpitations. For a minute, I thought I needed nine-one-one, too."

"Poor Jimmy." Though Lucy only knew the man by sight, it seemed an awful fate. "I don't even know how that theater stays in business. There's hardly ever anyone there. There couldn't have been much cash on hand."

"Yeah, that place is just limping along," Edie agreed. "Goes to show how desperate some characters are. Not a common thing around here. But you never know." Edie's sunflower earrings bobbed around her head, flashing a colorful warning. "It makes you think twice about security. I've got lots more than a few bucks in my register at the end of the day. I'll tell you that much."

Lucy was sure that was true. The Schooner was one of the most popular spots in town and did a booming business in the summer.

Maggie looked less worried, but still concerned. "A crime like this is rare for our town, thank goodness. The police will find the culprit quickly. Still, it worries me. I hope you're careful when you lock up at night, Edie?" Maggie sat in a chair beside her friend. Lucy noticed a basket of yarn in bright summer colors and a pile of patterns, prepared for a class, on the small table next to her.

"Don't worry about me. I have alarm system on top of alarm system. My niece's son, Dale, is working at the diner this summer as a busboy, and Richard, his father, comes to pick him up and keeps me company almost every night while I lock up. Helping Dale take out the trash and all that. Richard is always working late in his shop, behind their store," Edie explained, "so I don't mind calling if I need a little backup."

Lucy knew the shop well; The Gilded Age, known for fine antique furniture. Edie's niece, Nora, managed the store, and her husband Richard refinished and repaired antique pieces, and made custom orders, too, in a small woodworking shop behind the store. It looked like it had been a separate garage or maybe even a one-horse barn. The buildings on Main Street were that old.

The antique shop was a few doors down from Maggie's store and practically directly across the street from the Schooner Diner. Lucy had heard that Edie had helped her niece start her business and Lucy didn't doubt it. Edie was crusty and even cranky at times, but could be surprisingly kind and generous, especially to her relatives, who easily accounted for half the population in town. Lucy could never keep the Steiber family tree straight.

Wasn't this the same niece who'd had such a tragedy in her life, about two years ago? Nora and her husband had lost a child, Lucy recalled. Though she couldn't remember the details.

"How are Richard and Nora?" Maggie asked, glancing back at Edie.

"Oh . . . up and down." Edie sighed. "It will take years for them to work through this. You never get over a loss like that," she added sadly. She glanced at Lucy. "My niece's older son, Kyle. He passed away in his sleep, just about two years ago. The doctor said a blood vessel in his head burst, some freak thing he'd been born with. No sign of it at all. Poor boy was a walking time bomb," she added quietly. "Such a shock for the family."

"Not to take away anything from Jimmy, but it's so sad to see such a young life cut short," Maggie added quietly. "How's Nora holding up? I see that she's back to work in her store," she added on a more hopeful note.

"Nora could hardly get out of bed for a while. But she's coming along. Slowly but surely. She's found some help, sort of talk therapy, you might say." Edie tilted her head to the side and shrugged.

"Is she seeing a therapist? Or is it a grief support group?" Lucy asked.

Edie settled her bulky body into a wicker armchair alongside Maggie's. Her cotton flowered dress settled around her, like a picnic blanket spread on a soft lawn.

"Oh, I wouldn't call this person a therapist . . . though goodness knows, she might call herself that."

Lucy could tell Maggie's curiosity was aroused. She'd been casting a row of bright orange stitches on a medium-size needle, but paused to meet Edie's gaze. "Is she a minister or a . . . oh, what do they call them now . . . a life coach?" She delivered the last term in a tart tone, as if she thought the idea both amusing and bogus.

"No, no . . . nothing like that." Edie sighed, clearly reluctant to explain. "This person Nora is seeing calls herself a psychic medium. Claims that she can communicate with loved ones that have passed on. Nora believes that her son Kyle is sending messages through this psychic lady."

Lucy leaned back on the porch rail, understanding now why Edie was so hesitant to tell all.

"Hey, I don't believe in any of that stuff," Edie quickly added. "But my niece is hooked on it. She goes a few times a week. It must cost a fortune. I'm sure this Cassandra Waters isn't cheap. And she knows an easy mark when she finds one."

"Cassandra Waters?" The stagey, contrived name alone would have tipped anyone off, Lucy thought.

"That's right . . . and I have to admit, I feel a little responsible for them getting together. They met in the Schooner. This Cassandra comes in and sits at the counter almost every day, and sooner or later, starts chatting up the customers. So one day, she starts on Nora. That was that. Snake charmer. I've thought of throwing her out, but I never wanted to make a scene. And no one's ever complained. But now see what's come of it."

"I understand," Maggie replied quickly. "I've had more than a few unreasonable customers I'd like to kick out of my shop. But you just have to grin and bear it."

Edie nodded and tossed up her big hands, covered with rings and bracelets—a mixture of costume and genuine, a thick gold antique watch she wore daily dangling from one wrist. "I told Nora right off the bat this woman is a huckster and you'd be foolish to give her a wooden nickel. But Nora is willing to try anything, poor thing. She misses Kyle so and his death was so sudden, out of the blue."

"What does the psychic tell her?" Lucy asked. "It must be good to keep Nora going back."

Edie shrugged. "I'm not really sure. It's hard to pin Nora down on the details. I do know that as soon as this Cassandra laid eyes on Nora, she claimed she had a strong feeling that a spirit wanted to speak to her. The spirit of a young man with a close bond, who had recently passed to the other side. That's just how she said it. I was standing right there. I heard every word." Edie sounded a little unnerved, even now, Lucy noticed. "How did she know that? Spooky, right?"

"That does seem uncanny." Maggie turned her knitting over and checked the stitches. "But there are many ways she could have known Nora lost a son. If she's lived in town a while, she may have even heard some gossip."

"Maybe. She's told her other things since, too. More personal things she couldn't have heard around town. Nora doesn't give me the details, but seems convinced it's legit and she keeps going back for more. I'm worried about her," Edie admitted. "I don't know what to do. The only upside is that these visits have done wonders for Nora's mood. It's like a big cloud just lifted. She's definitely more like her old self. Everybody in the family says so."

"I guess it's given her closure," Maggie replied. "Everyone wants that after they've lost a loved one. Especially when it happens suddenly. I've often felt that way about Bill," she admitted, talking about her husband, who had died five years ago. "But I don't think I'd visit a psychic."

"You're the smart one, then. There are plenty who do and pay good money, to boot," Edie said.

Lucy didn't know much about the subject, but knew that was true. You could turn on the TV and see psychics at work in front of huge audiences, almost any time of the day. "Maybe you should go with Nora sometime, Edie, and see what goes on there."

"I've been thinking about it. This Cassandra has been working on me, too. She keeps saying she sees spirits all around me, just dying to chat it up. No pun intended."

Lucy saw Maggie smile, focused on her needles again. "It might satisfy your curiosity."

"That's true. I have to tell you, I don't know how she knows all this stuff. It really rattles me."

"About Kyle, you mean?" Lucy asked, though Edie seemed to be thinking of herself now and the spirits who were flocking about, *dying* to talk to her.

"Oh, sure, about Kyle. What else would I mean?" Edie reached into her knitting bag, fished around a moment, and pulled out a dark blue card, about the size of a postcard. She leaned over and handed it to Lucy. "Look this over. You'll get the idea."

The cursive white lettering was a bit hard to make out, but Lucy decided to read the text aloud. *"Let the voices of your past open doors to your future. A psychic reading will answer these questions, and more! Are my loved ones who have passed at peace? Can I speak to them? Is my lover faithful to me? Is there good fortune in my future? What must I do to remove all obstacles to my happiness? Schedule a private or group reading. A corporate event or private party. Other services: Channeling, Aura reading, Spiritual cleansing."*

Lucy couldn't help smiling by the time she'd come to the end. She turned the card over to find the psychic's address, phone number, and e-mail address. "She lives in the Marshes, right near me," Lucy told the others. "On Ivy Lane."

"Convenient. I wonder if she does house calls," Maggie murmured.

"Looks like it. Though there's no emergency number," Lucy quipped back. She examined the photograph of Cassandra Waters—a dramatic head shot against an appropriately misty background, her long dark hair blowing around her shoulders. With the help of a fan, Lucy had no doubt.

A crystal pendant and a simple, sort of Grecian-looking draped garment—the perfect shade of celestial blue—completed a mystical, ethereal impression.

Lucy had not imagined her quite so attractive. She looked very slim, with high cheekbones and large eyes, ringed by exotic makeup. It was hard to guess her age; no more than forty, probably. Though the photo could have been touched up?

"You have to give her an A-plus for marketing. She's got it covered on one little postcard," Lucy said.

"Soup to nuts," Edie agreed.

"What does Richard think?" Maggie asked.

"So far, he's signed on for the whole enchilada. He just wants to see Nora feeling better. A lot of marriages fall apart under a weight like this. But Richard's the solid type. Nora's been lucky that way at least." Edie sighed. "I guess they ought to put an extra alarm or something on their shop now. They have a lot of valuables in there. Never mind having their pockets picked by Miss Waters."

"We all need to be careful. At least until the police figure out how this happened to Jimmy," Maggie said.

Lucy twisted the top off her water bottle and took a long drink. "I still can't believe he's gone. Who would ever want to hurt Jimmy? He was a sweet old guy. And he did those funny magic shows before the children's movies. I took Dara to a matinee there a few weeks ago," she added, mentioning her boyfriend Matt's nine-year-old daughter. "Jimmy was great with the kids. I wonder if he was ever a professional magician. Or maybe an actor."

"He did seem to be a pleasant man; a little shy. It's surprising to me he liked to get onstage like that. But some people are like that, shy one-on-one, but not afraid to perform. Maybe they assume another personality." Maggie's nimble fingers moved along the needles swiftly, finishing another row. Lucy wondered what she was making. A sample for her morning class? "I don't think he belonged to the Chamber of Commerce or Main Street Business Owners. I never saw him at the meetings." She glanced at Edie. "Did you know him at all?"

"He came in the Schooner now and then, for coffee or a bite to eat. But we didn't talk about personal stuff. I don't remember if he ever mentioned a wife, or family." Edie shrugged. "My niece's boy Kyle worked at the theater one summer, a while back. He always liked Jimmy, said he was a real easygoing boss. I guess he was nice to the kids who worked there. He seemed sort of a people pleaser to me. Always left a big tip at the diner, and sometimes free tickets to the theater. The waitresses liked that."

Lucy glanced back at the theater. A uniformed officer crisscrossed the glass doors at the front of the building with yellow crime scene tape. The sight gave Lucy a chill though she stood in full sun. She rubbed the goose flesh on her bare arms.

"I guess we have to hear what the police say," Lucy said finally.

"I guess so," Maggie agreed.

"The officer who answered the call asked me a few questions," Edie offered. "I locked up around half past eleven. Richard was there, helping me close and picking up Dale. We didn't hear anything unusual going on at the theater. Or see anything on the street," she added emphatically. "I guess the theater had just closed after the late show. Jimmy was probably still alive. I wonder what time he was killed?"

Lucy wondered, too. "The medical examiner might have an idea by now. But the police don't always release that information. Even to the media."

"I expect the police will canvass the neighborhood," Maggie said. "But most of us close around six. Except for the theater and your place, Edie, this side of Main Street is very quiet at night. Even on the weekends. It will be hard to find witnesses."

Lucy thought so, too. Though the village was busy on summer nights, all the action was concentrated near the harbor and green, where boaters docked and walked into town, filling the cafés, bars, and ice cream shops clustered in that area.

She glanced at the psychic's card again, then gave it back to Edie. "Maybe Cassandra Waters will know what happened. Maybe Jimmy will come back and tell her."

"That would be good publicity for her," Maggie replied with a laugh.

"Oh, geez . . . I hope not. I'll never be able to convince Nora she's being hustled if that happens." Edie stuck the postcard back in her knitting bag and rose from her chair, the wicker creaking and sighing as it released her bulky body.

"Well, life goes on. I've got work to do. People need their big, cholesterol-packed breakfast specials," she added with a light laugh.

No explanation needed there—the rich scent of bacon, eggs, and home fries wafted in a lethal cloud from her diner every morning.

Not to mention toast, Lucy mused, her appetite piqued. She was hungry and could practically smell the buttery rye or whole wheat. But she was steering clear of carbs right now, especially the toasted, buttery kind. And the Schooner breakfast specials. At least until her birthday.

"Take care, Edie. Keep us posted," Maggie murmured.

"Yeah, you, too." Edie waved over her shoulder, her gaze focused on the brick path as she trotted down to the street with a surprisingly lively step. Lucy watched her rock from side to side on white walking shoes that looked a lot like very large marshmallows with Velcro straps.

"I guess I should get to work, too." Even though it was Saturday, Lucy had to get home to work on a project with a tight deadline. A graphic artist, Lucy had left a job at an advertising firm in Boston and set up her own home-based business several years ago, when she'd moved out to Plum Harbor. She loved being her own boss, though sometimes she had to lock herself in the house to meet her deadlines. Matt, who was a veterinarian, worked most Saturdays, so it was usually an office day for Lucy, too.

"And I should have some students here in a minute." Maggie glanced at her watch, then back at Lucy. "I'm just curious, how are the dogs taking to all this bike riding? Don't they miss their morning stroll with you?"

Lucy usually walked her two dogs into town almost every day, checking off exercise for all three of them. But she'd been biking a lot lately, wanting to step up her own workout.

"They're a little confused, to tell you the truth. I'm still haunted by those baffled, mournful looks when I leave without them," she admitted. "But I make it up later, after dinner. It's not as hot out, either."

"That's true. But that's quite a regimen for you. I'm impressed. Biking and walking every day."

"*Almost* every day." Lucy knew she wasn't that disciplined. "You know what they say, 'No pain, no gain.'"

"Do you know who first said that? Benjamin Franklin," Maggie replied, answering her own question. "I wouldn't hold him up as any model of physical fitness and I've always hated that expression anyway. It's not even true. I've had plenty of gain without pain. What about 'No joy, no gain'? I'd like to see that one on a T-shirt sometime."

"You should tweet, Maggie. You're a natural." That was true, but Lucy was teasing her, knowing how Maggie shunned social media and still thought tweeting had to do with birds.

"Twitter. Flitter . . . Fritter . . . what do I know?" Maggie shrugged, counting out the pattern instruction sheets in her folder. "What's going on with all this bike riding anyway? Are you practicing for the Tour de France?"

Lucy had been cycling a lot lately, though she hadn't realized anyone had noticed . . . aside from her dogs.

"Hardly. I just want to reduce my carbon footprint . . . and my butt. A bit," she added, glancing over her shoulder to check her rear view. At least the requisite black spandex bike pants packed everything in neatly.

Maggie laughed. "I don't know about your footprints but the rest of your body looks fine to me. Perfect, in fact. I wouldn't trouble yourself. What does Matt think?"

"Oh, he's all for saving the ozone and the polar bears, and all that." Lucy could tell from Maggie's expression that her answer had been avoiding the real question. "And he doesn't have any complaints about my bike seat, either. This isn't about Matt. It's about me. I just want to get into better shape this summer. I have a big birthday coming. Matt and I are going into Boston for my birthday weekend. I bought a special dress."

"Really?" Maggie looked interested. But Lucy knew that would grab her attention. Among her friends, Lucy was known as Woman Least Likely to Shop, her daily outfits selected for comfort and easy clean up after dog care.

"What's this special dress look like?"

"Little and tight," Lucy replied. "And blue. I could have bought it in black, the proverbial little back dress? But it made me feel like I was in mourning for my lost youth."

Maggie laughed. "I get it. But I make it a rule to never buy goal-oriented clothing. I don't think new clothes should pressure you. Life's complicated enough."

"Most of the time. Yes, it is." Lucy checked the strap on her helmet. She did like biking clothes and accessories, the colorful tops and the gadgets. It was always fun to have a hobby that required a cool outfit or two.

"Your birthday is sometime in July, right? You're Cancer the Crab, through and through," Maggie added, citing Lucy's horoscope sign. "Artistic, generous, sensitive, and loyal. To a fault. But moody at times and if you feel threatened or hurt, you tuck right into your little shell."

Lucy laughed and set the helmet on her head. "Exactly. I'm putting my shell on right now, see?"

Maggie smiled and touched her arm. "Lucy, you have nothing to worry about. You're totally young and gorgeous. Ask *me* about big birthdays. I've got a few years on you, kiddo."

Lucy wasn't sure of Maggie's exact age, but knew she had

to be getting close to sixty—though she looked fantastic, at least ten years younger. Lucy knew age was just a number . . . but she couldn't help the way she felt.

"I guess there are worse fates. But it's a big number for me. I didn't give a thought to turning thirty. Some people totally freak over that one. But this seems . . . heavier somehow. More of a milestone." Lucy sighed. "It's practically forty."

Maggie smiled wistfully. "An awesome age for a woman. You're just hitting your stride. Look at Dana and Suzanne," she added, calling up examples of close friends in their group, both a few years older than Lucy: Dana Haeger, a psychologist with a busy private practice in town, and Suzanne Cavanaugh, a supermom and super real-estate saleswoman.

Lucy had met both women, years ago in a beginner knitting class, that Maggie had taught. Their chemistry was instantaneous and irresistible, and Lucy knew very quickly she'd found lifelong friends. When the class ended, they decided to meet once a week, to knit and chat. But they talked and met much more than that, with Maggie's shop turning into their unofficial headquarters.

"They're both at the top of their game," Maggie continued. "Their kids are grown and they have time for themselves again. They can really focus on their careers and passions."

"Yes, I know. And they both look terrific, too," Lucy agreed. "I'm not saying my reaction is logical. It just . . . is." Maggie seemed to have forgotten that she didn't have any children yet, and by the time her theoretical babies were grown she'd be fifty . . . or even older?

Lucy fiddled with the chin strap of her helmet, thinking it was definitely time to go.

Maggie had finished several rows of orange yarn and now

snipped the thread and attached a new one, bright yellow. She shook her head and looked up at Lucy with an apologetic expression. She was about to say something, but Lucy interrupted her.

"What are you working on? Is that a sample for a class?" Lucy was genuinely curious, though also trying to change the subject.

"Yes, a simple summer tote. All one piece, a bit shaped at the top. Fold it, felt it. Add some handles. Voilà." Maggie showed her the photos of casual, roomy totes, in summer colors and stripes. The pattern lent itself to interpretation, which Lucy liked.

"Nice. Even I could make that." Lucy loved to knit but still gravitated toward quick, easy projects.

"I'm sure you can. But you're also trying to change the subject. All this bike riding and birthday stress . . . it isn't really about your birthday, is it?"

"Why do you say that?" Lucy shrugged. "What else could it be about?"

Maggie met her glance but didn't reply. Lucy's older, wise friend wasn't buying. But Lucy definitely did not want to get into a discussion about her lady parts and biological clock. And that whole annoying conversation about expired eggs, as if her organs were stamped like items in the dairy aisle.

That conversation inevitably led to back to her relationship with Matt—which was perfectly happy and wonderful—despite the elephant that had started pacing around their TV room, one with a big sign around its neck that said: GOT COMMITMENT?

"Oh, Lucy . . ." Maggie began.

Luckily, the sight of a blue and white cruiser pulling up in front of the shop drew her attention. Two uniformed officers got out and stood checking a list on a notepad. Preparing to check in with the shopkeepers on Main Street about Jimmy Hubbard, Lucy guessed.

"Here they come, right on time. I hope they stop here first," Maggie said quietly. "My statement will be short and sweet."

"And for once, we weren't anywhere near the scene of the crime. And we barely knew Jimmy," Lucy pointed out.

"For once," Maggie agreed with a small laugh.

Lucy understood perfectly. She and Maggie, along with their knitting group pals, often found themselves in the thick of a police investigation. They didn't mean to get involved; it just happened. And once they were part of some tangled situation, it seemed only natural that they'd try to . . . well, untangle it. Though the police department failed to see their well-intentioned interest in such a benign light.

One police officer in particular, a detective in fact, Charles Mossbacher, could not understand how it kept happening. Even though that's how he and Maggie had met a few months ago, while he was working on a case that involved a college student who had disappeared. The young woman was a close friend of Maggie's assistant, Phoebe.

He and Maggie had been dating ever since and right now, it seemed the only thing Charles and Maggie didn't agree on was her curiosity about his cases. But this time, Maggie was home free.

"I don't know anything at all about this tragic event. And I don't want to know. Nothing beyond what I hear on the news or read in the paper. You heard it first—my snooping days are over." Maggie looked her squarely in the eye.

Lucy was surprised. And a little doubtful Maggie could keep this pledge. But she didn't want to undermine her friend's willpower; Maggie did seem resolved.

"Charles will be happy to hear that."

"He should be. He's the reason I'm going cold turkey," Maggie admitted. "I've learned my lesson. It obviously upsets him and it's not worth risking our relationship."

"That sounds . . . serious."

Maggie shrugged and picked up the basket of yarn and the pile of patterns. "'Serious' is a serious word. Let's just say, so far so good. There's a lot of potential here and I'm not going to toss it away. Besides, he's also my alibi on this one," Maggie added with a grin.

Lucy guessed she meant that they'd been together all evening. Before she could reply, one of the police officers had walked through the gate and called up to them.

"Excuse me, ladies—were either of you in this shop yesterday? Or last night?"

"I was, Officer. I own the store." Maggie introduced herself. "This is my friend, Lucy Binger."

"I wasn't in town yesterday at all. I was home, working. I live out in the Marshes," Lucy added.

Lucy's neighborhood was just beyond the village and near the beach, the roads lined with stretches of tall beach grass and wetland meadows, known by the local nickname.

The officer looked down at his notepad. "You can go, Ms. Binger. But I do need to ask Mrs. Messina a few questions."

"I was just on my way." Lucy said goodbye to Maggie and walked down the steps to get her bike.

She had to admit, it was fun to see her inquisitive pal on

the other end of some questions for once. And she'd wriggled out of Maggie interviewing her any further about her dreaded birthday.

As Lucy pedaled down the driveway, she could hear the officer's questions and Maggie's replies, describing her whereabouts the night before, and her relationship to Jimmy, a distant acquaintance at best. Maggie certainly didn't seem to know anything that would help solve the poor man's murder.

Lucy wondered who did.

Chapter Two

The Schooner was hardly Dana's ideal choice for breakfast after a long bike ride Sunday morning. Lucy knew her health-conscious friend would have preferred a mango and whey powder smoothie at the Health Nut Café. Or even sitting at the harbor with a takeout seaweed salad and marinated tofu. How many times had Dana reminded them that in Asia, everyone eats fish head soup for breakfast, packed with protein and omega-3s?

But a text from their mutual pal, Suzanne, had saved Lucy from all three of those unappetizing fates. Lucy and Dana had just finished riding out to the beach and back to the village, when Suzanne spotted them on the road.

> Meet me at the Schooner? I have a little break between clients.
>
> Need iced coffee. Bad.
>
> Bet Dana has info about Jimmy H by now . . .

Lucy showed Dana the text. Dana squinted at the phone a minute. "Oh sure . . . let's meet up with her. Jack didn't hear much yet about Jimmy. But he did tell me a few things."

Dana's husband, Jack, had been a detective for the Essex County police force at one time, though he now practiced law in town. He still had connections on the force and heard a lot of inside information. Since he wasn't in law enforcement any longer himself, he didn't seem to mind sharing the gossip with Dana. She in turn shared it with her friends. Lucy wasn't sure if Jack could get in trouble for passing on the interesting tidbits. A lot of it did eventually come out in the media. As her friends often reminded her, it was such a small town, everyone knows everything, sooner or later.

"I was hoping you'd say that." Lucy quickly tapped a text back to Suzanne.

"Oh, is that why you invited me to go riding this morning?" Dana tried to sound injured, but was laughing a bit, too.

"Of course not. I thought it would be fun. Even if you do have a much nicer bike, and I could hardly keep up with you," Lucy teased back.

"Sorry. I think you need the derailleur checked or something. I'm surprised the chain didn't fall off." Dana glanced down at the gunky gears and Lucy did, too.

"I'm surprised, too. It happens all the time. I bought this bike at a yard sale. It is time for a new one."

She and Dana had dismounted at the harbor and were now rolling their cycles along the sidewalk on Main Street.

"Too bad the shop isn't open. I'm sure Maggie would be up for taking a break with us," Dana said. "Should we call her?"

"I think she's spending the day with Charles on his sailboat. Besides, the less she knows these days about an ongoing police investigation, the better. She's sworn off amateur sleuthing. She claims. Or did she say snooping?" Lucy couldn't remember. "It's a touchy subject with Charles."

"I guess his feelings are more important to her now. I think that's nice." Dana smiled.

"I do, too," Lucy said, though she was fairly certain Maggie's curiosity about such matters would persist, even if it did cause friction in her romance.

As they locked up their bikes in front of the Schooner, Lucy spotted Suzanne sitting at a booth near the window. Once they were inside, she noticed that Edie was not at her usual post, behind the big old brass cash register, posed like a bouffant Buddha, watching over her kingdom.

Suzanne waved wildly, as if bidding farewell from the deck of an ocean liner. "Lucy! Dana! Over here!"

Dana slipped into the seat next to Suzanne and kissed her cheek hello. "Good work, Suzanne. You grabbed a good table."

Good for people watching, Lucy knew she meant. One of the major perks of a visit to the town's favorite café.

Lucy sat across from them and picked up her menu.

"Wow. Look at you two in your spiffy biking outfits. You both look so cute in those little pants. I'd pay good money to fit into a pair that weren't meant as control-top underwear. Did you ride very long? It's so hot out there."

"Just to the beach and back. We did about ten or twelve miles?" They'd set out early, but it had been hot on the way back. Lucy was grateful for the glass of ice water that suddenly appeared, with the help of a very efficient busboy.

"*Only* ten miles? Excuse me." Suzanne shrugged. "What do you call a long ride? From here to Cape Cod?"

Lucy laughed. "That would be a trek," she conceded. But ten miles on a bike was not a long ride at all. Suzanne obviously didn't get out pedaling much.

"There is a great bike trail on the Cape now, on the path of an old railroad track," Lucy told her. "It's very smoothly paved and goes all the way from Brewster to Provincetown."

"I tried a stretch last summer. It is great. Most of it is shady and flat. We have to go out there together sometime . . . but not on that bike, I hope. You'd be in bed for a month." Dana took a long drink of water, too, and stared at Lucy over the top of the glass.

"What's wrong with your bike, Lucy?" Suzanne sounded concerned. "It is broken?"

"It's old and clunky and the gears don't work. Otherwise, it's perfect." Lucy glanced at Dana. "I can't help it if some people around here are cycle snobs."

"My bike is lighter and you don't need to kill yourself riding uphill," Dana explained. "That's all I'm trying to say."

"And it has about three hundred more gears than mine . . . and it was handcrafted in Italy. You forgot that part," Lucy reminded her.

Dana shrugged, trying not to smile. "Okay, you got me. But I didn't pick it out. Jack and the boys are the cycle snobs, I guess. They bought it for me as a surprise." When Lucy didn't answer she added, "I think they got a good discount. I can find out the name of the store for you."

Suzanne glanced from one friend to the other, following the debate as she perused the open menu.

Lucy sat back and opened her menu, too. "That's all right. Matt's buying me a bike for my birthday. A really good one.

Custom fit." She was not usually the type to brag, but Dana's teasing had struck a nerve.

"Wow, that's a nice gift. Very thoughtful." Dana was clearly impressed. "You should have told me, I wouldn't have gone on about it."

Suzanne put her menu down and just stared. Lucy knew her wide-eyed expression had nothing to do with bicycles.

"A bike? *Really?* What are you . . . nine years old? How about he custom-fits a diamond ring to the third finger on your left hand? Did that suggestion ever come up?"

"A good bike costs almost as much," Dana said quietly.

"And I don't even like diamonds," Lucy reminded Suzanne.

"That is so not the point and you both know it. How about a ruby? A sapphire? An emerald? Precious gems, a symbol of eternal, precious love. Sorry, honey—a bike just doesn't cut it. Even a super-duper nice one from Italy."

Lucy sat back, totally put on the spot. Suzanne could be outrageously outspoken at times, but this had to be one of her all-time over-the-top moments.

Before Lucy could reply, Dana jumped in. "Suzanne . . . what a thing to say. Where are your boundaries? It's absolutely none of our business."

"Thank you, Dana," Lucy said quietly, completely forgiving her now for having a better bicycle.

Suzanne rolled her eyes. "Okay . . . bad dog, Suzanne. Hit me on the nose with a rolled-up menu or something. It's fine. I just have one tiny question, Lucy. And I ask this as a dear friend. . . . You can't deny that you must think about it. Or don't you want to marry Matt after all?"

"Objection! Leading the witness," Dana said, in a court-room voice.

Suzanne sighed. "For goodness' sakes, we're just trying to have a little conversation here, Dana. Get a grip."

She stared at Lucy again, leaning across the table and speaking in a much softer tone. "If you don't want to answer me, it's fine. No worries. But we are your closest friends in the world. If you don't tell us, who can you tell? And of course you know, I only share because I care."

Lucy sighed. She glanced from Suzanne to Dana, who now gestured with a fingertip over her lips, as if she were zipping up her mouth.

"Guys, calm down. You don't need to come to blows. Truth be told . . . yes, I do want to marry Matt. I do think about it. A little," she admitted. "And I think Matt does, too. We just haven't had time to talk it all out yet."

Suzanne was obviously encouraged. "All right. That sounds good. For now. But you can't wait for him to initiate 'the conversation,' Lucy. Men never want to do that."

"That's not true, Suzanne," Dana quietly contradicted.

Suzanne glanced at her. "Not on your planet, maybe. But here on Earth, we all know men are from Mars, and women are from Venus. Or did you miss that memo?"

Lucy sighed. She'd never read that book and now wondered if she ought to.

"To tell the truth, I was hoping he'd do that. Or just propose or something? If I have to persuade or pressure someone into marrying me, what's the point? That's no fun at all."

Suzanne shrugged. "I didn't say it would be fun. But at least you'll know what page of the romance novel he's on."

"I know what you're trying to say, Lucy," Dana cut in. "But

there is a difference between drawing a line in the sand, and owning and airing your feelings. If this issue is bothering you. Then again, if it's not, maybe you don't need to have that conversation right now. Or ever. Maybe you and Matt could live together happy as clams forever, without taking the conventional path of marriage, et cetera."

Suzanne sighed. "Of course it's bothering her. Of course she expects marriage, *et cetera*. And by that I think you mean babies? Why else would she be riding her bicycle all over town like a maniac?"

"I just want to get into better shape. I bought a special dress for my birthday," Lucy insisted. "It has nothing to do with Matt. Or our relationship."

Lucy truly believed that. Yet, protesting so passionately to her friends gave her pause to wonder. Was she really upset about this question?

"Okay. Have it your way. I had my say." Suzanne raised her hands in surrender. "But to borrow a phrase from Dana's playbook, 'I think you need to process this conversation.'"

Dana laughed. "Is that what I say?" She smiled at Lucy and shrugged. "Suzanne's right. We both shared our thoughts. Enough said."

"Fine with me." Lucy didn't need to talk about this anymore, either. Did she really have to corner Matt and pressure him?

Whine, persuade, set out her logical points like a politician hoping for his vote?

She was definitely not that woman . . . and never would be. If that's what it was going to take, they very well might end up spending the next twenty years or so happily unmarried, et cetera.

The truth was, she'd always imagined that one day, when she least expected it, he would pop the question in some extremely original and adorable manner—surprise her with a ring in her morning cup of coffee? Or a glass of champagne? Or maybe it would appear as she unwound a ball of yarn? The way romantic actors always do in the movies.

"Maybe I just have to make him watch more chick flicks with me, and he'll get the idea," Lucy suggested to her pals.

"Maybe." Dana was studying the menu now and glanced at her over the top. "Our Netflix queue is filed with documentaries—Jack's favorite. The rise and fall of rock bands, mainly. Oh, and the Nixon era. Ask me anything about Watergate. I'm your gal."

"Ugh . . . talk about a mood killer." Suzanne shivered. "Kevin's not so bad. I can get him to snuggle up with a good chick flick from time to time, or even some *Downton Abbey*. Those smoochy movies will definitely give Matt ideas. But not the kind you need right now," Suzanne advised knowingly.

The waitress arrived to take their order. Lucy was grateful for the break in conversation.

She glanced out the window. The prime people-watching perch was paying off. Lucy noticed a familiar face approaching and about to enter the diner: Nora Gordon, Edie's niece. She did look much better than the last time Lucy had seen her, about a month or so ago. She'd cut her hair and dyed it a lighter color. She was talking and smiling in an animated way, and her orange and white striped T-shirt was positively cheerful.

Nora was walking down the street with another woman, whom Lucy didn't recognize. But when they came into the Schooner, Lucy knew the identity of Nora's friend, too. The pair paused a moment, looked around for an empty table, then headed for the far side of the diner.

"Don't all look at once—but Nora Gordon, Edie's niece just walked in, and the woman with her is a psychic medium, Cassandra Waters. At least, she claims to be," Lucy added in a hushed tone.

"A psychic?" Dana seemed amused. "Who told you that?"

"Edie. She was at Maggie's shop yesterday morning, and started talking about Nora. How she'd been so depressed after she lost her son, and the only thing that's helped her so far is visiting this psychic."

"I've heard of her. My boss brought her advertising cards into the office." Suzanne pulled the paper off a straw and stirred up her iced coffee. "He hired the psychic for a party. He said she was very good."

"Very *entertaining*, you mean," Dana clarified. "Saying she was 'good' would infer that she could really predict things."

Suzanne shrugged. "I don't know. I wasn't invited. But I have to admit, I do believe that some people have some sort of sixth sense. I'm not saying everybody who hangs out a fortune-teller shingle is for real. But there are some weird and unexplainable things going on in the universe, ladies. Grandma Bella, for instance, would have dreams about people in the family that really came true." Suzanne shrugged. "You never know, right?"

Dana tilted her head. "I don't count out psychic abilities or events entirely, either," she said. "For one thing, I've had too many patients tell me about intuitive feelings that come true. Or even prescient dreams. Carl Jung believed in extrasensory perception, synchronicity, and a collective unconscious that connects everyone. He studied and wrote about those topics extensively."

"Yes, I've heard that." Lucy took another sip of water. She was listening to her friends, of course, but also watching Cassandra Waters and Nora.

"I did not understand half of what you just said, Dana. But I *think* you sort of agreed with me." Suzanne looked pleased by this small victory.

"I do. But I also agree, most people who sell themselves as psychics—and I do mean sell—are total fakers, merely expert at reading people by appearance and body language and their reactions to certain key questions."

The food arrived: a yogurt and fruit parfait for Dana, a breakfast burrito for Suzanne, and for Lucy, an egg white omelet with mushrooms, a slice of tomato, and sprig of parsley. She forced a smile and dug into her dish, reminding herself of how lean and mean she was going to look on her birthday.

"I could practically claim to be a psychic myself. I have to practice all those techniques in my practice," Dana added.

Suzanne tucked extra napkins into the neckline of her hot pink tank top. "I never thought of it that way. A new career for you, Dana, in your retirement years."

Dana laughed. "You never know."

"Let me test your powers . . . will this burrito give me heartburn? I have a lot of houses to show today."

Dana closed her eyes and theatrically pressed her fingertips to her forehead. Then turned to look at Suzanne. "The spirits say . . . save half for lunch."

"Good call," Lucy agreed, around a bite of omelet that was actually quite tasty. "But that's just common sense."

Before Suzanne could reply, another voice cut into the conversation. "Hey, ladies, how are you doing? Need anything? Ketchup, napkins . . . more coffee?"

Edie had snuck up on her big white shoes, a stack of menus tucked under one arm and a coffee canister in hand.

"It's all good, Edie," Lucy replied. "How are you? How's your angina?"

Edie waved the coffee canister. "My ticker's fine. Just took a few extra pills last night. I haven't heard any more news about Jimmy Hubbard. Have any of you?"

Poor Jimmy . . . they'd forgotten all about him, distracted by Cassandra Waters and Suzanne's unsolicited relationship advice.

"I did hear a few things from Jack," Dana replied, in a quiet tone.

"Wait a minute . . . slide over, Lucy. Let me get in there. My hearing aids are buzzing with the racket."

Edie set the coffeepot and menus on the table as Lucy slid toward the window to make room. The diner owner squeezed most of her puffy body under the table, her legs angled out into the aisle.

"Okay, go on, dear. I'm all ears." Edie cocked her beehive hairdo in Dana's direction.

"Jack didn't say too much. But there was no sign of a struggle. And no sign of forced entry. The police are assuming that Jimmy opened the door to someone he knew, or had no reason to fear. And there was just one other thing they found out right away that might be important: Jimmy had a record of arrests and spent several years in prison. Serious time."

Lucy was the most surprised to hear that. "Really? He seemed like such a nice guy. No weird tattoos, or anything like that. It's hard to believe he was a hardened criminal. Maybe he'd made some mistake and paid his debt to society. It doesn't mean he was an awful person."

"Whatever it was, he seemed to have reformed. The police couldn't find anything else amiss since his release. Not even a parking ticket," Dana said.

"Lucy's right. People make mistakes. Though most of us don't screw up that badly," Suzanne conceded.

"So, what was he in for?" Edie asked. "Must have been something big to get locked up a long time."

Dana shrugged. "Jack wasn't sure. But it's possible Jimmy's death is somehow connected to his past. It's one lead for the investigation."

"Just goes to show, you never know about people, do you?" Edie sat back and shook her head. "Maybe he was messing around with the wrong types again. It's not ours to judge the man. We all have some dirty laundry in the back of the closet we wouldn't want to show the world. You can bet on that, girls."

"Everyone has secrets. That's certainly true," Dana agreed.

"Speaking of—here comes the Queen of the Secret Guessers. Right on cue," Edie whispered. "I just have to introduce you. I want to know what you think."

Before Lucy or her friends could reply, Edie had pushed herself to her feet, effectively blocking the path of her niece, Nora and Cassandra Waters, who were headed toward the register, check in hand.

Edie waved to them. "Nora, come on over. Say hello to Lucy and her friends."

Lucy leaned close to her friends and whispered, "Do you think the psychic heard us taking about her? We were pretty discreet and she was sitting far away."

"But maybe she read our thoughts?" Suzanne teased her.

"More likely, our lips. I bet she knows a lot about that, too," Dana whispered back.

Good point, Lucy thought. But there was no chance to reply. Nora and Cassandra Waters were suddenly smiling down at Lucy and her friends as Edie made some quick introductions.

"You know Lucy and her pals, don't you, Nora? They all hang around the knitting shop with Maggie."

"Sure I do." Nora cast a small but friendly smile at the group. "Nice to see you."

"I love your store," Suzanne said. "I don't go in enough. I could buy everything in there. But my husband won't let me."

Nora's smile grew wider. "Stop by anytime. I'll give you the friends-and-family discount."

Edie slung her arm around Nora's shoulder. "She'd give the store away if Richard didn't watch her. Doesn't take after me that way," she insisted, though Lucy did see Edie pluck the table check from Nora's hand and stick it in her apron pocket.

"This is my friend Cassandra." Nora stepped aside so that Cassandra could come closer. So far the psychic had stood by quietly, her slim white hands clasped loosely in front of her, almost in a pose of meditation.

She looked a bit different from her photograph, Lucy thought, but no less attractive. Just less glamorous. Her long dark hair was parted in the middle, framing her thin face and large blue eyes. She wore a pale blue tunic with long bell sleeves and gauzy skirt, printed with a blue and white batik design.

Lucy noticed the same pendant she'd seen in the photograph, a hunk of raw crystal on a chain, hanging from her neck, and a big ring on the middle finger of one hand, a large pink stone set in silver.

Except for the exotic jewelry, Cassandra Waters's appearance didn't give much hint at her profession and she didn't seem nearly as pushy or enterprising as Edie had portrayed her. At least, not yet, Lucy thought.

As Lucy and her friends greeted Cassandra, Lucy tried to act as natural as possible and suppress the impulse to treat the woman as if she were visiting from another solar system. Which was difficult, considering all that she'd heard.

Dana was doing a fine acting job, smiling and extending her hand. Suzanne, however, looked quite curious, even suspicious.

"I think I've heard of you, Cassandra. Aren't you a . . . psychic or something?" Suzanne asked boldly.

"Yes, she is and a totally amazing one," Nora said before Cassandra could answer. "She's been a great blessing in my life."

Cassandra seemed flustered by the compliment, her gaze dipping down a moment. "Thank you, Nora. But I've been blessed to be able to help you."

Edie stood behind them; she met Lucy's gaze and rolled her eyes. Can you believe this load of baloney? Lucy could almost hear her say.

"I find it fascinating, questions of clairvoyance and intuition," Dana said. "I'm a psychologist and I've observed these phenomena firsthand. How does the information come to you?" she asked. "Do you see things? Or hear things? Do you use cards?"

Dana's tone was curious and even respectful. Though Lucy knew how she really felt.

If Cassandra Waters felt put on the spot, she didn't show it. She was used to being interviewed this way, Lucy realized.

"I'm mostly clairvoyant. Meaning, I see visions," she replied with a small smile. "Though I will say I receive messages in many forms—through spirit voices and dreams, reading tarot cards, even animal messengers."

Lucy found the last interesting. She wondered if her dogs had any messages from the "other side" for her. Aside from "I need to go out. ASAP!" and "How about a biscuit?" her fur friends didn't appear to possess any extrasensory canine perception.

"I wish I could hear voices, to help me sort out the buying clients from the lookie-looks just wasting my time," Suzanne confessed.

Cassandra smiled gently. "We all have these powers, if we choose to acknowledge and develop them." She reached into her shoulder bag, a tapestry fabric sack, and pulled out a handful of her cards. "Here's some information about my services. Contact me anytime. I'd love to help you with your questions. This is my path, what I've been sent here to do. To use my gift to help others." Her warm voice and gaze were as sincere as any minister who had taken vows. She clearly thought of herself as one. Or wants us to, Lucy thought.

As they each took a card, Cassandra's gaze came to rest on Lucy. She smiled down kindly and Lucy felt a bit mesmerized by her startling eyes. "I'd love to do a reading for you, Lucy. There are spirits all around you, eager to communicate."

"Me?" Lucy's reply came out in a squeak. She laughed nervously. "What about?"

As soon as she answered, Lucy realized how silly she sounded. Walked right into that one.

"Your life's path, your future . . . your relationships." Cassandra nodded, the last category said in a definite tone.

The psychic's soft smile melted to a more serious look. She gently shook her head. "I'm sorry . . . that's all I can tell you right now. The energy in here isn't right. Too much tension and negativity flying around."

"Oh, sure." Lucy nodded, as if she knew all about the type of energy that made spirits kick back and get all chatty. Thinking about it, she doubted the menu at Edie's diner would encourage clear communications with the spirit world. It was enough to cause indigestion on any plane of reality.

"I often do group readings. Some people prefer that. Especially a group of good friends," Cassandra added, smiling again, as if she had easily sensed their close bond.

"Thanks. We'll think about it." Dana also held a card and glanced at Lucy across the table. Lucy wondered if she was serious after all. Maybe just curious? Or deciding to unmask a faker, since Dana did seem to know a great deal about how psychics operated.

Cassandra continued to smile with warm confidence. Their doubts and suspicions seemed to roll off her back, Lucy noticed. Or, perhaps more accurately, off her aura?

Cassandra stepped back from the table as Nora began to say goodbye. "Nice to see you all. Tell Maggie I said hello. I really have to get back to knitting again," she added.

"We meet on Thursday nights," Lucy added, "if you'd ever like to join us."

Lucy knew that all her friends liked Nora and none would mind her extending the invitation.

"Thanks. I might take you up on that sometime." Nora smiled. "I'll let you know."

A busboy came over to the table and offered the group more water. Nora reached out and ruffled his hair. "Hey, Dale, too busy to say hello to your mom?"

The boy acknowledged Nora with an embarrassed smile. "Sorry, Mom . . . I wasn't covering your table and I didn't have time to talk. Aunt Edie doesn't like that," he added, glancing at his great-aunt.

"That's right," Edie agreed. "You two can catch up at home. He's got tables to clear—nine and three. The dirty dishes are just sitting there, honey."

"Got it covered, Auntie."

As Dale dutifully ran off, Lucy couldn't help noticing how Nora's gaze followed him. She could only imagine what Nora was thinking each time she set eyes on her only boy. Of course, she had to be thinking of Kyle, the child she'd lost.

At least the two didn't bear much resemblance. Dale was on the fair side, with light brown hair and a broad-shouldered, athletic build. He looked about seventeen, a junior in high school, Lucy guessed. One who played a lot of sports: football or basketball? Maybe even lacrosse?

She remembered Kyle with his dark hair and slim build. More intellectual looking. He'd been a senior in high school when he passed away, and was headed for a prestigious college. His unexpected death had been a real tragedy. It was surprising that, even now, two years later, Nora was able to emerge somewhat from her mourning—which she credited to her sessions with Cassandra Waters.

Nora did seem back to normal, if you didn't look too deeply. But Lucy also sensed a lingering sorrow and a certain fragile quality. She suspected that just beyond the surface, Nora's healing had a long way to go. Certainly this was the kind of loss that one never truly recovers from, and which made people like Nora even easier prey for people like Cassandra Waters?

As Nora and Cassandra left, Suzanne checked her phone and began tapping out text messages.

"Good—my first appointment is held up in traffic. They're coming out from Boston to look at a waterfront listing. Just came on the market, sort of a faux French chateau with solar panels? Mine is not to judge. Just to sell. Sell, sell, sell."

The house sounded sort of hideous to Lucy. But Suzanne had definitely sold worse-sounding properties.

"Did you really mean what you told Cassandra, or were you just baiting her?" Lucy asked.

"Of course I meant it. What salesperson wouldn't want to read their customer's mind?" Suzanne laughed. "Do I think she can really read minds? That's another question."

"How about you, Lucy?" Dana asked. "Do you think spirits with special messages for you are hanging out in Edie's diner, hovering over our table?"

Dana was partly teasing, Lucy was sure. But partly serious, too.

Lucy laughed. "No. I don't know," she said honestly.

"No offense, Lucy. But I think Cassandra just sniffed out the weakest link. Dana and I give off alpha energy," Suzanne added, "and you're so sweet and nice."

"I'm an easy mark, is that what you're trying to say?" Lucy was laughing but also a bit insulted.

Suzanne shrugged. "If the crystal pendant fits . . ." she said in a tiny voice.

"I don't know about you guys, but I'm definitely curious. I think we should book a reading with her. All of us, together.

That will make it easier to observe her techniques. While she's focusing on Lucy, for instance, we can figure out her scam."

"I don't know. She seems pretty smooth to me. But a reading would be fun. I wouldn't mind doing it." Suzanne picked up the card and her phone and stashed both in her purse. "And let's not forget Maggie and Phoebe."

"Of course not. I'm sure they'll want to try it, too," Lucy said.

Edie appeared beside the table again. "So, what did you think of that swivel-hipped Svengali?"

"We're going to book a group reading, Edie. We want to see what really goes on. Want to join us?" Dana offered.

"I had the same idea. I'm seeing her tonight," Edie replied.

"She kept saying that spirits want to talk to me."

"Just what she said to me," Lucy cut in. "That must be her standard bait."

"Well, she also tossed a few tidbits, you might say. Nothing specific. But did set me back on my heels. How does she know this stuff?" Edie looked perplexed a moment, then she resolved again. "But it's no big trick to toss a lot of stuff at the wall and see what sticks, right? Let's see if she can keep that up for half an hour, or more. I bet I see through this gal's game pretty quickly."

"If you do, let us know. We won't call her until tomorrow. No use wasting our money, ladies, right?" Suzanne asked the others.

"I can tell you right now not to waste your money," Edie replied emphatically. "Though I will say it's the only thing that's helped Nora. God knows, she and Richard made the rounds of a hundred therapists, and must have dropped thousands on that trail. Is this really that much different? . . . No offense, Dana," she quickly added.

"No offense taken. Though I will say that sessions with a qualified therapist or grief counselor are a lot different than seeing a psychic. It can hardly be compared in the same breath."

"Yes, yes. Of course. I'm just talking off the top of my head." Edie waved her hand in apology, her bracelets jingling. "The bottom line is I know this woman is up to no good and she's got my niece wrapped around her little finger. My sister is gone. I'm all the mother Nora has left. I can't sit by and watch her conned by some charlatan."

"It's sweet that you're concerned, Edie," Lucy said. "Nora is lucky to have you. You tell us how it goes. Maybe we'll visit with Cassandra anyway, and see if we can help you debunk her."

"I like that word, Lucy. De-*bunk*," Suzanne echoed. "It sounds like just what it means."

"We could help derail her, Edie. We'd be happy to try." Dana put a second to the offer. "What will you do then? Tell Nora?"

Edie's wrinkled face puckered; it appeared she hadn't worked out this part of her plan yet.

"I'm not sure. Maybe I can just persuade the woman to leave Nora alone and my niece may never have to know she'd been bamboozled." She looked back at Lucy. "Let me have my session. I'll figure it out from there."

"Fair enough," Lucy replied. "In the meantime, if spirits want to get in touch with me that badly, they'll find a way, right?"

"Very true," Dana said. "As Emerson said, 'Heed the still, small voice inside of you. It rarely leads you astray.'"

Edie considered the words with a thoughtful expression.

"That's a good one. I like it. See you, ladies . . . and don't worry about the check, it's on me."

Before anyone could protest, Edie slipped the check off the table and stuffed it in her pocket. Certainly the first time that had ever happened to Lucy while dining at the Schooner. Edie obviously appreciated their offer to help her unmask Cassandra Waters, a strange but interesting assignment.

Chapter Three

After hobbling painfully into the shower and then downstairs for a breakfast of coffee and ibuprofen, Lucy realized she'd done enough bike riding over the weekend—more than enough, probably. She downed more coffee and decided to walk her dogs into town. To get the kinks out.

The trio soon arrived at the knitting shop. Maggie was outside, watering the abundant flower beds that bordered the picket fence and both sides of the path—petunias, snapdragons, swaying blue statice, pink echinacea, black-eyed Susan, and other colorful blossoms. Rosebushes and heavy-headed hydrangeas. She definitely had a green thumb, along with her other, crafty fingers.

"Hey, how are you doing? Hard at work already, I see."

Maggie turned and smiled, gently patting the dogs and pushing aside their licks of greeting until Lucy pulled them back.

"Just wanted to poke around out here before it got too hot. I should have weeded a bit this weekend," Maggie said.

"The price we pay for having too much fun. Rarely your problem. I think sailing agrees with you."

Maggie's cheeks were touched with color; her short curly hair looked beachy and windblown. She looked happy, too, Lucy thought.

"We did have a nice time. I've forgotten how relaxing being out on the water can be. My father had a boat and he taught us all to sail, but Bill never really liked it. He was more of a tennis or golf type," she explained, talking about her late husband. "Charles has a beautiful cruiser, thirty-one feet," she added. "We sailed up to Newburyport and back. It was a lovely day."

"Sounds great. You did miss breakfast at the Schooner yesterday. Dana and I met up with Suzanne . . . and Edie picked up our check."

"That is a notable event." Maggie laughed as she stood up and pulled off her gloves. "I guess Dana gave a full report about the investigation of Jimmy's death?"

"Jack hasn't heard that much. Only that there were no signs of a break-in or struggle, so the police think Jimmy knew the person who attacked him. The big news is that Jimmy had a criminal record and served a long prison sentence. I don't know about you, but I was really surprised to hear that," Lucy said honestly.

"Me, too. You never know, I guess. What did he go to jail for?" Maggie asked curiously.

"Dana didn't know. But she did say the police think his death might be related to something in his past, some connection with criminal associates."

"Yes, that makes sense. Charles didn't mention a word about it. He didn't catch that case. Which was why he had off the entire weekend, for once. Just as well that I wasn't around for that get-together," Maggie added. "You know what Oscar Wilde said, 'I can resist everything but temptation.'"

Lucy laughed. "Never heard that one, but I'll have to remember it. You did miss another interesting moment—one that has nothing to do with police work," she added. "Edie's niece, Nora, was there with Cassandra Waters and Edie introduced us to the psychic. Edie wanted to see what we thought of her."

Maggie gave her a curious look. "What's she like?"

"From what Edie said about her, I was expecting some loud, brassy woman in a gypsy costume, pushing a crystal ball in my face. But she was very smooth."

"Really? That's interesting. I got the same impression from Edie's description, too." Maggie headed up to the porch and Lucy followed, tugging the dogs, who were more interested to sniff the freshly watered lawn and shrubs.

"She was just the opposite—calm and quiet. Sort of New Agey? Very . . . sympathetic. Though she did press her hand a bit, pushing us a little to call her for a session." Lucy tied the dogs to the porch rails and set up their portable water bowl. "She also said there were a lot of spirits who wanted to talk to me, to give me advice about my life."

Maggie looked surprised, her smile growing wider. "Hard to resist a teaser like that."

"Yes, it is," Lucy admitted.

The comment had struck a nerve, with so many big questions looming now—her major birthday coming up, and wondering where her relationship with Matt was really going. Or not going.

She'd been thinking about it more than she wanted to admit. Lucy looked back at Maggie. "Edie already told us that was the way Cassandra got Nora hooked. She's sure that

Cassandra Waters is exploiting Nora. She's very concerned about it. She went to a session with the psychic last night, just to see what it was like."

Maggie nodded, heading for the storeroom at the back of the shop, which doubled as a kitchen. Lucy smelled fresh coffee and followed.

"Eddie mentioned she might do that the other day," Maggie replied. "I'm glad she followed through. She seems convinced that Cassandra is exploiting Nora."

"Suzanne, Dana, and I thought we should set up a session, too. In fact, we more or less promised Edie that we'd help her debunk Cassandra. We thought we should all go. What do you think? Want to try it?"

Maggie had poured them each a mug of coffee and handed Lucy one, no milk or sugar, just the way Lucy liked it. Maggie poured a spot of milk in her own mug and took a quick sip.

"Why not? I've never been. It could be fun. Why don't we ask her to come to the shop on Thursday night? We're supposed to meet here anyway this week."

Their knitting group met every Thursday night at seven, rotating between everyone's house and the shop. Lucy thought it was a good suggestion.

"Good idea. We already know that's a night everyone can make it. As long as you don't mind having a séance in your shop."

Lucy was teasing Maggie now a bit, though it would seem a little weird, sitting around the worktable—so far reserved for knitting, eating, and gossiping—and summoning up spirits.

"Oh, I don't mind at all. Do you think she'll make us hold hands or any of that silly stuff? Maybe we can knit while she does her thing," Maggie mused. "It will be just like a regular meeting—except we'll be chatting with voices from beyond."

"Whoa . . . what am I hearing down here?" Phoebe's apartment on the second floor was connected by a stairway in the storeroom, and she came down the last few steps two at a time. She landed in front of Maggie.

"You are not seriously planning to hold a séance in our shop, are you?" Phoebe turned her wide brown eyes first on Lucy, then Maggie.

Maggie sighed and handed Phoebe a mug of coffee. "Calm down, Phoebe. We're positive the woman is a phony. We're trying to help Edie debunk her."

"Fine, fine . . . easy for you to say. But I'm the one who has to sleep here. This house must be a zillion years old and some wacky psychic could stir up all kinds of nasty energy."

Poor Phoebe. Lucy found her reaction amusing at first, but quickly realized she was truly alarmed.

Maggie touched Phoebe's shoulder. "Don't worry. Nothing like that is going to happen. You've been watching too many scary movies."

"Easy for you to say. I *already* hear spirits wandering around down here at night. What if knitting needles start flying around?"

Maggie's serious, sympathetic expression melted into a smile. "I'd like to see that; it could be very amusing. Maybe the yarn swift will wind a few skeins for me. My least favorite job. Maybe the needles will grab some yarn and start knitting some pattern samples? Do you think I could leave them a to-do list?"

"Okay, be like that. You won't think it's very funny when this place is totally haunted by dead people knitting."

"Don't worry, Phoebe. If the spirits of knitters past decide to take over the shop, you can stay in my guest room until we get a ghost exterminator. I've heard that most ghosts are totally harmless. And you have Van Gogh. Cats are very sensitive to spirit energy. Van Gogh can let us know if any restless spirits are hanging around."

Phoebe had an active imagination, that was for sure. But Lucy still sympathized with her. It might be fun to have the psychic here, but not if Phoebe was lying awake every night afterward.

"I'm pretty sure she can just read some cards and make predictions about the future. No knitting ghosts or spirit messengers involved. Would that be all right with you?"

Phoebe looked calmer but still not convinced. "Like tarot cards, you mean? Not a Ouija board . . . right?"

"I draw the line at a Ouija board myself. That is creepy and it's all just your own nervous energy," Maggie said.

They all turned at the sound of someone coming into the store.

"Yoo-hoo! Anybody home in here?" Lucy heard Edie call out.

"We're back in the storeroom, Edie. Be right out," Maggie called back. "Would you like some coffee?"

"I'm good, thanks. Already filled my tank," she reported.

They walked back into the shop to find Edie settled in an armchair, rummaging through her knitting bag. "I just ran in for a little more yarn for my project." Edie pulled out a sweet little baby hat and held it up to show everyone. "Yellow, yellow, yellow. I'm about to puke, but what can you do? These young gals never want to know the sex of their babies. When did that go out of style? I'm getting sick of making yellow hats and booties and blankets . . . or boring old white."

"I hear you," Maggie agreed. She was already checking a cubby near the counter for the yarn Edie needed. "But once the baby arrives you can make something to match, in blue or pink," she suggested.

"By then I'll have some other pregnant relative to knit for. On to the next baby. That's the motto in our family—very prodigious."

"How did your session with Cassandra go?" Lucy asked. "Did you see her?"

"Did I ever." Edie's head tilted back, her small eyes growing wide behind glasses.

Phoebe jumped forward from behind the counter, where she'd been sipping her coffee and scanning Maggie's laptop.

"Tell the truth, Edie . . . does she conjure up troubled spirits?" Phoebe seemed to be bracing herself.

Edie shook her head. "Nothing like that. She does all sorts of silly things to put you at ease about that ever happening—waves white feathers around your head and then she burns a bunch of dried leaves and fans the smoke all over. I tell you, it smells like a bathing suit fell in a campfire. Nearly scared me off, too."

"Sounds very reassuring." Maggie's sarcasm seemed to go unnoticed by Edie. And Phoebe, too, for that matter, Lucy noticed.

"What did she tell you, Edie? Did you figure out her tricks?" Lucy asked.

Edie looked uncomfortable at that question. "Oh, she said a lot of stuff. A lot about George," she added, mentioning her husband, who had passed away more than ten years ago. "Passing to the other side must have really loosened his vocal cords. The man could barely string three words together when he was alive—'What's for dinner?' 'Where's the remote?' 'Get me a beer, hon?'"

Maggie laughed. "George had been a man of few words," she agreed. Without adding that Edie talked enough for both of them, Lucy thought.

"Now it seems he's got a lot to say. He's proud of the way I've been running the diner and doesn't want me to give any more money to our son, Chad. Not until he can get his act together."

"Did she really say that? That specifically?" Lucy asked.

Edie cocked her head to one side. "See . . . that's where it gets a little fuzzy. It's more like she gets some feeling or hint about something and has you filling in the blanks."

"Interesting. So you're feeding her information without realizing it?" Maggie said.

"Sometimes. I guess you are. You must be. Otherwise . . . well, how would she know?" Edie picked up the skein of yarn Maggie had found, and checked the label. "The thing is, from time to time, she does come out with the darnedest things. She knew some stuff about me I couldn't have been just giving away. Stuff from way back." Edie shook her head, clearly confounded as she opened her coin purse and picked out a few bills to pay for her purchase. "I tell you, it spooked me."

Phoebe looked uneasy again. She glanced at Lucy. "See . . . what did I tell you? Do we really want to mess with this stuff?"

Lucy felt a bit alarmed, too, though she didn't want to admit it. "Like what? Can you just give us a hint?"

Edie sighed. She looked like she wanted to confide the specifics but something was holding her back. It was probably too personal, Lucy realized. Which made the whole question of Cassandra's credibility even more complicated.

"You have to see for yourself. I can't explain." Edie snapped her purse shut and dumped it in her knitting bag.

"You're going to book a session with her, aren't you?"

"Yes, we want to have it here at the shop, on Thursday night if she'll come," Maggie replied.

"Oh, I have a feeling she'll come," Edie said. "I have to admit, I didn't really figure out how she managed to pull the wool over my eyes . . . and has been doing that to poor Nora for weeks now. But maybe you gals will," Edie said hopefully. "I'm counting on you now."

"We'll try our best, Edie," Lucy said.

"I might be out that night. But I'll be cheering for them," Phoebe added.

Maggie patted Edie's arm as she walked with her to the door.

"Don't worry, Edie. I'm sure there's a logical explanation for Ms. Waters's extraordinary powers of perception, however spooky they may seem. We'll get to the bottom of it. The more people who try to observe her objectively, the better, right?"

"I hope so. Nora won't hear a word against her. And I couldn't catch the woman doing anything all that suspicious with me. But I still smell a rat," Edie said finally. "And it's not just that funky incense she uses."

The door closed behind Edie, and Maggie let loose a sigh. "I've known Edie a long time. I've rarely seen her this worked up. I wonder what Cassandra said that got her so rattled. Edie is usually so forthcoming. She'll tell you anything. I mean *anything*. Too much information, most of the time." Maggie shook her head. "She doesn't seem to know the meaning of the word 'discretion.'"

Lucy knew that was true. "It must be something very sensitive and private. A *real* secret for Edie."

"Which makes it even stranger that Cassandra knew . . . and asked about it," Maggie added.

"Don't you mean, that the spirit voices told Cassandra to ask Edie about it?" Lucy was just pushing her buttons a little.

"Ah . . . yes, the spirit voices. Almost forgot about them." Maggie turned to Phoebe, who was working at the counter on the laptop again. "You don't have to come Thursday night, Phoebe, if you don't want to. We all understand and no one wants to push you into anything that you don't want to do."

Phoebe looked up. "It's all right. If I get freaked, I'll just run upstairs and watch *I Love Lucy*." Phoebe had found a set of DVDs at a yard sale, which had quickly become her go-to for instant stress relief. "I guess I'm curious, too, to hear what's in my future. With my new business and love life, and all that."

Phoebe had been dating but hadn't met any guy that she really clicked with in a while. She definitely wasn't rushing into anything, after her long-standing relationship with a musician had fizzled out last winter. Her energies had constructively been focused on her online entrepreneurial venture—selling her knitted socks and other handmade creations on the Crafty Cricket website for independent artisans. Socks by Phoebe was catching on and she was branching out to headbands and bikinis. The Black Sheep were very proud of her.

"Love and money. I guess those are the top two subjects most people ask about," Maggie mused.

Lucy agreed. "With a few questions about health thrown in here and there."

"Exactly. I just googled that routine with the burning herbs and white feathers that Edie told us about," Phoebe reported. "Standard procedure for clearing negative energy. This website says it's very potent and reliable."

Lucy could see Maggie force a serious expression. "I'm glad that sets your mind at ease. We should try it sometime, when we get a nasty customer in here."

"Yeah, we should," Phoebe agreed brightly. She shut the computer and headed to the worktable, where Lucy saw a few open cartons of yarn that needed to be unpacked.

Lucy glanced through the bay window at the front of the shop and checked on her dogs. They stood side by side, tails wagging as they watched activity on the street. They'd soon be bored, she knew, and start putting their noses—and then paws—on Maggie's window. Never a good idea to leave them out there that long.

"I'd better go. I'll get in touch with Cassandra Waters and ask for an appointment Thursday night around seven. I'll let everyone know if she confirms," Lucy added.

"Perfect." Maggie was looking over the contents of a carton that sat open on the counter, checking it against a long white order sheet. "Even though I've sworn off sticking my nose in police investigations, helping Edie this way is almost as much fun. And Charles never has to know."

Lucy was already at the door, but turned to reply. "Unless we find out that Cassandra Waters is up to something illegal. Then we will have to tell the police."

"Right. I didn't think of that." Maggie looked at her a moment, then shrugged. "We'll cross that Ouija board when we come to it."

"Good plan."

Out on the porch, she untangled Tink's and Wally's leads from the wooden rails, and wondered if they really would debunk Cassandra Waters. The psychic had been able to fool a lot of paying customers for a few months now in this town. Not to mentioned many other places she must have set up her crystal ball. Why would they be the ones to unmask her?

The answer popped into her mind. "'You can fool some of the people some of the time and all of the people some of the time. But you can't fool all of the people all of the time,'" she said aloud. Lucy glanced down at the dogs as they headed home. "Remember that, the next time you decide to sleep on the sofa."

Lucy was working on a project that was due on Wednesday, by five o'clock—a full-color brochure for a company that sold paving stones. It was not the most artistic project she'd ever taken on, but the client was easy to deal with, paid well, and didn't expect a masterpiece. Just a well-designed, easy-to-read catalog that showed off the stones in pleasant settings, mostly set in paths around swimming pools, where smiling model moms and children frolicked. Or close shots of curving paths that cut through sumptuous green lawns. Proud homeowners, in designer sportswear, stood cheerfully admiring their property . . . and their choice of deluxe pavement.

She'd once known a talented sculptor who earned the larger part of his living from carving excruciatingly cute bears from chunks of wood. He would sell these creations at a hefty profit to garden centers and landscapers. Hence his term, "lawn bears"—and his philosophy that most artists need to "carve the lawn bears" in order to make ends meet and no shame in it.

Lucy knew that jobs like the paving stone brochure were her "lawn bears"—and a small price to pay for freedom from office cubicles. She'd spent her fair share of time enclosed in those padded walls, poking her head up from time to time, like an anxious gopher or meerkat. Those years seemed another lifetime ago now. Making a living outside the cubicle maze required scrambling at times, but she had a steady client list these days and would never return to a corporate job again.

She'd moved out to Plum Harbor from Boston several summers ago, a few months after her divorce, and very soon after her aunt Claire died and left her cottage in the Marshes to Lucy and her older sister, Ellen. Ellen was married with two adorable girls and lived a short distance from Boston, in historic, upscale Lexington, her life much like one pictured in the paving stone brochure.

Lucy's sister didn't care much for the cottage or Plum Harbor and was happy to have Lucy living there so the property wouldn't get run down by renters.

Lucy hadn't made too many changes in the cottage since she'd moved in, except to paint some walls and rearrange the furniture to make room for Matt and his belongings when he moved in about a year ago. Including a collection of retro electric guitars, that had started out front and center, on a prominent wall in the living room . . . but had slowly worked its way into the TV room and then out to the enclosed porch.

The frat house decorating touch was a small price to pay for living with the man she loved and had been amazed to find loved her. She liked to think of herself as a person who knew when to focus on the big picture and not the lint of life, things that didn't really matter. Retro guitar collection? Lint. Matt's love and companionship? Big picture.

This week, for some reason, Suzanne's needling about engagement rings and commitment conversations—which to Lucy's thinking was definitely in the lint category—was still distracting her, as if the probe had struck a filling Lucy hadn't even realized was loose. Many a harmless dental exam had set off a toothache, that was for sure.

Whenever her mind wandered back to the annoying topic, she forced herself to focus on paving stones. And by Wednesday at four, she found herself finished with the project. She happily delivered it via e-mail, with time to spare for a quick spin around the neighborhood before Matt got home.

When she returned to the cottage, Matt's truck was in the driveway and she found him out back, cleaning the grill.

"Hey, honey, have a good ride?" Matt looked up and smiled at her as he scoured the grate with a wire brush.

"Short but fun. I've been at the computer all week. It was good to get the kinks out." Lucy often found herself alternating between exercising too much and sitting too much.

"Wait until you get your new bike. Did you decide on the model? We need to order it soon if you want it for your birthday. Wait till you see the water bottle I found. State-of-the-art. It even has a charcoal filter."

Lucy met his glance and forced a smile. A few days ago, such a comment would have elicited a big, happy "Aren't I a lucky gal?" sigh. But Suzanne's pestering had tainted that perception and Lucy was silently mad at her pal . . . and yes, she had to admit it, feeling cranky with Matt about the entire subject.

"I'm not sure yet," she said quietly. She took a long drink of water while he watched her. Then she forced a smile. "I'm going to take a shower. Be right out."

"Take your time. I'll start dinner."

She touched his arm and kissed his cheek as she walked by. He watched her, sensing she wasn't quite herself. While a little voice in her head wished that Matt would ask her what was wrong, another, more persuasive voice, didn't want to go there and hurried her into the house and up the stairs.

When Lucy came down, she quickly fixed a salad, then joined Matt on the patio, where the table was set for two and a platter of perfectly grilled chicken and vegetables took center stage. Her troubled thoughts melted into the soft, purple dusk and the flash of fireflies in the garden, as she and Matt shared the events of their day.

Matt had operated on a hamster, his first time performing surgery on such a small, delicate creature. "It was tricky but looks like the little guy is going to make it."

Lucy could tell he was proud. She was proud of him, too. He took his patients very seriously and went the limit for them.

"That's great. What's his name?"

"Horace. Horace Hamster, I guess. We'd better get the surname straight before we send the bill."

"You really need to double-check that," Lucy agreed. She happily reported that she'd finished the masonry catalogue. "An entire hour before it was due. I'm definitely getting better with deadlines. I didn't want to drag it out and miss my knitting group tomorrow night. A psychic is coming to Maggie's shop."

"A psychic? You mean like a fortune-teller? She's coming to knit with you?"

"To do a reading," Lucy replied. "Her name is Cassandra Waters and she claims she can contact the spirits of people who have passed on. We met her at the Schooner Sunday morning. She said there were a lot of spirits waiting to speak to me."

Matt laughed. "Interesting. What do you think they want to tell you, Lucy?"

Lucy shrugged and looked down at her plate, separating

bits of chicken she planned to give the dogs. "I don't know . . . that's what I'm going to find out."

Matt smiled and watched her. She hated when he did this, staring her down until she cracked.

Finally, she looked up. "What?"

He shrugged, his smile growing wider. "I didn't say anything."

"Why are you staring at me?"

"Can't I stare at you? You look pretty with your hair wet." He leaned over and flicked a curl off her forehead.

Lucy resisted his attempt at distracting her. "I know when you're trying to change the subject, *hon*."

"There is no subject, *hon*. You were talking about some fortune-teller at the knitting shop. Cassandra something?"

"Waters. And she's a psychic, not a fortune-teller."

"Oh, is there a difference?"

Now that he'd brought it up, she wasn't sure. Lucy stood up and began clearing the plates. "I don't know. I have to check. We really just want to see how she works. We told Edie Steiber we'd try to figure out if she was a fake. Edie's niece Nora has been visiting the psychic a few times a week. She's been giving her a lot of money."

"Oh . . . I see. It's sort of a favor to Edie then, having this woman read your fortunes at the shop?"

"Uh-huh." Lucy nodded and continuing clearing. "Edie's very upset. I guess we're curious, too," she admitted.

"It could be interesting. Aren't you curious to hear what she tells you?" Matt seemed to be taking her seriously now. Or was he just teasing? She wasn't sure.

"I guess so. I guess it depends on what she says," she added. "You cooked, I'll clean up." She picked up the stack of dishes and headed to the kitchen, the dogs following her every step.

Matt leaned back in his chair and watched her, still wearing that little smile. As if he knew something that she didn't know. And didn't want to tell her. About her future?

Probably just amused that she was seeing a psychic. He was very rational and logical, being a doctor. He didn't believe in anything that had not been proven by controlled, scientific observation or written up in textbooks. That had to be it. He secretly thought this whole business was a load of bunk, but didn't want to make her feel foolish. Lucy more or less agreed with him. And yet, maybe she did expect Cassandra Waters to tell her something startling and true. Maybe Matt sensed that, too?

Lucy set a dish of chicken scraps for Tink and Wally on the floor and started loading the dishwasher.

She had no idea what Cassandra might say, but when she got home Thursday night, she'd give Matt a full report. And they'd have a good laugh. She was certain of that.

Chapter Four

"It feels strange, sitting here without my knitting." Suzanne gazed around the table and took a sip of wine.

"And for once, we're all here on time. Myself included," Lucy added. "But I did ask her to come at seven fifteen, just to be on the safe side." Lucy checked her phone, wondering if Cassandra Waters would be late.

Maggie had served a platter of cheese, fruit, and crackers and there was a bottle of wine and glasses on the oak cabinet nearby. No one was eating or drinking much tonight, anxious about the psychic reading, Lucy suspected. Though no one had admitted that.

"It does feel odd, sitting here, staring at each other. Let's knit while we wait. I don't think any spirits who are waiting to chat will mind." Dana put on her reading glasses and picked up her knitting bag.

"What are we watching for, exactly? Will she pull cards from her sleeve, or something like that?" Phoebe tugged a bright orange project from her bag. Lucy couldn't tell what it was it going to be; there were only a few rows done so far.

Phoebe had switched for the warmer months from marketing socks on her Crafty Cricket Web page to selling knitted bikinis. Lucy suspected she was a starting work on a new order—which would not take long, considering the garment's scant design.

"It's not exactly what the psychic does. It's what we do," Dana noted. "We'll be revealing information, usually without realizing it. And she'll give it back to us, and make it sound as if she's telling us something she shouldn't really know."

"I get it . . . I think." Phoebe turned to Lucy. "Do you?"

"She probably fishes around, tossing out scenarios that seem likely, and watches to see how you respond. Even a twitch of an eyebrow tells her something. Is that what you mean, Dana?" Lucy asked.

"That's it. Exactly." Dana nodded and started her knitting. "She'll read our facial expressions, our body language, even our breathing or eye movements. She'll also size up the way we're each dressed and which of us is wearing a wedding ring, that sort of thing. Then she works with those clues and drops some bait to see how we react."

"Speaking of bait, do we really have to wait until she leaves to eat dinner?" Suzanne had been digging steadily into the cheese and cracker platter. She'd skipped lunch again, Lucy guessed, and was ready to take a bite out of her knitting bag.

"I'm afraid so. I only had time for takeout. Sorry. There's some Chinese food in the kitchen, ready to go," Maggie said.

Suzanne sighed. "All right. I can make it. I just hope my stomach doesn't start growling. She might think it's angry spirits."

"Don't even go there." Phoebe was alarmed at the mere suggestion. A knock on the door quelled any more debate.

"That must be her, right on time." Maggie rose from her seat. "You'd better put your knitting away. I'm sure she wants us to concentrate."

The knitting needles, along with the wineglasses and cracker crumbs, were quickly cleared by the time Maggie returned with Cassandra Waters.

The psychic was dressed in the same long, flowing style that Lucy recalled from Sunday morning at the diner. But tonight's outfit was made from an even sheerer, shimmery fabric, a deep bluish purple that made her eyes look lavender blue, too.

A shawl, finely stitched with touches of mohair, was draped around her shoulders, like a lavender cloud, Lucy thought. Her dark hair and heavy eye makeup contrasted sharply with her pale white skin.

She wore the big crystal pendant again and the heavy ring, on the middle finger of her left hand, along with a placid, almost ethereal expression.

"I think you've met Suzanne, Dana, and Lucy," Maggie said, making the introductions. "This is my assistant, Phoebe," she added.

"Well, thank you all for inviting me here, to read for you. I already feel good energy in this room," Cassandra said, gazing around. "Have any of you worked with a psychic medium before?"

"No . . . none of us," Lucy replied, answering for all of them.

"Can you tell if there's any *bad* energy in the shop? Any angry spirits?" Phoebe asked quickly. "You're going to smoke them out with some sage and stuff, right?"

Cassandra smiled and opened her large handbag. "I will burn some sage if you want me to, and I always light a sacred candle," she added, setting a large candle in a heavy metal holder in the middle of the table. "I do feel good energy in this space. A lot of creative energy. Many people who otherwise have no outlet for their creativity and deepest expression of their soul come here and find that," she said, glancing at Maggie. "This shop is almost . . . a sacred space."

Lucy could see Maggie trying hard not to beam with pride. But Lucy could tell she wasn't buying it.

"We do hold classes here. The students seem very pleased. And productive," she replied.

"I feel that. You're doing good, sharing your gift. Good spirits are drawn to this place, and are helping you."

"Really? Like little guardian knitting angels, do you mean? What a nice thought." Maggie's tone was light. Not sarcastic, but almost. She took her seat, opposite Cassandra. Lucy and Phoebe sat on one long side of the table, while Suzanne and Dana sat on the other.

Cassandra reached into the bag again and pulled out a bunch of dried leaves tied together with string. She lit the candle first with a wooden match, then lit the bunch of leaves and walked slowly around the table, fanning the smoke up to the ceiling and down to the floor.

"I'm just clearing the energy. Nothing to be concerned about. Perhaps some of you are a little anxious about our meeting?" she suggested. "It's like static on a radio station. We won't be able to tune in clearly if I don't clear this off."

Edie had been right, it did smell like a bathing suit fell in a campfire. Lucy tried not to breathe too deeply while Suzanne coughed and covered her mouth with her hand.

"I'd better get a drink of water. Be back in a sec." Suzanne began to rise but Cassandra pressed her shoulder back into the chair.

"I'd rather you didn't right now. You'll break the circle. I just secured our auras."

Cassandra gave her a stern look and Suzanne made herself tiny in her chair. "Sorry. I didn't realize."

"That's all right." Cassandra's hand slipped gently from Suzanne's shoulder and she stood at the head of the table again. "Can we dim these lights a bit? It will be easier to concentrate."

"The switch is right behind you. It's a dimmer by the doorway," Maggie told her.

The light above the table was dimmed and then dimmed again. Darker than you'd set it for a dinner party, Lucy thought. Is that how she gets away with her tricks? Because you can't see what she's doing?

The candle glowed brighter and Lucy found herself focusing on the shimmering flame. She looked up at the faces of her friends, cast now in shadow.

"I'd like you to relax and clear your mind as best as you can. Focus on the candle and the sound of my voice," Cassandra instructed, her tone as smooth as silk. "Take in a deep breath and, very slowly, out again. Once more," she coaxed. Like a yoga instructor, Lucy thought. There was silence for a moment. All Lucy could hear was the sound of her friends, breathing in and out.

Then Suzanne yawned loudly. "Oh geez . . . sorry. It's been a long day."

Phoebe muffled a laugh, but Cassandra ignored the interruptions. "Put both of your hands out on the table, palms flat, spread your fingers, thumbs touching. Let's make a circle of our hands, that's right, just connect, pinky to pinky," she instructed.

Lucy and her friends all did the same, making a circle of their hands on the table. Lucy heard Phoebe muffle a giggle again and it nearly started her snickering, too. But she managed to keep a lid on it.

"Close your eyes and focus on your questions, the questions that have brought you to this place, this moment. It's no accident that you're here tonight, in this circle of energy, seeking answers. . . ."

Lucy thought of her questions. She couldn't help it, reminding herself at the same time that the woman was a total phony. Still, the questions rose in her mind's eye, like squadron jets in an air show, twisting and turning, looping across a clear blue sky. Skywriting in big, puffy letters: Will Matt ever propose? Do I have to force that stupid conversation? Will we ever get married? Have a baby? Live happily ever after?

Cassandra let out a long, noisy breath, and spoke with her eyes closed, her hands still stretched on the table.

"Spirit guides, spirit masters, spirits of our loved ones who have passed from this material realm, we gather seeking answers, seeking guidance to navigate this earthly plane. We are protected by the light of love and the circle of our auras from all lower entities."

At this phrase, Phoebe's head darted to one side; she stared at Lucy, looking nervous.

"We permit only positive, loving energy to come forth to speak with us," Cassandra continued. "Thank you, God. And so it is."

Lucy had snuck her eyes open already, but pretended they

had been closed just as the psychic sat back with a calm, satisfied smile. Another moment of silence passed.

"We're ready," Cassandra said finally. "I feel the presence. . . . Yes, they've joined us."

Phoebe gripped Lucy's forearm like a vise. "I thought there were only going to be cards?" she whispered.

Obviously, not quietly enough. "Yes . . . of course. You requested cards. I have them right here," Cassandra answered before Lucy could. "But cards are just a communication tool, like many others. Sometimes you speak to a friend on the phone and sometimes you send an e-mail, right?"

Phoebe nodded.

"It's the same with spirits. They speak to me through different modalities."

"Um . . . okay." Phoebe nodded. Lucy could tell she was still nervous.

"You can leave if you want, Phoebe. It's fine. You don't have to stay for the rest," Lucy whispered.

"Yes, Phoebe. It's fine. Please don't stay if this disturbs you," Maggie added.

"No . . . it's okay. I'll stay." Phoebe's tone was shaky but Lucy could see her curiosity had won out.

Cassandra took the thick deck of cards and shuffled several times, then passed it to Suzanne. "Why don't you start? Shuffle the cards a few times and think of your questions or concerns. When you're done, just set the deck down in front of you. I feel your energy," she added. "You have a powerful soul. A warrior's soul."

"Gee . . . thanks. I'm not exactly a pushover." Lucy could see Suzanne glow at the compliment—she did fancy herself as a tough cookie. With a heart of gold, of course.

Cassandra knew how to endear herself to her clients, didn't she? Lucy wondered what the psychic would say when her turn rolled around.

The room was silent and eerie in the shadowy light, the soft swishing sound of the cards like a bird's wing, gently flapping. Suzanne set the deck down and turned to the psychic.

"I'd like you to make three piles, facedown," Cassandra said. "They don't need to be even. Anyway you like."

Suzanne stared at the cards a moment, as if this was an important decision, then split the deck. She sat back and took a breath.

Cassandra smiled gently. "Don't be nervous. Even if I see a challenge, I'll explain it in the most positive light. There's a spiritual solution to every problem. And a new beginning in every ending. I want you all to remember that." Her soft voice reassured them as she flipped the top card of each pile.

Lucy had to admit, that wasn't bad advice at all. In general. She already expected to see a few challenges in her cards.

Suzanne leaned over to stare at the cards that were revealed.

Then she glanced at her friends. "I know zilch about the tarot . . . are those cards good or bad?"

Cassandra shook her head. "There's no such thing as good or bad. Think of it as information. It's your choice to take action on these messages, or not. There is no predetermined future for anyone, though we all have a path or goal our souls have chosen before our birth here on Earth."

Here on Earth? Were there any other planets to choose from? Lucy wondered. She decided it best not to ask. Cassandra was clearly in the card-reading zone now.

She picked up each card, puzzled over it a moment or two,

then pushed it to the center of the table. Then she flipped out a few more cards from each deck to make neat rows underneath.

Suddenly she pointed to the first card, a picture of three figures fighting in a field with wooden rods. Cassandra touched it with the tip of her index finger, her long lavender fingernail making a tapping sound.

"You're having some conflict at your workplace? Some . . . rivalry?" she asked Suzanne.

"Yes!" Suzanne sat up straight in her seat, as if struck by a cattle prod.

Cassandra did not react, her eyes on the cards. "The energy is very strong, masculine, I'd say. But it could be a woman with a strong personality. We all have both masculine and feminine energy," she explained.

True, Lucy thought. But that does get her off the hook from saying for sure if she sees a man or a woman, doesn't it?

"Perhaps there are two rivals? Or a boss and a colleague?"

"Well . . . I am in a situation like that. With another saleswoman. She stole two big sales from me this spring. I don't know what to do. I don't want to complain about her to our boss and sound like a crybaby."

"I can see that. . . . You're the strong, independent figure, on this side." Cassandra pointed again. "Your manager favors her? Is that right?" Cassandra glanced up at Suzanne to confirm this guess.

Suzanne shrugged. "Maybe . . . Walter, the broker, likes anyone who makes him money."

Oh brother . . . fish, fish, fish. Was Suzanne really going to fall for this? Cassandra already knew that she was in sales, from their conversation in the diner, and maybe had even learned more about all of them from Nora.

But Suzanne seemed to be eating it up. At this rate, she wouldn't have any appetite left for their Chinese takeout.

"I can see from the cards below . . . this man with the bags of gold at his feet," Cassandra explained, pointing out another card. "He's interested in his business flourishing, whatever the cost. His intentions are not good or bad. Just self-serving." She looked up at Suzanne. "He might promise to solve it. But he really doesn't want to."

"Ha! That's Walter, all over." Suzanne sat back and shook her head. "But what should I do? How can I keep her from poaching listings from me?"

Cassandra took a breath and focused on the cards again, turning a few more over in the next pile. "This second card, a man tending to rows of wheat. This is a card of patience. The harvest comes to those who wait and focus on their own endeavors. This is the card of what can be." She flipped over a few more cards in that pile and glanced at Suzanne again. "It appears this situation will clear of its own accord. If you focus on tending to your own rows, so to speak," she added with another small smile. "You have great things in store for you, real victories—coming in late summer, or early fall." She pointed to the last card Suzanne had turned over. A gladiator, riding a chariot with two wild-looking horses on the reins, one white and one black. "This is the chariot rider, returning from battle. He's victorious but still must control the two horses, all the divergent energies. You're a very busy woman, moving in many directions. Taking action on many fronts," Cassandra said, characterizing Suzanne perfectly as she flipped over more cards from that deck. "Just stay calm and keep things under control. You have the strength and will to be victorious."

"Wow . . . thank you." Suzanne definitely looked pleased.

"I guess I have more questions. About my kids, mainly. But maybe someone else should go."

"I'm game," Lucy piped up.

Under the table, Phoebe tugged Lucy's sleeve, her head subtly shaking. "Don't do it," she whispered.

Lucy glanced at her and winked. Most of her friends thought she was so gullible. But she'd always thought Suzanne was nobody's fool and she'd gotten sucked right in.

I'm going to show them that this Cassandra just plays you, works with what she observes, and then feeds back what you want to hear. I won't give her any clues at all, Lucy decided. *Then let's see what the cards say.*

The deck of cards was slid down the table. Lucy shuffled and split the deck into three piles, just like Suzanne had done.

Cassandra moved around the table and Maggie moved her chair aside to make a space. Lucy felt intimidated with the psychic hovering over her shoulder in the shadowy light. Her otherworldly expression and strange eyes seemed even spookier. But Lucy focused on the cards and held fast to her resolve.

"You're a bit tense. Just breathe, Lucy. Relax." Cassandra closed her eyes and took in a deep breath herself. Lucy did the same, her eyes open, though.

Cassandra studied the cards Lucy had turned faceup and nodded to herself with a small smile, as if acknowledging some private amusement.

"The Queen of Cups . . . fair and dreamy. Creative, sensitive, and gentle. Usually a water sign."

It was Phoebe who reacted with a loud gasp, turning quickly. "You *are* a water sign . . . Cancer the Crab. And she's an artist, too," Phoebe added.

Lucy sighed, mentally thanking her . . . not. So much for not giving anything away.

She glanced at Cassandra. "So that card is supposed to be me, the Queen?"

Cassandra nodded. "Yes, it is. You don't feel like a queen now, though. You are having some challenges in your kingdom. In your relationship sector."

Lucy forced a bland face, then realized she was trying to force it, maybe even sucking her lower lip.

Her friends shifted in their seats, too. Except for Dana, who sat perfectly still, her hands clasped in front of her as she observed, as if from behind a one-way mirror.

Hiding her own reaction was not as easy as Lucy had expected. At least she didn't reply, just glanced at Cassandra.

Cassandra looked at the next card. "Interesting . . . more cups. There's some challenge or obstacle you're facing in this relationship . . . maybe even a deception? This card, with the full moon and howling dogs . . . something is concealed. Things are not what they appear."

"That's often true," Lucy said quietly, feeling a little sting as that arrow hit its mark.

"This card sometimes brings the message of a clandestine relationship, or a secret. But it also signifies that the secret will soon come to light. The action is happening at night. But in the full light of day everything looks different." Cassandra turned, her blue gaze zeroing in on Lucy like a laser.

Lucy met her gaze a moment and looked away, feeling quite uncomfortable. She was determined not to react but could feel the color rising warmly in her cheeks. Her fair, dreamy cheeks, one might say.

She was facing an obstacle with Matt right now, wasn't she? Suzanne seemed to think so. She certainly hoped there was no deception and reminded herself not to react. At least not openly.

Matt was not deceiving her . . . was he? A clandestine relationship . . . did that mean an affair? Oh, he wasn't having an affair, that was for sure. But there might be a secret. Something concealed. They were happy together. But things were not as they seemed. He wasn't ready to get married and didn't even want to talk about it?

This is all baloney, Lucy. Don't get sucked in.

Cassandra flipped out a row of cards in the second pile. "There's a tall man . . . a suitable match. But some question hovers above. The Hanged Man. Indecision. Inability to take action."

Of course she'd guess that I'm involved with a tall man. I'm tall, right? And I'm not wearing any rings. Dead giveaway that I'm single.

But who can't take action . . . me or the "tall man"?

Lucy didn't want to ask the question; either choice would be disturbing.

But what in the world did it matter what Cassandra Waters predicted about her life? You're taking this much too seriously, she reminded herself. You promised that you wouldn't, remember?

Still, she couldn't help meeting Cassandra's gaze.

"What does that last card mean?" Lucy asked quietly, almost afraid to hear the answer.

It was a lonely-looking picture, a bit unsettling—a long, bleak figure wearing a hooded cloak and carrying a lantern.

"That's the Hermit. Isolation. The Hermit ponders important questions, searching with his lamp for answers. It could mean this question will be resolved . . . and you are alone." She glanced at Lucy, quickly turning more cards. "But the card could also signify a time of isolation and meditation is over and a resolution is about to be found. It could mean you should ready yourself to move out in public. Buy new clothes. Celebrate some event."

Lucy was about to reply, but Cassandra raised her hand. She closed her eyes and seemed to be listening to distant music . . . or distant voices. She quickly looked back at the table and turned more cards until she reached one that seemed satisfying.

"Here . . . that's what they said," she murmured to herself. She pointed to the last card she'd turned from the third deck. "This house with garlands and dancing women? There is a celebration in your near future, a gathering of friends and well-wishers. It will be in the summer. Very soon, most likely."

She looked back at Lucy, seeming satisfied she'd reached the right conclusion. Or the spirits had given her the full message? "Whatever this question is, it will be resolved. You will be at ease at this point, having decided your course."

Lucy nodded, but still didn't know what to make of that conclusion. Her birthday was coming, a likely date for a celebration. But she and Matt had not planned a big party, just a night in Boston at the theater and a good restaurant. Her friends had said they wanted to have a cake for her at a knitting meeting and give her gifts then.

Everybody goes to parties in the summer—do you need to be psychic to know that?

And everybody hopes that their questions will "soon be resolved."

Lucy sighed and looked back at Cassandra, who now stood beside Maggie, waiting for Lucy's response.

"Do you have any more questions?"

Lucy shook her head. "I'm good, thanks. That was . . . interesting," she added, feeling she should say something more.

She looked around the table, wondering who would go next.

Cassandra leaned over and gathered up the cards. She nodded, looking pleased and satisfied at the reading. If she sensed Lucy's doubt and suspicion, she gave no hint. She clearly had confidence in her powers. Another method that put her act over.

Lucy hoped her friends didn't jump all over this Queen of Cups thing now—but she doubted they'd be able to resist. She cringed, imagining future nicknames . . . Queenie, maybe? Cassandra had nailed her with that card, but it could have been the luck of the draw.

But it appeared that the psychic could quickly and deftly fashion an interpretation to any card that fit her eager listener, no matter which strange image rose to the top of the deck. That actually *was* a talent, Lucy reflected. Along with her considerable acting skills.

Maggie went next and after her, Dana. Phoebe decided to pass, having had enough contact with the spirit world from the sidelines. Lucy was not surprised.

Cassandra had already pegged Maggie. Her reading was fairly predictable, Lucy thought. The psychic focused on Maggie's creativity and how she shared her artistic talents with the world, but was not always a keen businesswoman. Lucy didn't think that was true, Maggie was very sharp at business. But always room for improvement there, right? And an issue the psychic might sense was a sensitive one. She also talked about past relationships, sniffing out Maggie's marriage to Bill, who she guessed had "passed to the other side."

Or had she done a little homework online or at the library and found Bill's obituary and local news of Maggie opening the shop a few years back and mentioned her recent widowhood?

The Internet had made it frighteningly easy to set yourself up as a psychic medium. Especially if you had good research skills.

Maggie's cards showed a new relationship, "a harmonious match." That had to be Charles, of course. But again, Cassandra could have gleaned this from gossip or talk between Edie and Nora. Or taken a guess.

Dana was clearly the hardest nut for Cassandra to crack. The only evidence of Dana's reaction: a tightening of her clasped hands, which she was soon conscious of and hid in her lap.

Dana's cards spoke about her "path" as a "healer" and the challenge of working with unstable energies. A card with twins, two faces—two sides of her personality, a public face and a private one.

All true, but easy to say about anyone—and Dana had told Cassandra she was a psychologist when they'd met at the diner, Lucy recalled.

Dana's final card pictured an acrobat, juggling two golden orbs in a balancing act. Once again, a card that would have suited just about any woman Lucy knew. But it did particularly fit their pal Dana.

Was this all just eerie coincidence, smooth and clever

improvisation? Or was it really messages from some other realm?

Lucy shook her head to clear the smoke and mirrors, remembering their promise to Edie.

Finally, Cassandra began to ease out of her trance. "I guess that's all for tonight. I'm feeling a bit drained. The connection is fading," she reported with regret.

Lucy glanced at her watch to see that precisely an hour had passed. The spirits were on a tight schedule, weren't they? Maybe they had a union.

"Thank you so much for inviting me." Cassandra gathered her cards and blew out the candle. As Maggie turned the lights up again, reality quickly set in.

Lucy walked Cassandra to the front of the shop and handed her a check in an envelope. "Thanks again for coming on such short notice. It was all very interesting," she added, which was true enough.

"Good night, Lucy. And don't worry. Things will work out for you. Eventually. You'll see." A misty summer rain had begun to fall. Cassandra drew her soft shawl around her shoulders and draped it over her head, in the exotic style of women in the Middle East.

Lucy didn't answer at first, annoyed that the psychic assumed her predictions had been correct and Lucy had good reason to worry. I am not worried . . . am I?

"Good night," was all Lucy managed to say. She watched from the doorway a moment as Cassandra darted out into the rain.

When Lucy returned to the back of the shop, she found her friends bustling around, quickly setting out plates and flatware on the table. Maggie emerged from the storeroom with a tray full of different dishes, and they were soon sipping won ton soup and passing around bowls of Chinese food.

And critiquing Cassandra's performance.

"She's good at stroking your ego with subtle compliments and flattering observations about your 'energy,'" Lucy observed.

"Very good," Dana agreed. "She had a wonderful knack for associating the pictures and symbols on the cards with the clues we gave her, just by our appearance and the little bit she knows about each of us. Even what she could tell from first impressions about our personalities."

"That's what she did to all of us," Lucy insisted. "It was so obvious after a while. I bet she has some set lines she pulls out of her hat, for the working-mom types and the thirty-something singletons, like yours truly."

"Lucy's right. And I wouldn't doubt she did a little research on a few of us," Suzanne added. "Maybe just by chatting up Nora after she met us at the diner? That would have been enough to help. She could have even googled our names. We all have a few bits of personal information floating out there on the Internet."

"Okay, I can buy all that," Phoebe agreed, picking through a pile of lo mein noodles on her dish. "But how did she know Lucy was a water sign?"

"That is a fair question, but she might have just taken a guess. She could have just tossed out water sign and if Lucy said it was something else, adjusted her reply," Dana suggested.

"Or maybe she did a little research and a copyright entry came up with my name on it. I do have a credit for illustrating a children's book. They put your birthday down in the copyright information . . . though I have no idea why everyone in the world needs to know that. Thank you, Library of Congress."

Maggie laughed at her dismay. "Oh, fear of turning thirty-five, rearing its ugly head again. You should be proud you have a copyright of something, Lucy. But she may have found the entry. That's very true."

"Well, folks, all I can say, is whatever she does, she's darned good at it. But I don't know that our observations really help Edie. We didn't really catch her at anything, did we?" Lucy glanced around at her friends.

"No . . . we didn't," Dana agreed. "It would be interesting, though, to write down all the predictions and see what really comes true, over the next few weeks or even months. Sort of an evidence journal, like an experiment."

"I like that idea. I'm going to do it," Lucy replied. "I do think once you try to write down what she actually predicted you'll find she didn't say anything that definitively. There was always some wiggle room. Some possibility of this . . . or that."

"Right . . . and that makes you want to see her again, and ask for clarification. Cha-ching." Suzanne added her cash register sound. "In my case, I already know that the Warrior Princess, yours truly, will conquer the Evil Marcy Devereaux, client-snatching Witch. But it's a comfort to know the universe is on my side."

Suzanne turned her attention to Lucy. "How about you, Queenie? How did you feel about Cassandra's predictions? I think the spirits pushed a few buttons."

"It was a lot of fishing. Matt and I are not facing any challenges," she insisted. "He's not even that tall. He's only five eleven."

Her friends didn't reply, just glanced at each other.

Maggie was the first to speak. She rose and cleared away some dirty dishes. "I'll talk to Edie and tell her how we think Cassandra manages her act. I'm not sure it will help her convince Nora to end her sessions. But maybe Edie will use what we've observed to confront Cassandra and ask her to leave Nora alone."

"That might be enough. Edie just wants to protect Nora," Dana said. "Not necessarily chase Cassandra out of town."

"True . . . though sooner or later, I think somebody will see through this game and get pretty angry about being taken for a fool." Lucy was happy to take out her knitting and forget all about Cassandra Waters. But it was harder than she'd expected.

She thought the evening would be an amusing lark. But the soulful, simpering Cassandra had gotten under her skin, as well as the eerie images of the tarot. Even chatting and knitting with her friends for a while after dinner didn't completely dispel her mood.

When she got home, she found Matt had gone up to bed early and was asleep with a book open on his chest, a memoir of a naturalist who stalked a wolf pack through the wildest regions of British Columbia for a full year. You had to love a guy who read books like that, didn't you?

Lucy lifted the book aside and turned out the light, relieved that she didn't have to answer Matt's questions about the session with Cassandra Waters right now. She was sure he'd have a lot of them.

She slipped into bed beside him, listening to the rain on the roof and windows, and the lonely sound of the wind rustling the trees. Images of the tarot cards filled her mind; was she really the dreamy Queen of Cups? Or the dreary Hermit?

Neither alter personality fit exactly, though a note of truth still echoed within.

Lucy turned to her side and plumped her pillow, willing herself to fall asleep. It would be easier to put a light, breezy spin on Cassandra's ponderous predictions tomorrow morning, in the full light of day.

Matt did not need to hear half of this.

Matt had to dash out early the next morning and didn't get around to asking about the reading until they were together again that night. The rain had cleared and they decided to bring dinner—and the dogs—to the beach. Not always a good combination, but the dogs loved the outing so much, it was hard to ignore their sad faces when they saw a picnic basket being packed.

"So, how was the fortune-teller last night? Should we buy a lottery ticket this weekend? . . . Mmm, this is good." Matt was in the midst of a thick sandwich Lucy had made with a few leftovers she'd found in the fridge, grilled vegetables and cheese and other odds and ends.

"It was . . . interesting. She did say a few things to each of us that seemed on target. But I still don't think she's really psychic," Lucy said. "There are so many ways to 'read' people and she's definitely very sharp and knows how to gain a person's trust."

Matt nodded thoughtfully. "Sort of sizes you up and lulls you in? Like a used car salesman?"

Lucy laughed. "A little more subtle than that . . . but yes, I guess that's her technique."

"So, what she'd say? I'd still like to hear some of it."

"Let's see. . . . She started with Suzanne, whom she called

a Warrior Princess. She guessed that there was an office rivalry. But with Suzanne's pushy personality, that was low-hanging fruit, right?"

Matt nodded and grinned. "Very true. Go on."

"She already knew that Dana is a psychologist and said she has to be careful of the dangerous energies of her clients . . . and that she has a public and private personality. She said Maggie was creative, but could improve her business skills. Oh, and the spirits were happy to see her sharing her gift with the world. Maggie looked very pleased to hear that."

Matt shrugged. "Who wouldn't be?"

Lucy laughed at him. "Now that I'm recapping all these pronouncements, it doesn't sound like very much. Does it? Her delivery adds a lot. She's very dramatic."

"Well, I'm not that impressed. I must admit. I could have dressed up in a turban and told you all that stuff for free."

"We'll take you up on that, honey. Next time," Lucy replied.

"What did she say about you?"

Lucy looked away from his curious gaze and focused instead on Tink, who sat calmly beside her, gnawing on a toy. "Oh . . . the usual stuff. She did see a tall man in my life," Lucy said, embellishing a bit. "Do you think she means you?"

She laughed at his reaction. "It better be. . . . What did she say about this tall, handsome guy?"

"She just said tall," Lucy corrected. "But a suitable match, I think."

"You think? You don't remember?" Matt was acting mildly insulted but she knew he was just teasing her.

"Yes, definitely suitable. I guess she said a few more nice things about the tall man, too," she added for good measure.

She picked up the other half of the sandwich; definitely a winning recipe, though she doubted she could ever reproduce the combination.

"This is good. . . . I don't even know what I put in here."

"Don't try to change the subject. What else did she say?"

Lucy wondered now how much she should tell Matt. Was this a good time to initiate that "No pressure . . . but what's up with our relationship, pal?" conversation that Suzanne had been encouraging?

Lucy wasn't sure. As good a time as any, she supposed.

"Let's see . . . first she told me I was a queen. Creative and dreamy."

"And beautiful," he added quickly.

"She did say that. I didn't want to brag." Lucy smiled at him, sipping a cold beer. "But she also said I was Hermit. Or even an upside-down hanging man . . . Or maybe you are? The tall, handsome man in my life, I mean. Hanging upside down."

Her explanation trailed off, treading in tricky territory now, she realized.

Matt glanced at her, still smiling, but his eyes squinting a bit with unease. "A Hermit? Or an upside man?"

Lucy nodded and took a breath. She said there's a question in our relationship. A challenge that needs to be resolved. Regarding our future. Our commitment? The words formed in Lucy's head, but she couldn't quite get them out. Tink had licked every possible tasty morsel from her toy and stuck her nose in Lucy's paper plate, investigating new possibilities.

Lucy snatched it away, but not before a pile of pita chips spilled over and the dogs both descended, like hungry gulls.

"Oh, dear . . . chips are bad, dogs. . . ."

Matt laughed. "Too late now. It won't hurt them."

True enough. She sighed, as big sandy paws tramped around the blanket and Matt's cell phone rang insistently as well.

He checked the number. "It's Claire," he said, mentioning his ex-wife. "I'd better take this. She was trying to reach me all day."

"Nothing wrong with Dara, I hope?"

Matt had an adorable nine-year-old daughter. Lucy had worried at first how Dara would feel about sharing her father. But she and Dara got along wonderfully, mainly because some part of Lucy had remained perennially ten years old. Everybody knew it. She loved to play kick ball, do crafts, bake cookies, and watch Harry Potter and Disney movies.

"No big deal. We still didn't sort out the camp thing and vacation time. I'd better talk to her."

Matt picked up the call and Lucy picked up the mess. The tide was going out very quickly now. Small tide pools reflected the fading sunlight and little children waded in the puddles, some trying to catch tiny crabs and fish trapped there. Lucy loved the beach at this time of night.

But the biting flies soon arrived. They loved dusk on the shoreline, too. Before too long, she and Matt ended up running to Matt's truck, blanket, basket, and dogs in tow.

When they got home, Matt had to call his ex-wife back and talk about Dara's summer plans in more detail. Lucy decided to take the dogs out since they'd missed a walk on the beach.

She wanted the exercise, too, feeling a little frustrated that she'd missed a good moment to have a serious talk with Matt. Maybe the spirits knew it wasn't the right time yet, she reasoned with a secret smile. Maybe they'll give me a sign when the perfect moment arises?

Lucy strolled the usual loop around her neighborhood, but when she came to the turn that headed home, she spotted a notoriously nasty shepherd mix approaching in the distance.

She quickly doubled back and turned her dogs down the nearest corner, Ivy Lane, glad for the escape route. Tink and Wally were normally gentle souls, but could morph into wolves of the wild when challenged. Lucy didn't feel like having her arms yanked out of their sockets, or even being knocked down.

The moon was full, shining bright and low above the trees and rooftops, casting the street in silvery shadows. Halfway down the block, she suddenly remembered, this was the street where Cassandra Waters lived.

She couldn't recall the house number, but it didn't take long to notice a small yellow cottage with a decorative flag hanging near the front door—a golden angel on a purple background. And as if there could be any doubt, a sign hung on a post halfway up the drive, CASSANDRA WATERS—PSYCHIC ADVISOR, with her phone number posted beneath.

The light was on in a front room and sheer white curtains were drawn tight over the window. But when she walked closer, the door opened. Lucy paused, holding her dogs back and stepping behind a tree.

She peered around and saw Cassandra in the doorway. She wore a long robe covered with flowers. Purple, her signature color. A man came outside and stood with his back toward the street as he spoke to Cassandra. He wore a baseball cap pulled low over his head, and sunglasses. Obviously keeping a low profile.

Cassandra's visitor suddenly turned and walked quickly across the lawn to the sidewalk, his back still turned toward

Lucy. Which she found most annoying. Lucy saw a van parked at the end of the street, in front of an empty, wooded stretch of property.

Cassandra watched her visitor depart for a moment, then shut the door. The van started up and drove down the street, headed Lucy's way. Just as it rolled by, she peeked around the tree and peered through the driver's-side window.

The driver had tossed his hat and glasses aside. Lucy could see very clearly that it was Richard Gordon, Nora's husband.

What was he doing here, skulking around, visiting Cassandra Waters? While she was dressed in just a bathrobe?

None of the possibilities that came to mind seemed entirely innocent.

Chapter Five

"I knew that she lived near me. Her address is on that card she gives out. But I didn't realize how close her house is. Until I was walking on Ivy Lane. Then I wasn't sure of the number, but she has a sign hanging near the front door, psychic advisor. Like a doctor or dentist."

"The neighbors must be loving that." Suzanne was clearly amused. "That knocks about ten thousand off your asking price. Maybe more."

Leave it to Suzanne to see everything through the lens of property values. Lucy hadn't even thought of it.

"I was just looking at the house and the front door opened. A man walked out and Cassandra stood there a minute, saying goodbye to him. I saw her lean forward and they got very close. She could have been talking to him, not wanting anyone to overhear. Or she may have kissed him. I'm not really sure. It was dark and his back was turned toward me. He also had his collar flipped up and wore a baseball cap and sunglasses," Lucy explained.

"Interesting," Dana said quietly. "Definitely flying under the radar."

"I wouldn't doubt Cassandra Waters has a few gentlemen callers in that category. She's very attractive, in a sinuous sort of way. Some guys really like that." Suzanne took a sip of iced tea and fanned herself with a pattern book that Dana was working from.

Lucy and Dana were wearing bathing suits, but Suzanne had dropped by on a break between appointments, and just had time to slip off her sandals and roll up her capris. It was Saturday, a busy day for her, especially in the summer.

Matt also had to work most of the day and Lucy had called Dana to see if she was up for a bike ride. Dana had persuaded her to come over and swim instead. "It's too hot to ride, we'll melt; and you'll use different muscle groups swimming," she reminded Lucy.

It was hot, and it didn't take much to persuade Lucy to grab her bathing suit and knitting and head over.

"Maybe she was telling him something. Like, 'Call me later, honey,'" Suzanne mused. "But it makes even more sense that she was kissing him goodbye, if she didn't have any clothes on."

"Suzanne, I did not say she wasn't wearing clothes. It was a kimono. Some people wear those over clothes . . . don't they?"

"Sure, bag ladies. They love a layered look. Actually, it's just the type of lingerie I'd expect a psychic to wear, lounging around the house. Or entertaining a male companion."

Dana ignored Suzanne's fashion analysis. "Did you get to see the man's face?"

"I couldn't at first. But he took his hat and glasses off after he got into his van—which, by the way, was parked about a mile down the street."

"Dead giveaway. That's how cheaters park when they visit a honey," Suzanne cut in.

"And I did see his face when he drove by." Lucy paused. Shards of sunlight reflecting off the clear blue water suddenly bothered her eyes. "It was Richard Gordon. Nora's husband," she said quietly.

"Richard? Are you sure?" Dana leaned forward on the chaise longue, her knitting slipping into her lap.

Lucy nodded.

"Wow . . . that's a bombshell." Suzanne sat back, fanning faster. "Now I understand why you're holding back on the kissing question. That is a game changer."

"Exactly. I'm just telling you . . . and Maggie, of course," she hastily added. "I don't want to start any gossip about him. I'm not even sure what I saw. Except that it was definitely Richard leaving her house. And looking like he didn't want anyone to know he'd been there."

"What time was this?" Dana asked.

Lucy shrugged. "I'm not sure. It was dark out, after nine I guess."

"That's late enough for me to be suspicious." Suzanne checked her phone and dabbed a bit of sunblock on her nose.

"Maybe he went there to pay for Nora's sessions. I bet Cassandra prefers cash." Lucy had given the question some thought last night and come up with a few—albeit slim—explanations that did not smear Richard's reputation as a loving, devoted spouse.

"I bet she prefers cash, too," Dana said. "Less to declare on her income tax. But then, why the disguise? Nora makes no secret of her relationship with Cassandra."

"Maybe he was having a session with Cassandra and felt embarrassed about it," Lucy offered. "It's one thing for Nora to advertise that she believes in a psychic. But maybe Richard likes everyone to think he's just humoring his wife and knows better."

Lucy picked up her knitting, the summer tote project that Maggie had showed them Thursday night.

"Oh, I think he was having a private session, but no tarot cards involved," Suzanne said decidedly. "That lame disguise and the car parked down the street? Come on, Lucy. Even you have to admit that MO has affair written all over it. Poor Nora. How weird is that? Your husband is running around with your psychic advisor? That's really twisted."

Suzanne picked up a carrot stick and chomped down noisily.

"That would be very sad. But we don't know anything like that has happened," Lucy quickly added.

"Lucy's right," Dana said. "Lots of people, especially men, would feel embarrassed to consult a psychic. Believe me, I get the same thing with patients feeling embarrassed about seeing a therapist." She laughed and glanced at Lucy again. "I don't think we know one way or the other what was going on there."

Suzanne shrugged and poured herself more tea. "Maybe you guys don't want to know." She suddenly sat up straight in the lounge chair and pulled her dark glasses down off her forehead. "Hey . . . wait. I just remembered something. It's just like that tarot card Cassandra pulled for you, Lucy—that really spooky-looking one with the big full moon and the two dogs, howling? And there were people in the background, doing something in secret at night, remember?"

"I do remember," Lucy said, though the card's eerie images and Cassandra's prediction had not come to mind until now.

"She said the card was about a secret about to be revealed. A clandestine relationship," Suzanne recalled. "I remember exactly . . . because it gave me the super-gooseflesh . . . which I am getting right now, guys. Even though you could fry an egg on the sidewalk today."

Suzanne held her arms out, showing off her reaction.

Lucy felt a creepy chill, too, though she wasn't nearly as dramatic about it. "I guess the connection didn't occur to me because I was trying to relate the card to some secret in my life," Lucy said. "But maybe I'm just the witness in the scene, and the card is really about Cassandra and Richard?"

Dana looked up from her knitting and met Lucy's glance. "You sound like you believe her now, in her powers to predict the future."

"No . . . not really." Lucy realized she'd been swept away in Suzanne's excitement. "But it is a strange coincidence."

Dana nodded. "Yes, it is. If you choose to interpret it that way."

They were all quiet a moment, even Suzanne. Then Lucy said, "I did think about Nora. Of course I would never tell her this. I don't want to gossip or make her suspect something that isn't true. But if turns out to be true and I didn't say anything . . . I guess I'd feel bad about that, too."

"It is a dilemma," Dana agreed. "Maybe you should ask Maggie. She knows Edie and Nora best."

Lucy thought that was a good suggestion and she certainly trusted Maggie's discretion.

"I think that's a good plan." Suzanne closed her eyes and tilted her head back. "Hanging out at your pool, Dana, is giving me a good idea. Why don't we all go away together for a night or two? It doesn't have to be very far. But we could have a total blast. Just lolling on the beach, knitting, and watching dumb movies . . ."

"Sounds like everything we do right now . . . except for the beach," Lucy replied, though she did like the idea. "What did you have in mind, a weekend on the Cape?"

"That's an idea. But I did hear of this great little beach house that rents by the week, out on Plum Island. Sleeps six, and it's right on the water. The tide is just lapping at your toes," she said.

Lucy loved Plum Island and sometimes wished she lived out there, except for the inconvenience in bad weather, when the road washed out. The tiny island, little more than a sandbar, was connected to the village by a small land bridge and some residents even traveled back and forth by boat.

Lucy and Matt drove out there often, whenever they felt a need for a change of scenery from the neighborhood beach. Once across the bridge, you felt as if you'd traveled some distance, to a desolate, remote spot, filled with funky beach shacks and long, empty stretches of shoreline.

"You've totally sold me. No need for a big pitch," Dana told her. "But can we find a weekend that we're all free?"

Suzanne had already pulled out her phone to check her calendar. "Let's see . . . I can do it the weekend of July eleventh. The kids will be at camp by then and I think Kevin is going on a fishing trip with his brother." She looked up, beaming with pleasure at the thought. "On second thought, I might just stay in the house alone all weekend."

"Hey, don't back out on us now," Dana said. "I'm definitely free that weekend. Jack is going to play golf with his brother down in Connecticut."

"Great. I'll let Maggie and Phoebe know," Suzanne said. "They can close the shop one day in the middle of the summer. Not exactly prime knitting weather."

"Only for the faithful. Like us," Dana said. "What about you, Lucy? What do you think?"

It was the weekend before her birthday, but she was sure they had no special plans. "I'd love to do it and I'm pretty sure I'm free. Matt won't mind. I think we were going to bring Dara up to camp in Maine that weekend. But she'll be with us for a few days before, so I'm sure he won't mind if I don't go."

"Perfect timing then." Dana slipped her glasses back on and picked up speed with her stitching.

Suzanne sat up and met Lucy's gaze straight on. "Speaking of Matt and former in-laws . . . how's it going with that birthday gift situation? Were you able to change the bicycle order yet?"

Lucy could not help but be amused by the way Suzanne had framed her question. And automatically assumed she really wanted to change her birthday gift from a bike to an engagement ring.

Which was not true.

But Lucy didn't want to get into that again.

"I'm working on it," she said honestly. Even her mere impulse to bring the subject up last night on the beach had to count for something.

Suzanne, however, did not look satisfied by that progress report. "'Almost' doesn't count, Lucy. Do you get paid if you *almost* turn in a project?"

Suzanne had a good point. "Of course not . . . but this is entirely different. You can hardly compare—"

"Yes, I can. No difference at all," she insisted. "You've got the weekend. Plenty of time. I expect a full report on Monday."

Dana laughed and stopped knitting. "I can't believe this conversation. Are you really giving her a deadline?"

"She needs one. She can rarely focus without it. Haven't you noticed?"

Before Dana could reply, Lucy jumped in to defend herself.

"That's not fair. Of course I can focus. I get all sorts of things done without a deadline." Lucy felt sure of that, though she could not think of a single one, offhand.

Dana glanced at Lucy, far more kindly than Suzanne did, but still seemed to agree. "A deadline does give structure. Even if you don't meet it."

Lucy didn't answer, feeling annoyed now at the both of them.

"Uh-oh, Queenie's lost that dreamy look," Suzanne murmured. She slipped on her sandals and rolled down her capris. "Sorry, Lucy. But you'll thank me for this later," Suzanne insisted as she grabbed her bag. "I'll let you know if the beach house is free. I hope you won't stay mad at me that long."

Lucy tried to act as if she would, but she couldn't help smiling at Suzanne's mock sad face as she waved goodbye and headed back to work.

"Suzanne gets carried away. Just ignore her," Dana said after a moment.

"I know. I'm totally ignoring her. She can't help herself sometimes," Lucy said.

"Good . . . ready for lunch?"

"In a minute. I'm just going to jump in the water and do a few laps." To cool off after getting so annoyed at our mutual, pesky friend, she might have added, though that detail was surely understood.

She had no intention of meeting this silly, arbitrary deadline. If she wanted to have a serious talk with Matt, she'd figure out when and how, entirely on her own.

No matter what her friends—or Cassandra Waters—thought she ought to do.

𝓜𝓸𝓷𝓭𝓪𝔂 𝓶𝓸𝓻𝓷𝓲𝓷𝓰 𝓪𝓻𝓻𝓲𝓿𝓮𝓭 and Lucy had not made any further progress in meeting Suzanne's silly deadline. If she bothers me about it, I'll just ignore her, or change the subject. Or needle *her* about some bête noir, Lucy decided. Suzanne's rivalry with Marcy Devereaux—that should distract her.

Armed with a plan, Lucy quickly pedaled the last few blocks to the shop, hunching down close to the handlebars as she sped up on the last stretch. She pulled into the driveway and skidded to a stop, gravel spraying in all directions.

"Goodness, you're a speed demon on those wheels now, aren't you?" Maggie was just coming up the walk with her purse and knitting bag and Lucy met her on the porch as she unlocked the door.

"That was a little daring," she admitted. "Nearly ended up in your garden." A small exaggeration. Very small, actually.

"Glad you didn't. For a few reasons." Maggie dropped her belongings on the counter and headed to the storeroom to make coffee, her usual routine.

"What do you think about that beach house idea? Can you do it that weekend?" Lucy asked, following her.

Suzanne had confirmed that the beach house was free the weekend of July 11, and Maggie and Phoebe had been in the e-mail loop, too, though Lucy had noticed only Phoebe's reply. She was definitely joining them, even if Maggie didn't give her the day off, Phoebe had claimed. Maggie had not answered yet.

"The house looks cute from the pictures, right on the beach," Maggie noted. "I'll have to move a class or two. But it won't kill me to close the store for one Saturday. It gets very quiet in here as the weather warms up."

Lucy knew that was true, though Maggie's work ethic was relentless. "And I'd hate to miss an outing with all of you. Who'll untangle your knitting messes?" She glanced at Lucy with a grin as she turned on the coffeemaker.

"Good point. We should cover your share of the rent for that service," Lucy mused.

Maggie was just about to measure spoonfuls of coffee but paused. "Do you really want hot coffee today? Maybe we should run across the street and get iced coffee at the Schooner?"

"Good idea. But I'll get it and bring it back. You have your flitting around to do. It's getting close to nine." She knew Maggie's routine well by now. She liked to roam around the shop, straightening the displays, checking the inventory, pulling out the necessary yarn and needles for her classes.

"'My flitting'? What does that mean?" Maggie wasn't really insulted but did look amused.

"Oh, you know . . . Skim milk, one sugar?" Lucy asked.

"Perfect. I'll just flit over to the counter and check the inventory, while I wait."

Satisfied by the reply, Lucy headed for the door, but it quickly flew open.

Suzanne ran in, brown eyes wide, her expression shocked. "Did you hear about Cassandra Waters? It's just awful. . . ."

Lucy and Maggie stared back at her. "What happened?" Lucy asked.

Suzanne took a breath, her expression grim. "Well . . . she's dead," Suzanne said flatly.

Lucy took in a sharp breath. She couldn't believe it. People were bound to gossip about someone like Cassandra Waters. Even contrive such extreme stories.

"Are you sure?"

Suzanne nodded bleakly. "I was just in your neighborhood, setting up a sign for a listing. I saw the police cars and I stopped to see what was going on. The husband of the woman who found her, one of Cassandra's neighbors, told me the whole story."

"Which is?" Maggie prompted her.

"This neighbor found Cassandra's dog wandering loose in her yard and went over to Cassandra's. When Cassandra didn't answer the door, she went around the back and looked in a window, to see if anyone was home. She saw Cassandra's body stretched out on the floor. In a back room where she gives private readings . . . *Gave* private readings, I should say," Suzanne corrected quietly. "She was already dead."

"Oh dear, that's terrible news," Maggie replied. "How did she die? Do they know yet?"

Suzanne swallowed hard, at a sudden loss for words. A rare moment, Lucy thought. "Oh yeah . . . it was pretty obvious. Someone had bashed her skull in with a huge rock, one of those geode crystal things that she wears around her neck? Except this one was the mother lode, about the size of a bowling ball," she added in a quieter voice. "They just dropped it next to her body. Like they wanted the police to find it—as if they were sending a message."

Was it a message? Or just the handiest, heaviest, deadliest object the killer could find in a fit of lethal passion?

Lucy had no idea about that, but could easily imagine the horrific scene, picturing Cassandra's body in a tangle of flowing purple fabric, spattered with blood.

"What a way to end a person's life. Who could do such a thing, face-to-face?"

"I'm sure she has some irate customers, who feel cheated. But you'd have to be enraged to lose it like that," Suzanne agreed.

"That's very true. But think of the very sensitive and intimate topics Cassandra was privy to," Maggie said. "A person's passionate response, positive or negative, would be relative to that."

"Good point. Maybe she gave someone advice and it didn't work out. To the point of ruining their life and they held her responsible." Lucy and her friends had not taken Cassandra very seriously. But she was certain some people did.

Nora Gordon, for one. But just as quickly as the thought popped into her mind, she brushed it aside.

Impossible. Nora is far too sweet and gentle. She just isn't capable of anything like that.

Suzanne dropped down in the wing-backed chair that faced the counter, clearly drained from her role of messenger of such unhappy news.

She looked up at Lucy. "Did you tell Maggie about Richard?"

"What about him?" Maggie asked curiously.

"I saw Richard leaving Cassandra's house on Friday night. He was trying to disguise himself with a baseball hat and glasses. But I saw his face when he drove past me. It was definitely him," she added.

"And? You left out the juicy stuff, Lucy," Suzanne said.

Lucy sighed, more reluctant than ever to convey the possibly salacious details. "Cassandra was wearing a kimono sort of thing. Was that all she was wearing? I don't know, I couldn't tell," she added, answering the obvious question. "And I saw her lean over very close to him, right before he walked away. Were they kissing goodbye? I don't know," she said, turning from Maggie to Suzanne. "All I know is that he was at her house and didn't want to be recognized."

"All right, fair enough. But I think you should tell the police. Let them figure out how innocent it was," Suzanne said quickly. "Don't you think, Maggie?"

Maggie sighed. "Considering Nora's devotion to Cassandra, I'm sure the police will question him, too. I think you should tell the police at some point, Lucy. When you're questioned," she added. "I think the police will want to talk to all of her clients. I'm sure that's at the top of their list."

"I was just thinking the same thing," Lucy replied.

Maggie nodded as she locked up the register, which she had unlocked just moments ago. She looked up at Suzanne and Lucy. "I'm just going to run over to the Schooner and see how Edie's doing. This is going to be a shock to her . . . and even more for Nora. Anyone want to join me?"

Suzanne stood up and checked her phone. "I wish I could. I have to get to the office for a sales meeting. I'm already late."

"I'll come with you," Lucy offered. She wasn't feeling any

work pressure today and had to admit she was curious to hear more about Cassandra's murder. As ghoulish as that seemed.

The usual morning rush filled the diner. There was a line at the takeout window and about half the tables and booths were filled. Edie was working behind the long counter. If she was distressed by the news of Cassandra Waters's death, she wasn't showing it.

Lucy and Maggie took seats at the end of the counter and Edie walked over to them. "Yes, I heard all about it," she said before they had even said hello. "Can I get you two anything?"

"Just iced coffee, Edie. We wanted to see how you were doing," Maggie said.

"Me? I'm fine . . . and I'm not at all surprised." She filled two tall glasses with ice. "Talk about your bad karma catching up, huh? Not that I believe in any of that bunk. But what goes around comes around. I do believe that's true."

"That's one way to look at it." A little harsh, Lucy thought. But Edie could be pragmatic.

"Karma, yes. Though the police will require a more specific explanation," Maggie added.

"They've got their work cut out for them. I'd bet you could line up her clients from here to the harbor . . . and half of them are pleased as punch to hear someone shut that woman up," Eddie asserted. "Think about it. She'd manage to weasel out a person's deepest, darkest secrets, before you even realized it. Claiming the spirit world wanted to help you solve your problems. And you paid her handsomely for the pleasure. Nice racket, right?"

Edie had gone to a private session with Cassandra, Lucy recalled. She sounded very cynical about the experience. But also as if she had found herself giving away some secret of her own?

"Probably true," Maggie agreed. She glanced at Lucy. "None of us were that forthcoming when she came to read cards, but I'll bet the regular clients, the true believers, poured their hearts out. Especially if a person kept going back. Cassandra was bound to learn about their private issues."

Edie shrugged. "My point exactly. She must have found out something she wasn't supposed to know. Or maybe she was trying to blackmail someone. I wouldn't have put that past her."

Edie served the iced coffees and Lucy took a sip. "I thought of that, too."

"It's no secret that I didn't like the woman. I didn't trust her. I wanted her to leave Nora alone . . . but not this way," she added, wiping a drop of coffee from the countertop. "Nora worshipped her. She'll be crushed. I'd hate to see Nora slip away from us again, back into her depression."

Edie's expression went soft with concern. She shook her head as if the worrisome possibility had already come true.

"Does Nora know yet?" Lucy asked.

"I spoke to Richard. He told me he was going to break it to her as gently as possible. The details are upsetting, though," Edie conceded. "It's not like the woman died peacefully in her sleep. I'd say someone was furious with her."

Edie straightened the sets of napkin holders and salt and pepper shakers in view, her thick, age-spotted hands trembling. Though Edie was acting very matter-of-fact about this news, Lucy thought that deep down, she was surprised and upset. More than she let on . . . and not just about Nora's reaction.

Edie suddenly looked up, staring at the door, her mouth hanging open. She quickly slipped out from behind the counter and Lucy and Maggie both spun around on their stools to see where she was heading so quickly.

Nora came through the door and Edie met her with open arms. Nora's face was tear-streaked, the front of her cotton blouse haphazardly buttoned. She stared at Edie and silently shook her head, then burst into heart-wrenching sobs.

Edie pulled her close against her pillowy body and patted her head. "I know. I know . . . It's a shock for you, honey. Just like that. Out of the blue," she said simply.

Nora nodded into her aunt's shoulder and slowly pulled away. Edie handed her a wad of napkins and she wiped her eyes.

"I'm sorry to make a scene here, Aunt Edie. I tried to call you but . . . I just can't believe it. I just saw her last night. Who could have done such a horrible thing to poor Cassandra? She was the kindest, most beautiful soul. . . ."

Lucy glanced at Maggie. A kind, beautiful soul? That was not the impression anyone in Lucy's circle had come away with. But Cassandra and Nora did share a special, deeper bond. One of codependence and exploitation, according to Edie.

But to Nora, their bond was clearly much more elevated than that.

Edie sighed, holding Nora's shoulders. She stared into her niece's eyes, trying to hold her attention. "I know it's hard for you. But you have to think of Dale now . . . and Richard. They both need you. We all need you. Please try to be strong."

Nora nodded. "I know."

Richard walked in the diner, looking relieved at the sight of his wife. "There you are . . . I didn't know where you'd gone." He glanced at Edie. "She scared me," he confessed.

"She's had a shock. But she's going to be all right. In time," Edie insisted.

She more or less transferred Nora to Richard's hold. He wound his arm around his wife's shoulder to take over comforting her, maybe even to keep her standing upright, Lucy realized. Nora looked dazed and unsteady on her feet.

"I've called Dr. Plesser. She can see you this afternoon. We'll close the shop and I'll drive you over."

Nora glanced at him and nodded. "All right. I guess I should see her. Though it won't be the same as talking to . . ."

She swallowed hard and shook her head, unable to say Cassandra's name, Lucy guessed.

"Of course not. But try not to think about that now, Nora," Richard said, coaxing her.

"I just feel so tired. I want to sleep," Nora murmured, almost talking to herself now.

Nora's son, wearing his busboy uniform, rushed up to his parents. "Mom, are you okay? Maybe I should get you a glass of water. Why don't you sit down?"

Dale looked frightened, Lucy thought. He'd gone through so much with the loss of his brother. A family crisis that was still not entirely passed. Lucy was sure he felt afraid that the drama was welling up all over again.

Nora touched his cheek. "I'm all right, Dale. Don't worry. I'm just sad," she said. She glanced at Richard. "I guess I'd like to go home and rest."

"Yes, of course. I'll take you home right now."

"I'll come by later to check on you, dear," Edie said to Nora as Richard led her away. "Call the doctor again, maybe she needs some pills," she added quietly, to Richard.

"Don't worry, I'll take good care of her," he promised, opening the heavy glass door to let Nora pass through.

Edie watched a moment then sighed. She turned back to Maggie and Lucy. "I've got to admit, I didn't think much of Richard when they first got together, way back when. I didn't think he was good enough for Nora. She could have her pick. But he's turned out to be a peach. He sticks by his wife, thick or thin. I'll say for that him."

Lucy nodded, biting down on her lip without realizing it. Maggie glanced at her, then back at Edie. Lucy had the feeling that Maggie felt burdened now, too, by the compromising sighting of Richard at Cassandra's house.

"We'd better go, too. If you need anything or just want to stop by and knit awhile, you know where to find me." Maggie gently patted Edie's arm as she passed by.

"I'll do that. And thank you, ladies," Edie added in an unusually meek tone, "for letting me vent. I know you won't tell Nora what I really thought of her idol, will you?"

"Of course not," Maggie assured her.

Lucy did not reply, her agreement understood. She smiled at Edie, then led the way to the door.

But even though Nora might never know how her aunt felt about Cassandra Waters, the police soon would. Lucy was fairly certain of that.

Then again, just as Edie had pointed out, there were probably many in Plum Harbor who held the same low opinion of Cassandra. If her killer was among her clients, the police would be working overtime to sift through the long list of possible suspects.

Lucy walked Maggie back to the shop and grabbed her bike.

With no customers in sight, Maggie lingered on the sidewalk. "Nora is taking it hard. Edie has good reason to be concerned," she said.

"Yes, she does," Lucy said. "Nora really depended on Cassandra." Lucy had not realized just how much until this morning. "She was Nora's lifeline. I didn't feel one way or the other about Cassandra, though I certainly didn't trust her. But even if she was a faker, maybe she did consider her profession a form of therapy for people like Nora. Or even entertainment, for customers like us? It's still awful that she was killed. She was so young. I think it's very sad."

"I feel bad, too. No matter what you thought of her—a phony baloney, or the real thing—no one should meet their end in such a violent way. I hope Cassandra's spirit is at peace," Maggie said sincerely.

Lucy felt the same. She adjusted the strap on her helmet, then looked back at Maggie. "I have to admit, it was hard to watch Richard and Nora. I feel even worse about seeing him at Cassandra's house the other night. It makes me feel so . . . responsible. As if I know this big secret. When the visit could have been perfectly innocent. My brain isn't set to 'auto-smear' like some people we know," she added quickly, meaning Suzanne. "But what if he *had* been fooling around with Cassandra? I don't think Nora would be able to stand that. She's already so fragile. I definitely don't want to be the one to topple their entire marriage. It looks like a balancing act already."

Maggie nodded, her gaze sympathetic. "I don't envy you. You're in a tough spot. But I do know it will do no good for anyone if you withhold this from the police. You have to trust that they won't damage the Gordons' marriage unnecessarily. If he was being unfaithful to Nora, well . . . it certainly isn't your fault. You can't worry about protecting him. Or Nora. We have to give the police their best shot at catching Cassandra's killer."

"Yes, I know." Lucy set her helmet squarely on her head and closed the clip under her chin, then glanced at Maggie with a small smile. "But can I ask you something totally random? When you and Charles went sailing last weekend, did he offer you any cold beverages . . . that looked like Kool-Aid?"

Maggie looked confused a moment, then smiled and tapped Lucy's helmet with her knuckles. "No, he did not. And that was pretty fresh, *Queenie*."

"Just sayin'." Lucy shrugged and swung up on the bike, pausing to wave goodbye as she pedaled away.

Secretly, Lucy was sure that her good friend had been as surprised as anyone to hear herself touting the official line about cooperating with the police, "letting them do their job . . . blah-blah-blah . . ."

Jimmy Hubbard was one thing, poor fellow. No one had known him very well, and his death, though violent and a bit of a shock around town, had not been all that interesting. Most likely it was just what it appeared to be, a robbery that had gotten out of hand. Even the local newspaper and TV stations grew bored with the event very quickly.

But Cassandra Waters, a professed psychic, whom they had met with only days ago and who had been such an important figure in the lives of people they knew well . . .

That was another box of crackers entirely, as Edie might say.

Not taking anything away from Maggie's powers of self-discipline, Lucy doubted Maggie would be able to keep her promise and avoid poking around in this investigation.

Lucy hoped so, anyway. She and the rest of her friends had no such scruples and she knew it would be hard to avoid speculating and even sniffing around the Internet.

In fact, once she got back in her office, she decided to do an online search on Cassandra and see what came up. The inspiration gave her a sudden jolt of energy as she pedaled hard to climb back up the dreaded hill on Main Street.

No pain, no gain, she reminded herself.

Chapter Six

aggie had expected to hear from Charles at some point in the day, but his visit to the shop surprised her. It wasn't even lunchtime, though it might have been for him, she realized. He sometimes started a shift at 6 a.m.

She was standing by the counter and met his gaze as he walked in. He looked around, concerned about interrupting her with customers. He was very considerate that way.

"The coast is clear," she said with a smile. "There was a class this morning but they're all gone and it's too nice outside for much traffic today, I think."

"I guess that's to be expected, when you've got sort of a seasonal business?"

"Yes, it is," she said. "Unlike your line of work. Now the police have two murders to investigate."

"You heard about Cassandra Waters."

Maggie shrugged. "It was all over town by nine this morning. Suzanne happened to be on Ivy Street and saw the police cars and even spoke to the neighbors."

"So you know the full story already. As usual," he teased her.

"I wouldn't call it the full story. But a few of the gruesome details. Suzanne just happened to catch the husband of the woman who found the body. A neighbor who had been returning Cassandra's dog . . . or something like that."

She shrugged again, acting nonchalant and playing down her interest.

Charles saw right through her. She could tell instantly by the way his eyes crinkled at the corners, suppressing a laugh.

"Something like that," he echoed.

"Would you like a cold drink? Iced tea, or cold water?"

"Sounds great. Yes, I would."

He followed her to the back of the store and watched while she rummaged around the storeroom. He leaned on the counter and smiled at her.

Charles wore a suit or at least a sport coat and tie, no matter the weather. He looked very handsome in a jacket and tie, too, she'd always thought. Perhaps it was the department dress code for detectives on duty, but Maggie had a feeling he would have dressed up anyway. He didn't even look uncomfortable, or bedraggled by the heat, though he did slip his jacket off and neatly drape it on the back of a chair when they stepped back out to the worktable.

Maggie handed him a glass of iced tea and took a seat nearby.

"Are you on this case?" she asked quietly.

He nodded. "Yes, I am."

"We had her here Thursday night. For a reading. Cassandra, I mean," Maggie reminded him.

"Right. You mentioned that she was coming." Charles nodded, still smiling at her. "We'll be talking to everyone who's met with her since she came to town. She kept records. They look very complete."

"Records of appointments, you mean?" Maggie suddenly wondered if he meant notes on the people Cassandra met with, research she did before the meeting in order to sound clairvoyant.

Charles nodded again. "That's right, her appointments. What did you think I meant?"

"Oh, I don't know. Maybe she kept notes about her clients. She must have done a little research before appointments when she could. Just to sound like she was really tuning to the spirit messages."

"So you don't believe she was really psychic?" Charles seemed amused. He squeezed the slice of lemon on the top of his tea and took a long sip.

"Of course not . . . do you?" Maggie stared at him, sure he must be teasing now.

He sighed and set his glass down. "I don't believe in that sort of thing. Though a lot of people do. Her profession does complicate the situation."

"I'd think so." Maggie paused, wondering what questions she could ask.

She'd found out the hard way there was a fine line between interest in Charles's job and being a pesky snoop in police investigations. She'd crossed that line a few times too many . . . with unhappy consequences.

"Do you think her murder is related to Jimmy Hubbard's death?"

Charles shook his head. "Not likely. Of course, we have to consider that possibility. We're looking at her client list first. But I'm sure you already guessed that."

"Yes . . . I did."

He waited a moment, wondering how freely he should talk about the case with her, Maggie suspected. But she was going to be officially interviewed and he was investigating the event. And he had already admired, many times in fact, her amazing powers of observation and memory. What else would a detective want in a witness . . . or a girlfriend, she secretly assured herself.

"What did you think? Aside from suspecting she was a fraud? Do you know any reason why someone would want to kill Cassandra Waters? Have you heard any gossip?" he added, more to the point.

Maggie set her tea down, the ice cubes tinkling against the glass. "No . . . not really."

Charles smiled. "What does 'not really' mean?"

"The way she was killed . . . someone must have been very angry with her, very upset. Disappointed or feeling betrayed, perhaps? If you plan to kill someone, you don't just grab the first heavy object in the room and bash their head in. You find a more methodical, premeditated method. A gun maybe, or even poison. But of course, you know that," she added quickly.

He nodded. "Do you know of anyone who might have been angry at Cassandra Waters?"

Maggie shook her head. "The only person I know of who met with Cassandra on a regular basis truly idolized her. Believed in her powers totally. She's very distraught over Cassandra's death."

Charles lifted his chin, his brows drawn together—his alert look, Maggie secretly called it. "And who is that?"

"Nora Gordon. She owns the Gilded Age Antique Shop, down the street. I'm not telling you anything you won't find out quickly, or maybe already know," Maggie added. "You'll see from the appointment list that Nora visited Cassandra several times a week. And I'm sure Nora will tell anyone who asks her, how she felt about the psychic—absolutely devoted. She called Cassandra a beautiful soul and believed that she was channeling messages from her son Kyle. The boy died in his sleep about two years ago, from a brain hemorrhage. He was a senior in high school, just eighteen years old."

Charles pursed his lips. "That's rough. I can understand how she got drawn in. But this Cassandra wasn't such a sweetheart, was she, to take advantage of a grieving mother?"

Maggie shook her head. "No, she was not. Although Edie Steiber, who's Nora's aunt, says that Nora was so depressed before she met Cassandra, she would hardly get out of bed. Her husband was afraid to leave her alone, afraid she might harm herself. The 'messages'—if that's what you want to call them—were like therapy for her. The only kind that seemed to do her any good."

"I get it. Complicated. This phony psychic did some good while lining her pocket."

Charles had an amazing way of boiling matters down to the bone. It was really a gift. "Exactly. A conundrum, you might say."

"*You* might say. Though I would be laughed out of the station house if I used that in a report. I'll save it for Scrabble," he said.

"Thanks for the warning." Maggie laughed.

Charles liked to play Scrabble on his boat. He had a special set with ridges around the boxes on the board, so the tiles stayed in place if the sailing got rocky.

When the water got rough, she couldn't focus on the board anyway. But they'd had fun.

114 / Anne Canadeo

"Any good Cassandra did was an unexpected by-product of her tricks. I don't think that sort of do-gooding counts."

"Probably not," Maggie conceded. "If there really is anything 'out there' or 'up there' that eventually holds us to account."

"No one ever came back to say for sure. No matter what people like Cassandra Waters claim." Charles drained his glass, set it down, and smiled. "I'd better get back to the office. Probably a million calls coming in on this one."

"No doubt." And he'd be working late or even double shifts, until Cassandra Waters's killer was found. Maggie knew by now. "Don't worry about Wednesday; we'll figure something out," she said, following him to the door.

Wednesday night had become their midweek date night as the relationship had advanced. Maggie knew she would miss him. She had planned a special dinner, too. It was funny how she'd been so adept at living alone when they'd met, satisfied most of the time with her own company. And now, one canceled night together seemed a big hole in her week.

"I'll be in touch. It may not take us long to find the guilty party."

"You sound very confident. I guess you have a good lead or two." She was fishing a bit. Sheer reflex. She had to get a grip on that. She hoped he hadn't noticed.

"Oh, we do. Ruiz went to the toy store and bought a Ouija board. We're going to give it a full interrogation after lunch."

He dropped a quick kiss on her forehead and slung his jacket over his shoulder. Maggie, still smiling at the silly joke, watched from the window as he walked down to the street.

She saw Charles pass Phoebe on the path and tip his head hello. Phoebe bobbed her head back but kept walking. She liked him well enough, Maggie thought, but didn't like that he was a police officer. Phoebe did have a thing about authority figures, and the experience of being a person of interest in a case a few months ago, when her best friend from school disappeared without a trace, was still fresh in her memory.

"I guess Charles came to talk about Cassandra Waters— and make sure you are not sticking your nose in his case again." Dressed for the hot weather in a long gauzy skirt, tiny tank top, and rubber flip-flops, Phoebe slid behind the counter and set down a cup of frozen yogurt, which was covered with strawberries and granola.

Maggie thought the food choice was just an excuse to eat dessert instead of a real lunch, but Phoebe claimed it was perfectly nutritious. Maggie didn't argue; her assistant could certainly use some flesh on her bones. The ceiling fan turned on high was likely to lift her right out of her seat.

"We did talk about Cassandra. But he didn't mention a word about my nose. Do you have to eat that messy thing at the counter? It's going to drip on something."

"Oh right . . . sorry. I just wanted to get back in time. So you can go out if you want to," she explained, retreating to the table in back.

"Thanks, but I'm in no rush." Maggie did want to check on Edie but knew the diner was packed right now and Edie would be too busy to chat.

She also expected a uniformed officer to drop by at some point to ask questions about Cassandra, and she didn't want Phoebe to deal with that situation alone. "He said some officers would be coming by to take statements. They're talking to everyone who had sessions with Cassandra. We expected that," she reminded Phoebe.

Phoebe was twisting herself in a pretzel shape in the chair, still spooning up her yogurt. "Yes . . . I know. But I hardly said a word to her. I just sat there and listened. I don't really have anything to say to the police."

"Just tell them that. We'll all back you up. Your interview will be short and sweet."

"Not so sweet . . . all things considered," Phoebe murmured. Maggie knew what she meant. Cassandra was dead. Still hard to believe.

Maggie stood at the counter and leafed through a new pattern book. It was only late June and the fall patterns were already coming out. She would be ordering her fall and winter stock soon.

Something to look forward to.

"Do you think Cassandra will come back and haunt her killer?"

Maggie's head popped up; she stared at Phoebe over her reading glasses. "You have an amazing imagination, Phoebe. You ought to write novels, or movie scripts, or something. Not that your knitting patterns aren't wonderful, too."

"I'm serious." Phoebe had finished her lunch and wiped her mouth on a napkin, then dumped the drippy container in the trash bin near the stockroom. "She knew all about that realm. She knew how spirits operate. How they get in touch with living people. I think she could do it."

Maggie laughed and shook her head, setting the pattern book aside. "You have a point. I never thought of it like that. I just hope she doesn't appear in the shop and ask us to help her bring her murderer to justice. Now that would be a spooky plot for a story, don't you think?"

Phoebe froze in place. She stared at Maggie, bug-eyed. "Don't even say that. Now you really scared me."

"I'm sorry . . . you started it." Had she really said that incredibly childish thing? Maggie was appalled at herself. But Phoebe didn't seem to notice.

She really hadn't meant to frighten her assistant. She'd forgotten the poor girl spooked so easily.

"I'm so sorry, Phoebe. I was only making a joke. That could never, ever, *possibly* happen in a million years. You know that, don't you?"

Phoebe clearly did not; her gaze remained locked with Maggie's, her cheeks pale. Finally, she swallowed hard and took a breath.

"I hope not."

"Absolutely not. As in never *ever,*" Maggie said, relieved to see some color return to Phoebe's complexion.

But before Maggie could offer any more assurances, a basket of yarn flew off the top of the oak cabinet and bounced on the table, balls of lavender mohair unraveling in all directions.

Phoebe screamed and covered her head with her hands. "OMG! She's here. . . . It's Cassandra. . . . She heard us."

Maggie's heart skipped a beat. She forced herself to look up at the top of the cabinet, staring at the empty spot left by the basket.

Then she shook her head and nearly laughed out loud. "Don't worry. Cassandra is not back. Unless she's returned as a cat. But I think we know this one."

Phoebe looked up, too. "Van Gogh . . . bad cat. You nearly gave me a heart attack."

Phoebe's unmistakable, tattered alley cat had been strolling daintily along the top of the cabinet, but now stopped in his tracks and sat, peering down with vague interest, though not the least bit impressed by Phoebe's scolding. Phoebe looked back at Maggie.

"I'm sorry, Mag. He snuck out today. I didn't even realize it."

"That's all right. I'm happy to see him. This time," she said. She laughed and headed to the front of the store; a customer had come in.

"I think there's some tuna in the fridge. Just get him up-stairs again," she whispered, "before anyone with an allergy comes in?"

Maggie's one firm rule was no cat in the shop; Phoebe could keep him provided he stayed in her apartment. But Van Gogh was certainly a welcome sight downstairs today, considering the possible alternatives.

Lucy had intended to search the Internet for tidbits about Cassandra as soon she got home, but a note with attached files from a new client, Bleckman Paper Products, had appreared in her in-box. She'd been hired to design their company directory, an extremely mundane project. But it paid well. Checking the files and formatting the document was her first priority.

But, quickly bored with the work, Lucy decided to take a break and poke around the Internet for information about Cassandra Waters.

She typed in a search to find several references to that name in Cape Ann—a child psychologist in Newburyport, an insurance broker in Rockport, and an exotic dancer (at least that's what she called herself) available for bachelor parties and private performances.

None of those photos matched the Cassandra Waters she had known, though she did come across two online listings for the psychic's services, the text a verbatim copy of her advertising card. There was also a fluff piece about her in the Lifestyle section of the *Plum Harbor Times*, dated a few months back, when she'd come to town, buffed up her crystal ball, and set up shop on Ivy Lane.

Lucy had hoped for more and felt frustrated enough to request a simple search of the psychic's name on a background check website, at the cost of a mere ten dollars. Only to receive the two bits of information she'd already found, spit back at her.

She returned to designing the directory, which included photos of all the employees. Staring at names, titles, and phone numbers inspired her to try the reverse look-up site.

She found the window and tapped in Cassandra's phone number, then the cell phone service was quickly located—a red dot on a map of Plum Harbor. When Lucy paid the fee to receive more information on the user—under ten dollars, which seemed worth it—she found the service was billed to someone named Jane Mullens. Lucy wondered if she'd made some mistake with the street name or house number.

But of course, Cassandra Waters was an alias . . . Duh.

Otherwise, what luck to have been given the perfect name for a psychic and then turn out to be one. Unless Cassandra's mother had been graced with the powers of predicting the future as well?

Lucy's fingers itched to turn her considerable research skills on Jane Mullens. But she heard the thunder of dog paws downstairs. Tink and Wally, galloping to the front door to greet Matt with happy barks and whines as he walked in from work.

Matt called up to her from the foyer. "I'm home, Lu. It's so nice out. Want to take the dogs to the beach?"

Lucy went to the top of the stairs and peered down at him. "I had the same idea. I'll just change my clothes."

The hot day had cooled off, and it would be cooler still on the beach once the sun went down. Lucy was ready to get some circulation back in her legs. The background check of Ms. Mullens—aka Cassandra Waters—would have to wait.

As she tugged on her running sneakers and a sweatshirt, she guessed the police had already unearthed this choice tidbit about Cassandra's real name. Probably their first order of business was a check to see if the victim had any criminal record or other identities.

Still, it didn't hurt to have some interesting information to report at the next knitting meeting. Even if Dana arrived with something juicier—passed on from Jack—stashed in her knitting bag, too.

"Did the police get in touch yet, about an interview?" Lucy asked Maggie.

"Not yet. How about you?"

"Someone left a message on the home phone last night, while we were out. I'm supposed to call back before noon."

Lucy felt a little nervous about the interview. But she was sure Maggie had already guessed that and knew why.

She sat on the porch steps in front of the shop, watching Maggie hover over the flower boxes with a watering can, occasionally picking off a shriveled bloom or two. The sun was still low in the sky but it promised to be another hot, sunny day. She was glad she'd gotten her bike ride in early, but did not look forward to pedaling back to the cottage.

Lucy did not know much about gardening but had learned from Maggie it was important to dead-head the flowering plants—pick off the spent blooms—so they would make more flowers even faster. Maggie's petunias flourished, no matter the scalding weather. She clearly knew something about it.

"Charles stopped by yesterday for a few minutes. He asked me some questions, nothing too intense. I told him what I thought might help. I don't think you could count that as an official interview."

Maggie set down the can and straightened up, rubbing the bottom of her back with one hand. "I guess we're not high on the list."

"Guess not. I wonder if they have any ideas yet. It's barely twenty-four hours since the body was found."

"They don't have a clue," Dana said, coming up the walk. Lucy hadn't even noticed her there. "Well, maybe a clue. But no solid leads yet. Not that Jack has heard of."

"Did the police contact you yet?" Maggie asked.

"Nope, not yet." Dana carefully stepped around Lucy and gently patted her head hello. "You went riding without me."

"I was going to call you, but figured sweaty spandex was not ideal attire for appointments with patients."

"Very true. We'll go out this weekend, though, okay?"

"Absolutely."

Dana smiled. She chose a wicker chair in the shade and took her knitting out. "What's up, ladies? Are we chatting about the Cassandra Waters case yet?"

"Not yet," Lucy said, "but since you mentioned it, the police left a message for me last night. They would like me to call back before noon, for an interview."

"We knew they'd probably call soon," Maggie said. "I didn't hear from anyone yet, though. Did you, Dana?"

Dana shook her head. "Maybe they called Lucy first because her name begins with *B*? Alphabetical order?"

"Or because I booked the appointment with Cassandra?" Lucy said.

"That could be." Maggie nodded. "I guess they'll catch up with the rest of us soon enough."

"I found out something about Cassandra yesterday. I guess I'll tell the police later." Lucy's friends both turned to look at her. "I think her real name is Jane Mullens."

"Good work. Jack thought her name was an obvious alias, but he didn't hear that yet." Dana turned back to her knitting; she was also making a tote, but on a smaller scale, beige nubby yarn with brown stripes. Neutral tones that would harmonize with most of Dana's wardrobe, Lucy noticed. "I think we all had the feeling that Cassandra Waters was a stage name, so to speak."

"It definitely sets the right tone for her work. Much better than Plain Jane. And the Mullens part . . . well, that doesn't sound psychic at all," Lucy said.

"True. But how did you find her real name?" Maggie tugged off her gloves and sat in a chair near Dana.

Lucy explained about the reverse look-up site, where she'd typed in Cassandra's address.

"I'm assuming it was her service. She's the only person who lived at that address, right? I guess it's possible that the last person who lived there was named Mullens and never changed the address on her account," she added. "But I'm going to run a check of that name and see if I can find a photo."

"You could freelance for private detective agencies now, too, if you get bored with your usual projects," Maggie suggested.

"I'm thinking about it," Lucy said.

"You're keeping pretty good pace with the police depart-ment," Dana said. "Though they have the advantage of all her client lists and investigation software that just spits this stuff out. I do wonder why they didn't call us yet. You'd think they'd check on the clients she'd seen closest to her death."

"We were pretty close . . . but Nora was probably the last to see her. She had a session on Sunday night," Maggie re-called. "She said so in the diner. Remember, Lucy?"

"Yes, I do. She didn't say what time it was," Lucy said. "So maybe she wasn't the very last. But I bet the police spoke to her by now. She was such a frequent visitor with Cassandra."

"Yes, they must have," Dana agreed.

"I'm sort of dreading my interview. I still feel uneasy about telling them that I saw Richard Gordon leaving Cassandra's house Friday night."

"You have to tell them. It could come back to bite you later. No need for that." Dana's tone wasn't scolding, just matter-of-fact.

"Yes, I know." Lucy glanced at Maggie. They'd been through this the other day.

"They may have already spoken to both Nora and Richard and he may have told them himself he was there on Friday night," Maggie reminded them.

"I thought of that, too." Lucy nodded. "I just feel like if he didn't, it's sort of a bombshell. I just don't want to get him into any trouble. . . . I'd feel so responsible."

"I understand," Dana said. "But if he was up to something, he's the only one who can be held to account for his actions. Not you. Not in any way."

"And now the police have two murders to figure out. They need all the help they can get," Maggie said.

"Yes, they must be overwhelmed with this case, on top of Jimmy Hubbard. Did Charles mention any progress with that?" Lucy asked Maggie.

"Only that the police have no idea yet if the two murders are connected. They're hoping Cassandra's client list lends a clue in that direction."

Dana suddenly looked up from her knitting. "I did hear something more about Jimmy. Turns out he went to jail for possession of narcotics and intent to sell. He was found guilty and sentenced to fifteen years. But he gave testimony in another case not too long ago, and got out early."

"Jimmy Hubbard? The guy who made balloon animals at kid's birthday parties? A drug dealer?" Lucy could not get her mind around the revelation.

"He went to jail for that offense. But that doesn't mean he was dealing drugs around here," Maggie reminded them. She suddenly looked over at Dana. "Was he?"

Dana nodded and picked off a thread from the bottom of her project. "They searched the theater soon after he died and found bags of meth in a film canister, hidden in the projection room."

"I saw the police going in and out for a few days," Maggie recalled. "I didn't think much of it."

"Why wasn't any of this in the newspaper, or on the local news?" Lucy asked.

"They want to keep this line of the investigation quiet. They still haven't abandoned the possibility of some former criminal connection tracking Jimmy down. For one thing, he did supply testimony that put other guys behind bars," Dana reminded them.

Maggie looked shocked. "He seemed so nice. I don't

know . . . gray and bland? A shy man. No hardened criminal, I'd say. But that must have been an act. Or maybe he had a split personality?"

Dana shrugged. "It could have been an act. Or he may have just been a bland, shy drug dealer. An amoral, criminal personality who was good at compartmentalizing and found a way to be a nice guy by day and make easy money by night. Or whenever opportunity presented itself."

Dana looked down at her knitting and shook her head. She looked sincerely upset by the subject. "I see so many adolescent patients with addiction issues, even in this town. Which we all know couldn't be a nicer, more wholesome environment. The families are torn apart. Our boys are grown now, thank goodness. But I worried all the time about them navigating that high school quicksand. I don't know if any kid is really immune."

"I've seen it myself at the high school. The art room draws those troubled, out-of-sync types who are often at risk," Maggie said. "It's such a waste. Kids just don't realize what they're getting into. Even with all the drug education now in the schools."

Maggie sighed and offered her friends more cold water from an icy pitcher out on the porch.

Dana took a glass and sipped quickly. "This tastes good. Nothing like cold water on a hot day. The simple pleasures of life are always the best."

She set the glass down and carefully rolled up her knitting, then slipped it into her tote. "Maybe the police will never call the rest of us for interviews. Maybe the investigation is already focusing on a hot lead. They've been pretty tight-lipped about Jimmy all this time."

"Speaking of tight-lipped . . ." Lucy turned to Maggie. "I'm sure Charles hasn't told you anything about either case."

"You know Charles. He's an original Sphinx."

The image of Charles's face superimposed on the Egyptian icon made Lucy smile. "I hope you don't feel uneasy talking about Cassandra with us. I don't want you to have another argument with him because we can't stop gossiping."

"Trying to prevent gossip in a knitting shop is like . . . well, trying to prevent people from salivating in a bakery. It's pure reflex. The autonomic nervous system and all that, right Dana?" Dana nodded and smiled as Maggie glanced her way. "No way could I ever control that. Charles can't possibly expect me to, either."

Dana laughed. "You're right, Maggie. Knitting and tongue-wagging go together like peanut butter and jelly."

"More like wine and cheese, in our case," Lucy noted.

Maggie laughed. "Very true. All I can control is my own behavior. Such as, no Internet searches for alias names or criminal records. Not that I'd be able to manage such a thing anyway," she added, laughing at her own lack of tech savvy. "Gossip away, my friends. Don't hold back on my account."

"Good to know. But I've had my daily dose for today. Time to go up to the office," Dana said.

"Me, too." Lucy stood up and put her bike helmet on. "Time to get back to the thrilling employee phone directory for Bleckman Paper Products."

"Which I hope isn't so taxing that you have no energy left for more Internet investigation." Dana prodded with a sly smile. "Maybe you'll find something juicy to relate about Cassandra on Thursday night?" Dana asked as they walked down to the sidewalk together.

"Maybe." Lucy thought she might but didn't want to say for sure, in case the next search turned out to be a dud.

She walked Dana a couple of blocks farther down Main Street, pushing her bike along as they chatted. She had a small package to mail at the post office and stopped to cross the street.

"Have a good day. I've got to run across and mail this," she explained to Dana. "I missed my mom's birthday back in May. It's just a card and a little gift. I'll give her a real one next time I see her."

"I'm sure she'll appreciate it anytime. How is your mom? What's she up to this summer? More world travels?"

"Of course," Lucy replied. "Though I have to check the big map I set up in my office, dotted with pins."

A joke, of course. But just barely. Isabel Binger, a professor of political science at the University of Massachusetts in Amherst, was a legend among Lucy's friends, owing to her adventurous spirit. Just about any spare time from her college schedule was spent traveling the globe—teaching, studying, or taking part in service work in far-off countries.

Dana laughed. "I think it's great that she's so active. She's such an inspiration."

"She's in Africa now. Researching a book about water use, and the political impact a water shortage could have in the world someday."

"Really? I'd be interested to read that." Lucy knew that if any of her friends did read it, Dana would be the one. Her taste in books ranged from light mysteries and women's fiction to heavier scientific topics. "You must be proud of her," Dana remarked.

"I am," Lucy said honestly. "I just wished we visited more

often. She was supposed to come this summer, for my birthday. But she won't be back from her trip by then. But maybe I'll go up to Amherst at the end of August, before the term starts."

"Good plan." Dana touched Lucy's arm. "We'll all do something fun for your birthday. A party at a knitting night meeting, right? Cake, champagne . . . the works."

Dana was so sweet and perceptive, Lucy realized she'd easily noticed that Lucy did feel glum about her mom canceling their visit.

"Absolutely. I'm looking forward to it. Though champagne and knitting doesn't mix well for me."

"Oh, I don't know if anyone will get much knitting done that night." Dana smiled, gave Lucy a quick hug, and started on her way again.

Lucy crossed to the post office, secured her bike to a parking meter, and went inside to mail the package. When she came out, the Gilded Age Antique Shop, just across the street, caught her eye.

Richard was outside, tugging on one side of the green and gold canvas awning. He checked it a moment, then disappeared into the shop.

Lucy guessed that Nora was not in the shop today, still too upset over Cassandra to leave her house. She wondered if Nora was sedated, or had seen her psychiatrist yesterday, as they'd planned. She crossed and locked her bike to a wrought-iron bench that decorated the shop entrance alongside a large antique urn of petunias and vines.

The shop was cool and dark, and the rich smell of freshly varnished wood and lemon oil filled her head. The air conditioner hummed, her footsteps muffled on rich red carpeting.

She didn't see Richard and wandered around, looking for him and at all the beautiful items for sale there.

She hadn't been inside the shop for a long time. She'd forgotten the atmosphere of abundant elegance. Everywhere she looked, the satiny sheen of mahogany, cherrywood, and tiger oak met her gaze. The curves and carvings, the tufted velvet cushions, and elaborate brass handles and knobs were a feast for any eye, and especially for antiques lovers, she was sure, who must mark this place on their treasure hunting tours.

Along with the writing desks and claw-foot closets, lamps, china dishes, and cups were scattered like colorful jewels. A few flirtatious, fringed piano shawls, lace-edged linens, and other vintage odds and ends were displayed in eye-catching arrangements. Nora had an artistic flair, there was no doubt.

And Richard was a wizard at reclaiming stained and damaged pieces with rich potential. Maggie had once told her that he picked up their items at garage sales, thrift shops, and flea markets for rock-bottom prices, and turned a handy profit reselling them.

Of course, that was not without hours of hard work put into the restoration. Richard made each wooden surface glow like satin. Nora's artful staging worked its own magic on their customers as well. The two were a well-matched team.

"Hello, Lucy. Can I help you with something?" Richard appeared from behind a high armoire, a chamois polishing cloth in one hand.

He looked tired and drawn, his complexion pasty, his eyes bloodshot, as if he'd been up all night, worrying, or taking care of Nora.

"I just stopped by to say hello. How is Nora doing?"

His sighed, wiping his hands. "Not well. She's beside herself. She still can't process it . . . this loss." He met Lucy's gaze. "I didn't think much of Cassandra Waters, but Nora had come to depend on her. I didn't realize until yesterday how much."

"That's too bad." Lucy paused. "Have the police spoken to Nora yet? I heard they were interviewing all of Cassandra's clients."

Richard nodded. "Yes, briefly. She wasn't in any condition to be of much help. I'm sure she doesn't know anything about this. Believe it or not, there are people in this town who visited Cassandra even more often than my wife did."

"She had a booming business, didn't she?"

Richard cocked his head. "Oh, that she did . . . and at those rates, she did well for herself." He folded the cloth and laid it on a table.

Lucy could hardly imagine the sum he and Nora had given to the psychic advisor. How bitter Richard must feel, believing it was worth any price to help his wife with those sessions, and finding Nora right back where she started. Or worse.

"Did the police ask you any questions?" She knew she sounded nosy now and was not sure of his reaction. "I'm just asking because I got a call last night from a detective on the case, and I have to call back around noon."

Richard's expression relaxed and he nodded. "Oh, sure . . . well, let's see. Yes, they did ask me a few. But I'd never gone to see her alone. Once or twice with Nora, at the start. I never believed in her powers, though she was a convincing actress," he added. "With the candles, and the cards, and all the lingo."

He waved his hands in the air, smirking again.

Lucy had seen the routine for herself. She knew that was true.

She wasn't sure what to say next, but pushed herself to continue. "Richard, please don't take this the wrong way . . . but I was walking my dogs Friday night and I was on Ivy Lane, where Cassandra lived. I saw you coming out of her house. About ten o'clock, I guess." Even in the dim light she could see his face drain of color, his pale blue eyes blinking nervously.

"Me? Are you sure? I'm usually home, snoring away at that hour." He tried to force a smile, but couldn't quite manage it.

"You were wearing a hat and glasses, but you took them off when you got in your van. You drove right past me."

He smoothed back his thin, straw-colored hair with his hand and sighed. "Well . . . all right. I was there. What of it?"

"I just wanted you to know that when I give my statement later, I have to tell that to the detective. I'm just trying to give you a heads-up. I don't care why you were there," she added quickly. "I know it's none of my business."

Now she did hear a genuine laugh, a short, sharp bark. "Ha . . . at least something's off-limits for you."

Lucy felt stung by that reply. She felt her cheeks grow red with a nervous flush, the curse of her recessive genes.

"I wasn't there on purpose. It was a coincidence. Other people may have seen you, too. Neighbors, maybe. To tell you the truth, I'm sorry that I did see you. I don't want to cause any trouble for you, or for Nora. Honestly. That's why I came to tell you first, before I have the interview."

Richard sighed, his mouth straight and tight as he peered down at her. "All right, guess I'm warned. Not that it will help much. This entire situation is the biggest debacle of my life. I bet you have your theories, too, about what I was up to with Cassandra. Don't you?"

Lucy straightened her shoulders. "I told you before, I don't want to know."

"I don't believe you. I'm sure you're curious."

Lucy knew it was time to go but her feet felt bolted to the floor.

"It's not my business," she said again, though she still didn't walk away.

"What's the rush? You've come this far; you should be the first to know. Everyone will hear about it soon enough. No secrets are safe for long in this town."

He shrugged, his demeanor that of a man who was worn-out, drained to the bone, physically and emotionally, practically giddy with exhaustion, the gears stripped on his powers of judgment and discretion, uncaring now of what he might say or do.

He seemed to be cracking before her eyes. Carrying a secret too long, she wondered? Or was it watching his wife relapse into her former mental state that had been the last straw for him?

Lucy was afraid now how he'd react if she did go. She took a deep breath, and met his gaze. Bracing herself for his confession.

His mouth twisted to one side. He glanced away. "It's too embarrassing to say out loud . . . but I'd better get used to it. I'll be telling the police soon enough. The whole pathetic story."

Chapter Seven

Lucy stood stone still; she didn't even breathe, waiting for him to continue. "What story?"

"The awful truth of the matter. Why Nora got so hooked on that damn psychic reader . . . I was feeding Cassandra information about my son, Kyle, so that she could help Nora during their sessions. She needed to say things that had the ring of truth. That were convincing. That gave Nora some peace and closure."

Lucy leaned back, resting a hand on a nearby table to steady herself; her legs had gone watery. She could hardly believe what she'd just heard.

"You gave Cassandra private, personal information about your son so she could devise convincing messages from him for Nora?"

He pursed his lips and nodded bleakly. "I'm not proud of it, believe me. But when I saw how Nora started coming out of her depression after those first few sessions with that woman . . . And without really hearing anything substantial.

Maybe a few bits of information Cassandra had strung together from news articles, or picked out from a high school
yearbook." He shrugged. "I don't know how she pulled off her
act. I never asked. But I did know even a tiny spoonful from
Cassandra was a miracle drug for Nora. She wanted more. She
needed more," he said firmly. "And I wanted my wife back. For
me, for Dale. Most of all, I wanted her to have her life back,
too."

"Whose idea was this, Cassandra's?"

He nodded. "Yeah. It wasn't mine. I'm not that diabolical.
No matter what you might think now," he added with a short,
harsh laugh.

Lucy took a breath. She didn't know what to think, her former impression of kind, supportive Richard all mixed up in her
head by this shocking disclosure.

"Cassandra got in touch with me a short time after I sat
in on a session with her and Nora. Nora was so eager to share
this wonderful experience. It cost so much, I wanted to see for
myself if it was worth it."

"Of course you did," Lucy replied.

"I guess Cassandra could tell I knew she was a faker from
the word go. But I was willing to play along and humor Nora.
The psychic smelled an easy mark, that's for sure. She'd probably rigged this deal before. I didn't agree at first," he added.
"But Nora came back one day from a session all upset and said
there were hardly any messages from Kyle that day. The connection was fading. She was torn apart again. I couldn't watch
that, when I knew how easy it was to fix."

"So the fix was in," Lucy murmured.

"It was. I would speak to Cassandra over the phone, once
or twice a week. She'd report on her sessions with Nora and

we'd figure out how the next session should go, what she would say. What private information about Kyle she could weave in. That sort of thing. She always acted like she was doing me a favor, not charging any extra for this service." Richard laughed harshly. "She knew she was getting Nora addicted and had set me up, supplying the drug my wife needed. A real sucker, wasn't I?"

Lucy didn't reply. What could she say?

He took a long breath and wiped his hand over his mouth. "I know now it wasn't just for Nora. It was for me, too," he said. "Selfish. I can see that now. A deal with a heartless conniving witch that was bound to come to a bad end. No matter how it unraveled . . . But I never expected this. Cassandra, murdered? Nora, traumatized all over again." He shook his head sadly. "No, sir, not in a million years."

Lucy stared at him, not sure what to feel. Repulsed by the way he'd deceived and betrayed Nora? Sorry for him as well? He did seem such a desperate and pathetic figure, looking like a scarecrow now in his baggy khaki work shirt and paint-splattered jeans.

Plain old adultery—Suzanne's suspicion, mainly—looked dull as dishwater compared to this revelation. Lucy almost wished now that's what his confession had been.

"You can't understand. I know." Richard raised his hand a moment, and let it drop again. "Unless you live my life. I wouldn't wish that on anyone," he added with a sad smile.

"I don't know what to say. I'm sorry for you. Sorry for both of you," Lucy said finally.

She'd come to unburden herself and give him fair warning before she spoke to the police. Now she felt doubly burdened, knowing the full meaning of what she'd seen Friday night.

"You've opened a Pandora's box now, haven't you?" His tone was low and flat. "I think the best thing for me to do is close the shop and go down to the police station and tell them . . . well, what I just told you." He shrugged. "It's not a crime. It doesn't have anything to do with the reason the psychic was murdered. I guess that's why I didn't tell the police in the first place. I didn't think it mattered, one way or the other."

That was not the reason. He knew it, too. But Lucy didn't bother to call him on that point.

"That's a good idea. You sound like you've been wanting to get this off your chest for a while, Richard," she said honestly. "It must have been very hard to keep that secret."

His pale eyes flashed with recognition of her sympathy. "It was hard. I didn't like lying like that to Nora. But when I saw how happy she was, I couldn't stop. If you loved someone and they were sick and you knew there was some magic potion that could cure them, but you had to lie a little to get it. Not hurt anyone physically, or steal or do anything that awful," he added. "Wouldn't you do that? To save the life of someone that you loved?"

"I understand what you're saying," Lucy said. But would the police understand his side of it? They might turn around and accuse Richard of scamming his wife. But he could prove he wasn't gaining anything from it. It would be a hard case to bring into court and the police had their hands full right now with bigger fish to fry.

He might be all right, she reasoned.

"I hope they don't tell Nora. Do you think they will?" he asked her suddenly.

"I don't know that it would serve any purpose. Maybe they won't have to tell her."

"I hope so," he said quietly. "I will let them know that we had this conversation. That you saw me at Cassandra Waters's house the other night and asked about it," he added.

She was thankful for the gesture. It would still be an awkward moment when she spoke to the police. They might ask why she didn't come forward sooner. But at least she didn't have to feel she was incriminating anyone.

"Well . . . I'd better go," she said quietly, finally turning away.

"I'd better, too," he replied.

When Richard said he was going to the police station, he'd meant right away. He walked with her to the door, shut the lights, and took a big ring of keys from his pocket to lock up.

Outside the shop, Lucy unlocked her bike from the post. She saw him walk to his van, parked in front of the shop. Down an alley beside the store, she saw a separate garage, Richard's workshop space.

She wondered what would happen to their business if Nora relapsed into another deep depression. It would be one more pressure on him, keeping everything afloat.

"How could you understand?" he'd said to her. "You'd have to live my life. I wouldn't wish that on anybody."

The way Richard had contributed to Nora's deception was unthinkable . . . maybe even unforgivable, but Lucy couldn't help it. She still felt sorry for him.

Lucy pedaled home slowly, the sun beating down like hot metal weights on her bare shoulders along with the pressure of Richard's confession. The dogs were glad to see her return and she let them romp outside in a gated space while she took a fast shower and gulped down more water.

She wanted to tell at least one of her friends about her disturbing visit to the antique shop. Maggie maybe? But it was almost noon and she had to call the police department and give her statement. A moment she'd been dreading. But a job begun is half-done, her mother always told her.

Lucy checked the number she'd jotted on a slip of paper on the kitchen counter and tapped it into the phone.

"Ruiz," a pleasant female voice responded.

"This is Lucy Binger. You left a message on my phone to get in touch today."

"Oh, Lucy . . . right. I was calling in regard to Cassandra Waters. You've heard about what happened to her?"

"Of course. Everyone in town has."

"The police are interviewing all of her customers. I noticed your name here. Looks like you saw her last week, Thursday night, June eighteenth. Is that correct?"

"That's right. I booked a group session with her and she came to the knitting shop. She read cards for all my friends."

"Oh, I see. Their names are in her notes, too. But I didn't realize you had seen her all together."

Lucy had made the appointment, so that made sense. Maybe Cassandra kept separate notes about people she consulted with, bits of gossip she ferreted out, or information she looked up on the Internet?

If Detective Ruiz thought it uncanny that Lucy and her knitting circle were in the middle of another of her investigations, she didn't mention it. They had first met the police officer years ago, when a rival knitting store owner had been found murdered in her shop and Maggie became a prime suspect. Of course her friends had felt obliged to rally to Maggie's defense.

But a few years later, when a blushing bride—who had knit her own gown with Maggie's help—had been tangled up in the mysterious death of her husband, Lucy and her friends had again become involved in police business.

Actually . . . it happened fairly often, Lucy reflected. And seemed to come as natural as knitting. If the police were ever honest about it, Lucy knew that she and her friends had helped them far more often than they had messed up any investigations.

She hoped that would be Detective Ruiz's perspective today. . . .

"So, why did you consult Ms. Waters? Any special reason?"

"We were all curious, I guess." Lucy paused. "And we were trying to do a favor for Edie Steiber. Her niece Nora Gordon had been seeing Cassandra very frequently but Edie didn't trust Cassandra. She thought the psychic was deceiving Nora, just to get her money. So we had a reading to see if we could debunk her."

Detective Ruiz didn't answer for a moment. "Did you observe anything during your session that supported this suspicion?"

"It wasn't any one thing. It was more like a combination of techniques, we thought made her so convincing. Reading a person's appearance and body language, for example, and their reactions to questions. Maybe even doing a little research about them before the session."

"That's generally how these hoaxes work." The detective didn't accuse Cassandra of operating that way, Lucy noticed. Just spoke in broad terms. That's how police detectives *generally* worked, with well-chosen words, holding their cards close to their vest.

"I guess I need to speak to all of your friends," Detective Ruiz said. "Did anything out of the ordinary happen at the session? Anything at all you thought was, oh I don't know . . . notable?"

"Nothing that remarkable. Her predictions and advice were pretty general and vague. Especially when we picked it over later."

Detective Ruiz paused. "Is that the only time you ever dealt with her?"

"Actually, I met her a few days before the session at the Schooner Diner. She was there with Nora Gordon, and Edie Steiber introduced her to everyone. She spoke to us a little while. That's when we decided to book a session and help Edie. Right after she left."

"I see." Lucy heard papers rattling. "I understand you had contact with her another night as well—not contact exactly, but you saw Cassandra Waters and Richard Gordon together, on Friday night, June nineteenth. That would be the day after the session at the knitting shop. Do you remember that?"

"Yes . . . yes, of course I do. I was just about to mention it."

"Good. Take your time. Tell me everything you can recall."

Lucy took a breath. Richard must have gone to the station as he'd promised and told his story. That's how the detective knew to ask her about it. It should have made it easier, but she still felt put on the spot.

Lucy had been sitting on a stool at the counter and now rose and paced the kitchen floor, from the magnet- and note-covered refrigerator to the sink and back again, a very small space, especially considering her stride.

"I was walking my dogs. I guess it was about ten o'clock.

I usually don't walk down Ivy Lane, but there was a big shepherd my dogs don't get along with on Fenwick, so I turned on the corner to loop around." She heard her voice rambling on nervously and tried to slow down.

"Yes, go on."

"I saw the sign near her driveway, advertising her services, so I knew it was Cassandra's house. I was standing across the street, a short distance down the street, when the door opened. I saw her in the doorway with a man, who was leaving. He had on a baseball hat and dark glasses, so that sort of caught my attention."

"I see . . . go on."

"They talked a moment and then he walked to a van that was parked down the street. When the van passed, he had taken off the hat and glasses and I saw that it was Richard Gordon, Nora Gordon's husband. But you probably know all this, right? Because I saw him this morning at his antique store, and he told me why he'd been there. And he said he was going to the police station to tell you, too."

"Yes, he came in. I didn't take his statement, but I read it a little while ago. I'd like to hear the story from you, too, Lucy. I know you only saw them together for a few moments and it was dark. But how would you describe their interaction? Arguing? Friendly? Anything more than just talking?"

Lucy stared out the kitchen window, seeing just a blur of green lawn and blue sky. She pushed a strand of wet hair behind her ear. Of course, the police would want her side of the story, just to see if it matched up. Maybe, despite the poignancy of Richard's words, that was not really what he was doing there.

"It seemed . . . intimate in some way. But I'm not sure I could say friendly. She had on a sort of bathrobe-looking thing—a kimono. So that seemed intimate to me. I don't know if she was dressed underneath," she said bluntly. "I couldn't tell at that distance."

"All right, go on."

"At one point, she leaned very close and whispered to him. Or even kissed him? He had his back turned to me, so I couldn't really see. But now I don't think they were involved that way. Romantically, I mean," she added. "Because of what Richard told me this morning."

"So you told him that you saw him that night. Just what you told me, more or less. What did he say when you confronted him? What was his explanation?" Detective Ruiz asked calmly.

Lucy guessed that she probably had a copy of Richard's statement in front of her, and was checking for any discrepancies in the two versions of the event. Lucy tried to remember exactly what he'd said.

"He told me that he had been in touch with Cassandra regularly, and gave her information about his son, Kyle, so that Cassandra could create messages from Kyle's spirit for Nora." The disclosure was difficult to relate. Such a twisted hoax to perpetrate on one's grieving wife. "He told me that he'd gone to a session with Nora, when she'd just met Cassandra, and started giving Cassandra information very soon after that."

"Did you believe him?"

"Yes, I did. For one thing, he seemed so regretful and disgusted by his own behavior. And what he said shows him in such a bad light . . . why would anyone make that up?"

Detective Ruiz didn't stop to answer that question. It occurred to Lucy that there could be possible reasons why such a tale would be contrived . . . to cover up something even more horrible?

"How did he sound when he told you this? Angry? Upset? Matter-of-fact?"

Lucy thought a moment. "He sounded sad. Pathetic. Burned-out. Like he was losing his grip. Disgusted with himself," she said again. "And even embarrassed. Made a fool of. I may have smelled alcohol on his breath," she added, "though I'm not entirely sure of that. He did look tired, as if he hadn't slept in days."

"Why do you think he told you? Did you pressure him in any way?"

"No . . . not at all. I told him that I had seen him and had to mention it in my statement today. I didn't want to blindside the guy. But I also told him, a few times, that he didn't have to tell me what he was doing there. I didn't need to know. I didn't really want to," she added.

"But he told you anyway."

"He insisted. He said he didn't want me to go without hearing him out. I don't know the Gordons very well. Just by sight around town. And a little bit through Edie. But he seemed like he really wanted to get this off his chest. Maybe he would have told anyone who happened to be there at that moment," Lucy added. "I think he wanted someone to hear his side of the story. I don't think he had any intention of hurting Nora. He sounded desperate to help her. He said the sessions made her so happy, it was like a miracle cure. Edie had said that, too. So he thought his interference was harmless. At least, at first. He also told me it had all been Cassandra's idea. She'd contacted him and suggested it. That's what he said, at least," she added.

Lucy wondered now if Richard had told the police the same story.

"All right. I guess we're done. Unless you have something else to add," Detective Ruiz replied.

"I know you can't tell me this, but I can't help asking . . ."

"Yes?"

"Do you have to tell Nora what Richard did?"

Detective Ruiz didn't reply for a long moment. "You're right, I can't tell you that, Lucy. Partly because I don't know. I can say that we need time to look into Mr. Gordon's story, and determine if his relationship to the victim is relevant to the investigation."

"Yes, of course." Lucy felt foolish now for asking. Luckily, the police were a little slower at jumping to conclusions than she and her friends were. And they also had this funny tic about needing to back up a story like Richard's with facts. No matter how convincing the delivery had been.

"Is there anything else you'd like to tell me? About the Gordons, or Cassandra Waters?" the detective asked.

"No. I can't think of anything." Lucy was eager to end the call. She felt exhausted and distracted, and wondered how she was going to get any work done today.

"Thanks for your time. If I have any more questions, I'll be in touch." The detective said goodbye and hung up.

As Lucy set down her phone, she realized she'd forgotten all about the dogs, still out in the yard. She found them worn-out from chasing squirrels and birds, and panting in the damp, cool shade of an overgrown holly bush. She brushed the dirt and leaves from their fur and with a collar in each hand, led them back inside, where they eagerly lapped at water bowls.

She picked out a ripe peach, grabbed her water bottle, and stomped up to her office, feeling frustrated about all the time lost in her workday.

If I never hear another word about any of those people, I'll be perfectly happy.

You say that now, a tiny voice chided. Let's hear what you say Thursday night, hanging with your pals.

As Lucy set about her work, answering e-mails and pushing along with the Bleckman directory, one part of her was tempted to at least send a quick text or e-mail to Maggie and give her a hint about Richard's startling confession.

But when she finally did, Maggie never texted back and Lucy got too busy again to contact any other friends. Matt came home early and she was happy to shut the computer and get up from her desk.

"So, did you get a chance to call the police back today?" Matt asked as they finished dinner.

"I did. I spoke to Detective Ruiz. She's very smart and easy to talk with, too. You remember her, right?"

"The woman detective, right? When that girl you know, who knit her wedding gown, got in trouble, she figured out who was really responsible, right?"

Maggie had actually figured that puzzle out. But Lucy didn't bother to correct him. "That's right. Rebecca Bailey. She still comes to knit with us sometimes, with her mother."

"What did the detective think of your fortune-telling session? Any big clues jump out at her?"

He was teasing now, but Lucy didn't mind. She had not told Matt much about that session, all the unsettling tarot cards that had turned up, resonating with her worries about their relationship. The less said about that right now, the better.

"That part was pretty cut-and-dried. But I did have something unusual to tell her. About Richard Gordon."

She quickly told Matt how she'd seen Richard and Cassandra a few nights ago while walking the dogs and what had happened when she'd gone to the antique shop this morning and told him.

"Wow . . . that's unbelievable. I only met Richard a few times. But he never seemed to me the type of guy who could lie that way. Sounds like he was desperate."

"I think so. I think he's really telling the truth about the situation, too," she said. "I felt awkward confronting him like that. But I didn't know what to do. I did have to tell the police when I called them. Even though he'd gone there and told them everything before I called."

"That was a sticky spot. But I think you did the right thing." He'd finished his dinner and took a last sip of wine. "Did Detective Ruiz remind you to not get mixed up in her case again?"

His tone was half-teasing but half-serious, too. She was eager to reassure him that that was not at all the situation.

"I have to admit, I'm curious. We all are, since we did meet Cassandra and saw how she operates. But I'm happy to leave this one to the police. I already know more than I want to."

Matt seemed satisfied with that reply. "What do your friends say?" he asked. Lucy had cleared the dishes and served a bowl of ripe strawberries. Matt picked one up and took a bite.

He had such strong, white teeth. She'd always liked that.

"I didn't tell them yet. You're the first to get the scoop."

"Wow, honey." He tilted his head and stared at her. "I'm honored. I didn't realize I was on the A-team. Does that mean I have to knit now, too?"

"Silly . . ." She laughed at him and picked out a strawberry for herself. "You're my friend, aren't you? My best friend," she added.

He smiled and took her hand, the teasing gone from his warm expression. "Of course I am. And you're mine. Among other esteemed titles I hold for you."

She met his gaze and held it. The perfect moment to bring up that nonchalant "just-wonderin'-where-our-relationship-is-goin'-pal?" conversation. The one her friends had been coaching her on. One friend, in particular.

Lucy sighed. Wasn't the quiet but complete understanding between them enough? It seemed to be all the reassurance she needed.

Or was she just seeing what she wanted to see? And maybe Matt—though clearly perfectly content in the moment—was thinking something entirely different about their future. Wasn't thinking of it at all?

He smiled, his gaze questioning. "Are you okay? Still rattled by talking to that detective?"

Lucy shook her head. "I'm all right."

She paused. A voice in her head that sounded a lot like Suzanne screamed from the sidelines: "Run for home plate! Run for home plate!"

"There is something I've been wanting to talk about," she said finally. "Our . . . our relationship."

He sat up straighter, his expression alert now, though he still kept hold of her hand. "Is this about my house stuff? I know I haven't been taking care of my chores," he admitted quickly. "I'm sorry. . . ."

They had split up the housework soon after they'd moved in together. Maybe even before that, as one of Lucy's ground rules. Matt wasn't very good about doing his "stuff" and Lucy often covered for him, because he worked such long hours and she was always home.

She slipped her hand away, smiling a moment. "Yes, come to think of it, you haven't been doing your *stuff*. But it's not about that."

"Oh . . . all right." He sat back and crossed his arms over his chest, wide-eyed and relaxed, assuming his "just trying to be open and interested" expression.

Set up like a wooden duck at a fair. All you have to do is pull the trigger, a little voice advised.

"I was just wondering . . . would it bother you if I went away for a night or two in July? Suzanne found this house on Plum Island and we want to do a girls' weekend. I just didn't know if you would mind, since you've been working so hard and we haven't really made any vacation plans yet," she rambled in a nervous rush.

You yellow-bellied, sap-sucking coward . . . you super-fried chicken.

If you get a bicycle for your birthday instead of an engagement ring, that's just what you deserve.

Matt sat back, looking a bit surprised. Then he smiled and shrugged. "Sure. Sounds like fun. What weekend are you thinking of?"

"We thought we'd leave on Friday night, July tenth. The weekend after the Fourth."

He walked over to the calendar they kept on the refrigerator, marked up with important occasions—invitations and appointments, Dara's weekends, dental visits, and knitting meetings. Of course.

"I guess it will be all right. Dara is coming the weekend of July Fourth and she'll stay for the week. I'm taking her to camp on Saturday the eleventh," he added.

Dara was signed up to spend two weeks at a very nice sleepover camp on a small, pretty lake in Maine, in a town just over the New Hampshire border.

"Sounds like it works out. What will you do after you drop her off, visit your brother?" Matt's brother Will and his wife, Jen, lived in Maine, not far from the camp. A family visit would give Matt something to do. And he did look a bit glum, as if he didn't like facing a weekend alone.

"That's a good idea. Jeff Solomon asked if I want to go fishing sometime. Maybe I'll call him," he added, mentioning an old college pal who lived in Boston but had a weekend home nearby, in Ipswich. "He just bought a new boat. A Boston Whaler with a flying bridge; it even has radar to find the fish."

"Radar? That doesn't seem fair. Doesn't your conscience bother you, taking such a big advantage over a bunch of poor, defenseless flounder? Being a vet and all that? Shouldn't you have more compassion?"

"Flounder aren't running in July. More like those crafty sea bass and cunning swordfish. Did you ever come face-to-face with one? Hardly defenseless. Fish are smarter than you think,

Lucy. Don't let those blank stares fool you." He stared at her, walking closer.

Lucy laughed and stood up. "What is that supposed to be? A fish imitation? Pretty lame." She covered his eyes with her hand and leaned over and kissed him.

"Not lame at all . . . if I got a kiss out of it," he said afterward. "There's a reason they call us slippery."

Chapter Eight

*L*ucy was glad that the Thursday night meeting was at Suzanne's house. She was next on the rotation and was relieved at her narrow escape this week.

She'd been swamped with work the last two days and could have never cleaned and cooked for the meeting in time. As it was, she'd rushed around the house just to make it out by quarter past, then remembered she'd offered to bring dessert, requiring a quick detour to the supermarket for fresh berries and gelato.

She hoped the contribution wasn't too spare but was sure that whatever the dessert lacked in wow power she'd more than make up for with the information she would share about the Gordons and Cassandra Waters.

Walking up Suzanne's driveway, she heard voices in the backyard and knew her friends were already out on the deck behind the rambling old Colonial, a bargain property Suzanne and her husband had snatched up before it had hit the official listings, a run-down wreck at the time with great potential and all the space their big family needed.

Slowly but surely, with patience that most mortals did not possess, they had restored and rebuilt the house to its present glory.

While Suzanne still complained of a few rough edges, even more bathrooms to update, and a basement "perfect for the set of a Harry Potter sequel," the old house was more or less a masterpiece. Suzanne, however, had recently admitted she'd love to sell the place and trade up for another fixer-upper, in an even better neighborhood. Something with a water view.

Knowing Suzanne, her family had best start packing. Once she homed in on a goal, she was pretty much unstoppable.

Lucy let herself through the gate and found her hostess nearby, wielding giant tongs and a hot mitt—shaped like a lobster—as she cooked on the grill, flipping heads of baby bok choy.

"Sorry I'm late. I stopped to pick up dessert. Just some berries and gelato."

"Perfect. We were wondering what happened to you. We thought maybe you rode your bike here."

Lucy ignored the teasing. "I'll put this in the fridge, be right out."

"Good idea. Grab that pitcher from the freezer, too. Raspberry mojitos. They should be just right."

Lucy was sure they would be. Suzanne was an awesome cook and Lucy knew the meal would be wonderful—well worth a few teasing remarks from her often outspoken, but beloved, knitting buddy. Suzanne always served the most interesting cocktails, too.

While Suzanne poured the frozen, pale pink drink, Lucy

settled in a comfortable seat at the round wrought-iron table. A big green umbrella was open above, not needed, of course, at night, but creating a cozy space together with small lanterns hanging from the spokes for extra light and an array of candles glowing on the table.

She greeted her friends—everyone but Phoebe, who Maggie happily reported was on a last-minute date with a guy she'd met recently at a craft fair. He was a potter and Phoebe thought his work unique and very inspired. Lucy thought the match sounded promising.

Her friends had already blazed a path into the appetizers— a platter of fresh mozzarella, tomato, and basil, she noticed as she pulled out her knitting and eyed the selections.

"How's your tote coming?" Maggie peered over at Lucy's project.

"Really good. I decided to enlarge the pattern, and use a mix of yarns. I'm almost halfway done." Lucy held up the patch she'd completed so far and showed them her progress.

Instead of using the yarn suggested, or even some self-striping, she'd mixed a selection of odds and ends from her stash, connecting them together as needed. The different colors, fibers, and weights were creating a very colorful and textural effect, she thought. One of her best projects so far.

"Wow . . . that's really stylish. I love it." Dana leaned in for a closer look. "So creative, too."

"I'm just having fun with it. I might give it to my mom as a belated birthday gift. She's still on her trip but should be back in August," Lucy told her friends.

"Oh? I thought she was coming to visit sooner . . . like around your birthday," Suzanne said.

"That was her plan but I just got an e-mail this week.

Some of her interviews and travel plans were delayed. So she had to extend her stay."

"That's too bad. But August isn't that far," Maggie said. "Julie will be back for a visit then, too." Maggie smiled at the mere thought of a visit with her daughter, who was in Barcelona most of the summer on an internship.

"How does she like living in Spain?" Dana asked.

"She loves it. Who wouldn't? She wants to move there permanently someday, she says." Maggie shrugged with a helpless smile. Lucy knew her friend would not be happy if her only child decided to live so far away. But Maggie was not the type to interfere, or try to make Julie feel guilty for her choices.

"She has plenty of time to figure it out. She still has one more year of school, doesn't she?" Lucy said.

Maggie nodded. "Yes, she does. Plenty of ball game left and a lot can change. And you have plenty of time to make another tote for yourself by the time your mother comes in August," she added. "I'd love to use this one in my window when you're done. The class is so successful, I'm going to offer it again in September. Your bag will be good advertising for me."

"My work, in the shop's window? Maggie . . . I'm honored." Lucy was half teasing her and half totally honest, beaming with pride. She sat up a little higher in her chair.

"That is a gold star. You never ask to show off my projects." Suzanne sounded pouty, her competitive side showing.

"You need to finish something first," Maggie murmured in return. "Then we'll talk."

Suzanne was a slow, unfocused knitter and a messy one. They all knew that. But she loved the therapy of just stitching and chatting to her friends. It didn't seem to matter if she ever produced anything usable.

"We each have our own style. No need to judge," Dana said, playing referee. She turned back to Lucy's bag. "I love the way you blended the colors, all in the same palette. Good planning."

Lucy had chosen mostly blues and purples, sprinkling in a few strands of yellow and hot pink here and there for a little pop.

"I had a lot of blue and purple bits in my stash, I guess. It's sort of my color." She looked over her work a moment and then back at her friends. "I have to admit, all I can think of now when I see certain shades of purple is Cassandra Waters."

"I know what you mean. I was thinking the same thing. Those are the only colors she ever wore. But I didn't want to say," Suzanne admitted.

Maggie's head popped up. She looked straight at Lucy. "That reminds me, what happened at your interview? You were going to let me know. Then you said you'd wait until we were all together."

"Did you tell them that you saw Richard and Cassandra together that night when you walked the dogs?" Suzanne asked.

Lucy took a sip of her cocktail, which was not too sweet but very strong. She needed some fortification for this conversation.

"Yes, I did. But before that, I had felt guilty, for some strange reason, at the thought of telling the police about that without telling Richard first. I didn't want him to think I had accused him of anything."

Her friends all nodded with understanding. "I know, it was weighing on your mind. You were in a tricky spot," Maggie agreed.

"So, pretty much on impulse, I stopped at the Gilded Age

on Tuesday morning. After I left your shop, Maggie. Nora wasn't there. Richard said that she was still too upset to come to work. But I ended up having a long talk with Richard."

Her friends immediately stopped knitting and leaned forward to hear more. Lucy quickly related the conversation and Richard's confession, as simply and accurately as she could.

Just as she expected, her knitting circle sat back, looking stunned.

"Mother of pearl! That's awful! That's the worst thing I ever heard any husband do to his wife . . . and I've heard about a lot of bad behavior," Suzanne railed.

"It is awful. Shockingly awful," Maggie agreed quietly. "It's almost worse than if he admitted having an affair with Cassandra."

"That's what I thought," Lucy said. "He did seem so sorry and confused, as if he had only done it to help Nora and had never expected the situation to get so entirely out of control."

"I believe he does think that's why he did it," Dana said. "You also have to consider that watching Nora in such a deep depression was painful for him, too. He rationalized, seeing a way to ease her pain—and his own—and get their life back on track." She sighed with sympathy. "Unfortunately, there are no shortcuts through the mourning process. I hear this story pretty often," she added. "A person looks back and says, 'I just meant to break the rule one time, for a good reason.' Or out of some desperate, overriding need. And they do believe the overall good it would do outweighs their transgression."

"But in the end it always catches up," Maggie finished for her.

"Usually. In one way or the other," Dana replied.

Suzanne was wandering around with the cocktail pitcher

again but everyone waved a hand over their glass. One raspberry mojito was more than enough for the evening, it seemed. "And now Cassandra is dead from unnatural causes, and their nasty arrangement is out in the open. . . . And it's going to be another, even bigger blow to Nora if she ever hears about it," Suzanne said, as she sat down again.

"Sad but true." Maggie shook her head and sighed. "I wonder if the police have to tell her the truth."

"I asked Detective Ruiz about that," Lucy said. "But seems it's too early to say. Even if she would have told me. She's very hard to read. I did get the feeling that she doesn't believe Richard's story. But why would he make up something so embarrassing and damning to himself, just to explain being spotted at Cassandra's house? There are a hundred things he could have said instead."

"I agree with you, Lucy. But it's also interesting that Detective Ruiz didn't take it at face value." Maggie was making a another tote, too. There was a thick section of rich, rust-colored mohair on the bottom and a smoother-fiber, dark orange yarn for the rest. "When you look at it from her point of view, even Richard baring his soul to you seems suspicious. He could have just acted insulted, or angry, and chased you out of his shop."

"I thought of that, too. A while after. When it happened, though, he just seemed so . . . distraught. I even smelled liquor on his breath and it was like, nine in the morning?" Lucy said. "He'd been through so much with Nora the day before, when Cassandra was found dead, and maybe he just couldn't take it anymore. Dreading Nora getting sick again." She glanced at her friends and took up her knitting once more. "I felt like he would have unloaded on anybody. I think he needed to get it off his chest."

158 / Anne Canadeo

Dana nodded. "That's very possible. I think Richard has caregiver burnout. He's been carrying a lot on his shoulders since his son died. His judgment probably isn't very sound right now."

Lucy could see that, too. "It's a total game changer for the Gordon family and for Edie, if she ever finds out," Lucy added, glancing at Maggie.

"Oh, Edie . . . poor thing. I nearly forgot about her," Suzanne said.

"She'll be crushed. She loves Richard. And she'll be broken-hearted for Nora. It's going to be hard to keep this from her," Maggie said.

Lucy had already realized that. "You are the closest to her, Maggie. If anyone tells her, I think you should. But maybe not right now. Maybe in a few days it won't matter one way or the other. Edie will be mad at Richard. But she'll be more focused on Nora and worried about her reaction. But if the police find Cassandra's killer, Nora may never need to know."

Maggie sighed. "Maybe so. But we all know. And the police do, too. It's hard to say if something like that can stay secret forever."

They knitted along in silence a moment, needles clicking in the flickering candlelight.

"I'm sorry, but someone's got to say it." Suzanne shook her head, brooding over her knitting. "Don't you think it's possible that Richard killed Cassandra? The police must be looking in that direction now. Maybe she wanted more money, more than the payments he was already forking over for Nora's sessions. Or maybe Cassandra threatened to tell Nora that he was feeding her information about Kyle."

"Blackmail, you mean," Maggie clarified.

"That's right. Or maybe he wanted Cassandra to start weaning Nora off these sessions and she wouldn't do it."

"Once you go in that direction, there are a lot of reasons that Richard could have become frustrated with Cassandra and wanted her out of his life," Dana added. "But I heard that he has a pretty solid alibi for the night Cassandra was murdered."

"Edie said he helped her close that night. But her dealings with him didn't cover the whole time frame of the murder," Maggie recalled. "What was the rest of his story? Was it verified by the police?"

"I'm not sure," Dana replied. "He does have a clearer motive now."

"Yes, he does," Lucy said. She'd thought of that while Richard was confessing to her. But somehow, she just didn't feel he was guilty. Was she too gullible? She wasn't sure of that, either.

"Do the police have any good leads, besides Richard? Except for sifting through Cassandra's client list?" Suzanne asked.

"Jack hasn't heard about anything solid," Dana reported. "The investigation is going in a few directions. Cassandra did have some customers in high places and the police are considering the possibility that she was blackmailing someone—and it all went sour."

Suzanne seemed interested in this track. "For instance? Any big shots we'd know?"

Dana glanced at her and smiled. "No specifics, sorry. But he did hear that the wife of a big politician was on Cassandra's list—Jack said we'd all know the name. The husband is thinking of running for Congress next fall."

"That narrows it down to about . . . twenty guys I can think of. But go on." Suzanne looked up from her knitting and sipped her cocktail.

"Just as an example. The equation sets a couple like that up perfectly for extortion. But no evidence of that has been found so far." Dana sipped her jewel-colored drink, too. "Wow . . . these are strong, Suzanne. What did you put in them?"

Suzanne laughed. "I'm just testing the recipe for our outing. We'll try one new cocktail at every knitting meeting and then we'll vote."

"Super plan. You bring the blender, I'll bring big bottles of pain reliever, antacid, and ice packs," Maggie said drily. "I could actually use some food to soak up my last gulp of that wicked brew."

"Oh shush . . . I'm not sure you should even come to the beach house, Maggie. You never want to have any fun," Suzanne scolded her.

But, prompted by Maggie's grumblings, Suzanne did jump up and run over to the grill. Lucy followed to help, and they soon returned to the deck with large platters of grilled shrimp and an array of grilled vegetables.

There was a loaf of warm, crusty bread and green salad, along with a pitcher of ice water. Lucy kept refilling her glass, eager to stop her head from spinning. Just before she put her knitting project away, she'd counted four knitting needles, instead of two. Not a good sign. She had never been a fan of argyle. That she knew for sure.

"I do have something else to tell you about," Lucy said as soon as a few bites had settled in her stomach. "Remember that online search I did of Cassandra's possible real name,

Jane Mullens? I had searched the phone service listed at her address."

"I thought that search must have been a dud. You never mentioned it," Suzanne said.

"The results came back on Tuesday, but with everything that happened with Richard, I didn't even want to look."

"The mood passed, I hope?" Suzanne pressed her.

"I knew you'd be waiting to hear what I found out. Interesting reading." Lucy pulled the report from her knitting bag. It was a few pages long.

Maggie leaned over her shoulder. "Goodness . . . does it go back to nursery school?"

"Almost. It shows her age, marital status, and closest relatives. Mullens is a married name. West was her maiden.

"Other aliases. Judy Waters. Judy West. Jackie West. Sister Cassandra, Sister Jewel . . . There are many colorful name combinations."

"Go on," Dana said.

"Then there are previous addresses. The lady picked up her tent and moved on a lot. That takes up at least a page. Then a list of arrests and convictions, the really juicy part, which pretty much convinced me, Jane West Mullens and Cassandra Waters are one and the same."

"What was she arrested for?" Dana asked.

"Let's see . . . Fraud, theft, larceny, wire fraud . . ." Lucy looked up again. "A few times for each of those. She seemed to wiggle away from the law pretty easily. Sometimes without doing any jail time. Or just paying a fine. It seems that as long as you label yourself an 'advisor,' you can charge for your *advice* and get away with a lot." Lucy looked up at her friends, their faces shadowed by the lanterns and candlelight. "Goes without saying, some people always want more. And if people are giving you money willingly, it's hard to prove in a court of law that it was stolen or given under false circumstances."

"Interesting. What makes larceny grand anyway?" Maggie asked curiously.

"I'm not really sure . . . do you know, Dana?" Lucy asked.

"I don't know what the law in Massachusetts says exactly. It does differ from state to state. I do know our state has some of the strictest larceny laws. I think grand larceny is any amount of stolen money or goods over two hundred and fifty dollars," Dana said. "Larceny basically means theft. But it's different from burglary, because the thief hasn't gone onto someone's property or used violence to commit the crime. And it also must be proven that the alleged thief intended to keep the property. Not just borrow it. Like a neighbor borrowing your fancy tractor lawn mower and forgetting to give it back."

"Or your new car?" Suzanne asked, in a tarter tone.

"Exactly." Dana turned to Lucy. "Is that what Cassandra did? Pretended to borrow money or expensive goods from her clients?"

"Yes, but in a crafty way. More or less persuading them to give her large sums of cash or valuables, for their own good," Lucy explained.

"Different from the way she was draining the Gordons' bank account?" Maggie asked.

"With Richard's help," Suzanne added.

"Yes, the scam was different. I searched some of these names and the words 'psychic arrested,' and added the locations and time frame. It was easy to find some local news stories about her exploits."

Lucy flipped the sheaf of pages to printouts of news

stories. "Just as she did with Nora, she would find a vulnerable client grieving a loss. But unlike the Nora situation, Cassandra would tell the client that the spirit was displeased, or died unhappily and was projecting bad energy. Then she'd persuade them that they needed to clear the bad energy. For a hefty fee, of course."

Her friends sat back. Maggie shook her head. "Who knows, maybe that part of her routine was yet to come for Nora and Richard."

"But how would she get hold of the goods?" Suzanne asked. "Would these clients just hand everything over? That seems too gullible to believe."

"You remember how persuasive she was. We went into the reading to debunk her but ended up talking about her predictions as if they were possibly true," Maggie reminded everyone. "Even you, Suzanne."

Suzanne looked humbled for a moment. "She did push my buttons," she admitted.

"She pushed everyone's buttons," Lucy said, not wanting to go there again. "To answer your question, though, Cassandra would say that some valuable piece of jewelry the client owned, or a large sum of money—maybe even an inheritance they had told her about—needed to be *cleansed* to release the bad energy from the unhappy spirit. She would promise to return the client's valuables once the energy was cleared. Of course, there was a lot of mumbo jumbo, pseudo praying and chanting involved over the tainted stash."

"Some smoky incense and feather waving?" Suzanne added. "Don't tell me . . . before the smoke cleared, she'd skip town."

"The woman was so brazen, sometimes she wouldn't even

bother. If the client complained, she'd tell them the valuables were still cursed and that they'd get sick or even die. Or say that someone close to them would die if they took back the money or jewelry before the energy was cleared. She had some good delay tactics," Lucy added, scanning one of the articles. "Like saying it needed to be purified by a full cycle of the moon. Or the valuables had to be kept in the dark in a sacred space."

"In a safe-deposit box with her name on it?" Dana suggested. Lucy nodded.

"People really fell for that?" Maggie shook her head, eyes rolling.

Dana shrugged. "She knew how to identify her victims. To find someone who was totally vulnerable, and prey on them."

"Like Nora, you mean," Maggie said quietly.

"That's right, someone who had suffered real trauma, a deep loss or disappointment, and remained desperate for answers and sympathy." Lucy leafed through the pages she'd printed out. "Here's a good one. The most recent clip I found, probably happened right before she moved east. In Scottsdale, Arizona, her last stop. She found a rich, older woman who told Cassandra she'd had a baby out of wedlock when she was a teenager, but had given the child up for adoption. The woman was still upset over this loss, wondering what had happened to the child and all that. A big part of the reason she'd gone to Cassandra."

"Gee . . . that would be a trauma. But why not hire a private investigator if you want to find someone from your past?" Suzanne asked.

"Perhaps she'd tried that and it didn't work." Maggie shrugged, helping herself to another spoonful of vegetables.

"People do turn to psychics as a last resort sometimes. When logical solutions fail."

"Very true, Maggie," Lucy said. "I'm not sure of the details here, but it seems that this event was a secret, one the woman kept from her family. Cassandra used that secret to manipulate the client, first wheedling money out of her to 'cleanse the bad karma,' and then trying to blackmail her. Her husband was a prominent minister in the area and it would have been a huge scandal for the couple if this information came out.

"The woman finally called in the police," Lucy added, "but never wanted to testify in court. She was afraid of embarrassing her husband. So the case fell apart."

"I wonder what happened to her marriage," Suzanne said.

Maggie sighed. "How heartless. How did Cassandra face herself every morning, that's what I'd like to know. She must have had no conscience at all."

"One salient trait of a sociopath," Dana agreed.

"Good job, Lucy." Suzanne looked up from her dinner, sounding quite impressed. "Lucy has held the floor tonight, Dana. Jack is going to lose his title as our favorite inside source if he doesn't step up his game."

"I can see that. I'd better warn him. He's left for a conference in California on Tuesday night. Conferencing on a golf course, mainly," Dana said, laughing. "He'd better get back in the loop with his law enforcement pals soon. I'm missing out on all the good stuff."

"At least we have Lucy," Suzanne replied. "But if you found all that out so easily," she said to Lucy, "I guess the police have uncovered it, too."

"In one-tenth the time," Lucy said. "Who knows, maybe it wasn't anyone from around here who ended Cassandra's long, sordid career. I bet there are dozens of clients in her past who still feel burned and would have loved some revenge."

"I was thinking the same thing," Dana said. "Personally, I have a strong feeling it was someone from around here. But the police still have to comb through all that out of state history and look for possible leads."

Maggie sighed and sipped her wine. "At this rate, Charles won't have a weekend off until Christmas."

"Take heart, Mag," Suzanne said, trying to cheer her. "I know Cassandra's dirty laundry is overwhelming. But maybe it's just what it looked like, a robbery gone bad. And the police will figure it out pretty quickly."

"Possibly . . . except that there was no sign of forced entry, or a struggle," Dana reminded them. "The police have said from the start that Cassandra most likely knew her attacker. Or had no reason to fear them. Which probably eliminates most of the burned and bitter clients from her past."

"The murder came calling and she let them in, without any concern. Same as Jimmy Hubbard," Lucy noted.

"That's right. . . . Do the police think there's any connection between the two murders? Even Charles should be able to tell you that, Maggie," Suzanne said.

"He should be . . . but he hasn't," Maggie said.

"At least I can jump in here," Dana said. "Jack did say something about that investigation before he left. The police found Jimmy's name on Cassandra's client list, too. It seems he visited her for at least two appointments."

"That's interesting." Suzanne had cleared off their dishes and was setting out bowls for dessert. "Maybe she was connected in some way with his drug dealing. It sounds like

Cassandra Waters knew no limits when it came to predatory behavior."

A sobering point, but very true, Lucy thought.

"I'm just curious, Lucy. You said Mullens was her married name. Where's her husband now, does it say? And were there any children?" Suzanne asked.

Lucy leafed through the pile of pages again. "Let me check. Barry Mullens was her husband's name. They divorced in 1995 and it says here he died a few years ago. But there was a daughter, Daphne. About twenty-two years old by now. She lives in Arizona, too. In Sedona." Lucy looked up at her friends.

"Sedona? Isn't that a real New Age hot spot?" Suzanne replied. "People say the mountains give off vibrations that make you dizzy, and space aliens are hanging around all over the place."

"Were you a travel agent in your past life?" Dana said, laughing. "That was some sales pitch."

"I've been there. The red rock mountains are very beautiful," Maggie said wistfully. "There are some New Age spas and all that. But wonderful hiking in the red hills, too. It is the perfect address for a psychic's daughter."

"I wonder if she'll come east to claim her mother's body," Lucy mused.

"Hard to say," Maggie said. "Even though they lived in the same state, I'm guessing that the self-serving Cassandra was not a model mother."

"That's putting it mildly." Suzanne's eyes rolled back as she dished out scoops of gelato. "Can you imagine it? Your mother is some sleazy, hustling psychic? Alexis is mortified if her friends catch me wearing mom jeans."

Lucy made a face. "Sorry, but those jeans are bad."

She didn't really think so, but couldn't resist a chance to get back at Suzanne for all the teasing she doled out.

"Seriously? I'm getting fashion advice from a woman whose shopping checklist is comfort, cheapness, and how well does this fabric wick perspiration during a workout?"

"Point made," Lucy said with a laugh. Those weren't her main criteria . . . but close enough.

"I like the way Lucy dresses. She definitely has her own style," Dana said, quickly coming to her defense. "But what you said about Cassandra is true, Maggie. Her sad history doesn't bode well for a mother-daughter relationship. I guess we'll just have to see if Daphne Mullens turns up."

Chapter Nine

As she had promised, Dana joined Lucy for another early morning bike ride on Saturday. They met at Lucy's house, planning to ride along the beach road, then down to the village.

"There's Ivy Lane," Dana called out soon after they started. "I just want to see where Cassandra lived."

Something in Lucy balked at the idea. She hated to be another lookie-look, and what was there to see anyway, but a run-down rented cottage? Most likely, still ringed by yellow police tape.

But when Dana swung around the corner, Lucy followed. Dana quickly picked out Cassandra's house—the unmistakable yellow tape was still up—and slowly circled in front. Lucy pulled up to the curb across the street and balanced there, waiting for Dana to glide over.

"There it is. The scene of the crime. Not much to see."

"Nothing," Dana agreed. "But I was curious. I wonder what the neighbors are saying. They must be very upset by what went on here."

"Upset . . . and maybe relieved that she's gone," Lucy said bluntly.

As the truth slowly emerged about the psychic, the way she'd manipulated and exploited the Gordons and the trail of ill deeds in her wake, Lucy felt she had escaped a close brush with a truly dangerous person.

"Look, a police car." Lucy followed Dana's glance to see a police cruiser coming down the street. A small green compact followed. As the vehicles turned into Cassandra's driveway, Lucy and Dana looked at each other.

"Let's go down the block a bit and watch," Dana said. "I don't want to stand here gawking."

"Good plan. We'll gawk from down the street," Lucy mumbled as she pushed off from the curb.

At a wooded stretch of vacant land, halfway down the block, Dana got off her bike and began fiddling with the clamp on her seat, moving the height up and down.

"Something wrong with your seat?" Lucy asked.

"Just acting like there is so the police don't come over and ask why we're hanging around here."

"Oh, right. I'll try to look thirsty." Lucy already had her water bottle in hand and took a long sip. She doubted the police even noticed them. "They're probably going back inside to check something. Or maybe take the tape down. They must be done holding it as a crime scene by now."

"Not necessarily."

Two uniformed officers had gotten out of the cruiser. One walked up to the front door and unfastened the large lockbox that was fixed to the doorknob, pulling down a strip of yellow tape or two in the process.

The other was talking to the driver of the green car,

through the driver's-side window. Finally he stepped back and the car door opened. A young woman emerged. Slim and petite, she had smooth dark hair, bobbed to her chin in a stylish, ragged cut. She wore large sunglasses and a white sundress.

It was impossible to spot a true resemblance from that distance, but something in the girl's build, the way she walked—her posture and the tilt of her chin—made Lucy feel absolutely certain that she was Cassandra's daughter.

"Daphne Mullens?" she said quietly, glancing at Dana.

"Highly likely." Dana was transfixed and didn't look back at Lucy until the door of the house closed tight. "She must have asked to see the house where her mother was living. Maybe the police will let her look through her mother's belongings while they supervise. If they don't need the house anymore as a crime scene."

"How sad. Can you imagine that? That poor girl."

Lucy sat on her bike again and started off. Dana did the same. There was nothing left to see.

"It is very sad. I guess they had some relationship, if she came all this way to sort out Cassandra's affairs," Dana said as she followed Lucy.

"What about Cassandra's belongings? Maybe her daughter is here to collect all her property."

"Yes, that, too," Dana agreed. "Though in light of the news articles you found, there're probably a lot of valuables in that cottage that didn't belong to Cassandra. And are probably logged in as evidence by now."

"Cash and jewelry with bad energy, in the midst of spiritual cleansing, you mean?" Lucy couldn't help her sardonic tone.

"Exactly. She was a regular spiritual money laundress,

wasn't she? Only there were no claim tickets, and only her clients' wallets got cleaned out," Dana added.

"How do the police handle that? I mean, if they found a lot of jewelry and cash in her house? Or, maybe she kept her stash in a safe-deposit box. How can they say what was legally hers and belongs to her estate, and what was stolen from clients?"

"That's a good question. I suppose any valuables are suspect. But clients have to come forward and admit that they gave things to her for that cleansing scam. As you noticed in those news articles, a lot of people are embarrassed to admit they've been taken advantage of that way and they never go to the police. But the police must have a list that includes some of those items. I don't think people like the Gordons, who paid for sessions and advice, can get any money back. I'm going to ask Jack about that," Dana added.

They had come to a steep hill and both women bore down on the pedals with greater intensity. Dana's smooth, superior gears and lighter bike helped her move quickly into the lead.

But Lucy took pride in the fact that she was barely a bike length behind, owing mainly to her muscle power.

At the top of the hill, Dana pulled over and took a sip of water. "That was a tough one. Now for the fun part."

Lucy eyed the perilous downhill slope that faced them and smiled. "Right . . . the fun part," she said, forcing herself to agree.

They rode on as they had planned and didn't talk about Daphne Mullens or Cassandra Waters again. When they reached the village, they decided to grab smoothies at the farmers' market, which was set up near the harbor every Saturday. Lucy chose fresh berries and yogurt, Dana ordered wheatgrass and greens. Balancing oversize cups on their handles, they pedaled up Main Street to the knitting shop and left their bikes in the driveway.

Knitting Camp had just finished and a pack of harried, perspiring parents had collected on the porch and path, waiting for the students to emerge.

Lucy always found the young knitters amazingly adorable, girls around Dara's age or slightly older, with soft, bouncing ponytails and braids, knobby knees, and here or there a smile full of braces.

They all seemed very cheerful and pleased with their projects—colorful knitted creatures, with ears, tails, wings, and funny fangs—stuffed and ready to be admired immediately by moms and dads.

Maggie had followed the flock and stood in the doorway, looking satisfied, but definitely tired—much more than she did after an adult class.

As the group drifted off, Dana and Lucy were able to make their way to the porch. "The cyclists have landed," Maggie declared. "Did you have a good ride?"

"We did." Lucy nodded and flopped in a wicker chair.

"A very good workout. Lots of hills. Lucy is going to kill in Boston, in her little blue dress." Dana took a chair nearby. She had remembered to pack her knitting and had stowed it in a small saddlebag that hung from her rear wheel. She set it on a table and started on her smoothie first.

Lucy had not brought her knitting, though she was eager to finish her tote bag project. She felt too hot to knit now anyway.

She wanted to tell Maggie about spotting Daphne Mullens, Cassandra's daughter. Possibly Cassandra's daughter, she corrected herself. They didn't know that for sure.

Just as she was about to bring it up, Edie called from the gate. "Hey, girls . . . I just had a minute, thought I'd run over."

"Hi, Edie. Do you need anything?" Maggie watched her walk up the path. "How's that baby jacket coming?"

"That little sucker is done. Working on the booties now." Edie sat in the porch swing, just about filling the love seat width. She fanned herself with a pattern sheet, left over from Knitting Camp.

"Want some iced tea?" Maggie turned to a large pitcher set up on a table nearby, along with some glasses and thin butter cookies.

"That would be delightful. I never get such good service back at the Schooner. Water, water everywhere. Never a spare minute for a drink," Edie murmured, mangling the famous scrap of poetry. She sipped gratefully on the cold tea, ice cubes, and lemon slices bobbing in her glass and then set it down.

"Well, I've got some news," Edie said finally. "You girls aren't the only ones in town with your ears to the ground."

Lucy smiled at her. "I think you caught the bug from us."

"Not from me," Maggie interjected. "I'm no longer contagious." She pressed a hand to her chest and offered an innocent look.

"What did you hear, Edie? Something about the investigation into the psychic's death?" Dana asked.

Edie shook her head. "Nope. About Jimmy Hubbard. You've all heard he was probably dealing drugs out of the theater, right? Charlene Vertucci, that reporter for the *Plum Harbor Times*, was just eating lunch at the counter. She told me the police have brought in a guy for questioning who may have killed him. They're calling him 'a person of interest,' but we all know what that means. They're only 'interested' when they think you're guilty."

"Not necessarily. But fairly often," Dana conceded. "Who is it? Did Charlene know?"

"I can't remember the guy's name. It's some fellow who works at a Quik-Stop sub shop near the highway. The police are looking for him right now. They say this guy was coming around a lot to see Jimmy, always at the back door. The boy who worked there told them that. They think the drugs were involved in some way. Either buying or selling them. And something went sour between them."

"Sounds like a strong lead," Dana said. "I guess we'll hear more on the local news tonight, if it pans out to anything."

"Do the police think this sub shop clerk is connected to Cassandra's murder, too?" Lucy asked.

"The reporter didn't say. But I hope so." Edie shook her head and put her glass aside. "I don't care who killed Jimmy," she said bluntly. "He was no good, getting kids hooked on drugs, and got just what he deserved, in my book. I just want the police to find the person who killed Cassandra. They're starting to ask my poor niece too many questions. I don't like it. It makes me very nervous."

With a hand pressed to her chest, she took a fast sharp breath. Lucy glanced at Dana, ready to spring into some emergency CPR.

But Edie soon sat back and sighed, swinging back and forth and fanning herself again.

"There's been a development there . . . between Nora and Richard. Very bad," she said quietly, shaking her head. "I don't know how they'll ever come back from this."

Lucy knew immediately what she meant. A knot of nerves

massed in her stomach. She stared at Maggie but her friend didn't turn her head to meet her gaze, her attention focused on Edie.

Edie sighed and stopped the porch swing. "Richard was telling Cassandra things about Kyle. Things the boy might say and do. So that Nora would believe her. To make her feel happier, Richard says," Edie slowly explained. "Did you ever hear of such a thing?"

She stared around at the women, who stared back with blank expressions.

"We know, Edie," Maggie replied finally. She glanced at Lucy. "Richard told Lucy the other day. It's a long story why. But Lucy told us the other night, at our meeting. I intended to tell you. But frankly, I think it's better that you heard it from Nora first."

"So you all knew before me?" Edie seemed shocked and maybe even angry. She stared back at Maggie.

"Just since Thursday night," Dana clarified.

Lucy felt most responsible for Edie being kept in the dark, since she had known the longest. "I'm sorry, Edie. We all thought Maggie should be the one to tell you. I guess she just didn't get a chance."

"No, I didn't. Yesterday morning when I came to the get iced coffee, I tried. But we got interrupted," Maggie reminded her.

Edie thought back, and her eyes narrowed. Then her expression relaxed and she nodded. "I did get the feeling you wanted to tell me something. And you never drink cold coffee in the morning, no matter how hot it gets outside. So that seemed fishy, too."

Maggie smiled a little. "Sometimes I do . . . but I was

really there to talk to you. I'm sorry I kept that from you. Even for a day. Can you forgive us?" she asked sincerely.

Edie sighed and shrugged. "Oh, whatever . . . I'm never one to kill the messenger. And you weren't even the messenger, were you? The one to be smoking mad at is Richard. And that wretched witch, Cassandra. I don't have much steam leftover after that."

"How is Nora taking this?" Dana asked.

"She's beside herself. She didn't even believe it at first, when he told her."

"Richard told her?" Lucy asked.

"He had to. The police called them both in for more questions and Richard knew that was the reason." Edie paused, smoothing out her big flowered dress. "Funny thing is, Nora had taken to her bed over Cassandra. She was practically catatonic over it. But now she's full of piss and vinegar. I hardly recognized her voice on the phone. She was down for the count one minute, then jumped back up, swinging away."

Lucy had expected Nora to fall into an even deeper emotional decline over the news of Richard's betrayal. She was glad to hear that hadn't happened.

"So the anger has . . . animated her?" Maggie said.

"That's right. Perked her right up," Edie replied.

"Interesting," Dana said, sounding curious. "Is she still seeing her therapist?"

Edie shrugged. "Said she didn't need that anymore. Though she may need to find a good marriage counselor. Richard's moved into the antique shop. Talk about a guy who has to sleep on the couch. He's got his pick. He can try a new one every night. Though those old sofas are lumpy and scratchy. I'd never have an antique couch in my house. What's the point?" Her rambling wound down and she sipped again at her tea.

Lucy and her friends exchanged glances. None of them spoke. "I'm just worried about Nora," Edie repeated.

"Because of this radical mood swing?" Dana asked.

"Because she was the last one to visit Cassandra. The last one on the list, anyway. Because she doesn't have a good alibi for the rest of the night. She went home and took a sleeping pill and went to bed. She didn't wake up until the next morning. Dale was out. He went to a party after work. Richard dropped him off, and went back to his wood shop. Then he went to get Dale at the party on his way home. Nora was home alone all that time. The time they say that Cassandra was murdered."

Nora's lack of an alibi was alarming. But what motive would Nora have to take Cassandra's life? She had no idea of the awful hoax Cassandra and Richard had been playing on her. Not at that point.

"What does Richard think about this—all the police attention focused on Nora? Are you speaking to him?" Maggie asked gently.

"I don't want to. But I don't have much choice. Dale is still working for me, and I can't help but see Richard, twenty-four/seven." She stood up and smoothed her dress and hair. "He apologized to me and explained his side of the story. Have to admit, I felt sorry for him. He did a damn stupid thing," she added quickly. "But the man's been sort of broken since Kyle died. Knowing how sick Nora has been, I don't entirely blame him. Is it fair to judge anyone by one stupid act?" She shrugged her big shoulders. "I know it's hard to believe, but

I've screwed up plenty of times. Times I wouldn't want people to judge me on."

"That's true, Edie," Lucy said. She felt the same about Richard. Some of the time, anyway. "But what does he think about the police questioning Nora?" Lucy asked again. Edie seemed to have lost focus on that point.

"He's worried. He doesn't want her to talk to them again without a lawyer."

"They haven't called a lawyer yet?" Dana asked. Lucy could tell she was trying not to sound alarmed. But she didn't do a great job of it.

"They will now. Even if I have to find one and pay the bill," Edie said.

"And what about Richard . . . are the police questioning him more?" Lucy felt uncomfortable asking the question. But she wanted to know. With this latest revelation, Richard had as much motive to kill the psychic as Nora did, if not more.

Edie met her glance, then looked away. It was hard to guess what she thought of speculation in that direction. "No. The police are not hassling Richard. Just Nora. He was here in town, working the whole night. After he dropped Dale off at a party, he went back to the shop to finish a dining table and chairs he had to deliver the next day. He was making so much noise that a tenant came down and had a talk with him. Just about the time they say Cassandra was killed. People saw him going in and out, loading his van with the furniture." Edie shrugged. "He's covered. It's poor Nora who's got no way to prove she was out like a light, all night."

Lucy nodded, feeling almost sorry now that she'd asked the question. Edie looked so upset all over again about Nora.

But at least, she knew. "I see . . . well, maybe something will turn up. Some way Nora can prove she was home all night."

"I hope so, though I don't know what that would be. Hey, I've got to go. They'll be sending a search party out for me in a minute." Edie glanced at her watch, a bubble-gum pink digital model with a rubber wrist strap. It looked as if she had borrowed it from a granddaughter. She squinted down at the face, then put her glasses on to double-check.

Lucy wondered what had happened to the watch she usually wore—a man's watch, an expensive one, too, with a thick gold band and large face with sweeping hands and Roman numerals. It had belonged to her father, Edie had told them, and Lucy had rarely seen her without it.

Perhaps the battery needed to be changed, or the band broke. It was an impractical accessory for someone who ran a diner.

Lucy and Dana said goodbye and Maggie walked Edie down to the gate, gently holding her arm.

"This has been a shock for Edie, too," Maggie said when she returned. "Never mind Nora. Our dear friend is not getting any younger."

"Do you really think the police suspect Nora?" Lucy asked her friends. "She wouldn't hurt a fly and would have never harmed a hair on Cassandra's head. I don't believe she'd be capable of bashing someone's head in with a big rock."

"Not the night Cassandra was murdered. Though she's probably feeling incredibly angry and betrayed now," Maggie said.

"I also think the police are on the wrong track, focusing on Nora," Dana said. "Even Richard had more reason to want to end Cassandra's life. She was practically extorting him. But he also needed her to keep the hoax going. Even though he may have hated her, and hated how she was manipulating him, I don't think he would have ended their charade so abruptly. Or so violently. I think he would have put more thought into it. Made it look like an accident maybe," Dana mused.

"Either way, it sounds like he has a solid alibi for the time Cassandra was murdered," Maggie reminded her.

"He does," Dana said. "Nora is the problem. She has no way to verify that she's telling the truth about where she was and what she was doing."

"Let's hope the person of interest in the Jimmy Hubbard case ties in to Cassandra's case in some way," Lucy said. "Maybe Cassandra was in on the drug dealing, and this disgruntled sandwich shop clerk took revenge on both of them. Didn't you say the police had found a connection between Jimmy and Cassandra?"

"Yes, he'd made at least two appointments with her. Maybe they were business meetings and not psychic sessions. Maybe selling and distributing drugs, and this store clerk, all fit into the puzzle." Dana returned to her knitting. "The police will be happy to solve two murders with one clean sweep."

"Will they ever," Maggie said. From her tone, Lucy could tell she was not seeing Charles tonight for their usual Saturday night date. Perhaps he'd be coming by very late, after work? But Maggie looked so out of sorts at the mention of the subject, Lucy didn't want to ask.

Lucy made a mental note not to miss the local news tonight. If the case was solved with the apprehension of the sandwich shop clerk, Maggie would be very happy, too.

Lucy rarely watched the news on Saturday night, but she and Matt had stayed in, watching a movie, and when eleven o'clock rolled around she suddenly remembered the sub shop clerk.

Matt was already on his way upstairs, collecting his sneakers and a denim shirt that was hanging over the back of a chair. "Coming up soon, honey?"

"In a minute. I just want to get the coffeemaker ready for tomorrow and check something." She did begin putting up the coffee, while listening to the newscasters' banter, trying to deliver the day's fairly dull events in a lively way.

Finally, a female anchor with a helmet of dark red hair said, "The Essex County police are looking for a man in connection with the homicide of a Plum Harbor businessman and resident, James P. Hubbard. Hubbard was found dead two weeks ago in the theater he owned and managed. Investigators are now seeking this man, for questioning. Twenty-one-year-old Quentin Kestler, a counter clerk at the Quik-Stop sandwich shop on Route One."

A photograph flashed on the screen. Quentin Kestler looked much like Lucy had pictured him, a skin-and-bones build with a white baseball cap on backward, a tattoo swirling down his neck and disappearing somewhere under the collar of a black T-shirt and the edge of a bright yellow apron, his Quik-Stop uniform. He was sticking out his chin, mugging for the camera.

"Police ask the public's assistance in establishing Kestler's whereabouts and have set up an anonymous tip line to receive information."

An 800 number flashed on the screen. Lucy found it disturbing that Quentin Kestler had disappeared into the woodwork. Disturbing and incriminating.

Maybe Edie's heartfelt wish would come true.

Maggie was thinking the same thing, having watched the same report. Charles was in the kitchen that adjoined her family room. He'd come in from work a few minutes past eleven and was enjoying a very late dinner; a dish of chicken parmigiana with spaghetti on the side, one of his favorites in her recipe repertoire. She'd just happened to have some in the freezer, along with some sauce, and had eaten just a salad herself, much earlier. She had been sitting with him, though, sipping a glass of red wine.

"I just want to check the weather," she said, when she noticed that the report about the sandwich shop clerk was coming on. "I'm meeting Lucy and Matt at the beach tomorrow."

That part was true, though the weather was incredibly clear and dry, with no threat of rain for the next week.

"It's all right, turn it up," he called after her. "I want to hear how much they decided to give the media about that guy, Kestler, anyway."

Maggie glanced over her shoulder, listening to the report with interest. Which was scant, she had to say.

She returned to Charles and sat across from him again. "So, there's more known about Quentin Kestler by now. I guess there has to be. That wasn't nearly enough to make him a wanted man."

Oh . . . dear. She was doing it again. And she had been so good these last two weeks, since Jimmy Hubbard had been found. Even Charles had remarked on it.

She glanced up to check his reaction. He sat back and smiled at her. "Of course there is. That's why we want him so badly for questioning. So far, he looks like our missing link. We can connect him to Hubbard and Waters. There's a ton of phone contact between him and the movie theater owner and visits to the back of the theater. The boy who works there, that Scotty Bailey who found the body, he can verify that and also says he overheard a big argument between the men just days before Hubbard was murdered."

Maggie tried to dampen down her reaction. Charles was on a roll. She'd rarely seen him this forthcoming about one of his investigations.

"Interesting," she murmured, just enough to encourage him, she hoped. "What about the psychic? Do you think the three were involved in a drug dealing partnership?"

"That's still a live lead. Kestler is noted in her client log about three times. He visited her cottage the morning she was killed," he added. "We haven't been able to pin any of the clients, who say they came to her for supernatural advice, as known users of illegal substances. But we're still not wiping that angle off the board. Maybe Cassandra Waters was just buying from him," he said with a shrug. "Her autopsy turned up negative for any junk like that, but you never know."

He shrugged and expertly swirled a last few strands of spaghetti onto his fork, then downed it in one bite.

"This is all inside information, Maggie. You know that, right?"

"Yes . . . I do," she said, nodding firmly. "And I'm honored that you trust me with it. But what in the world has loosened your tongue tonight, may I ask? Was it the wine?" She took hold of the bottle and examined the label, as if it held the mysterious answer.

Charles laughed at her. "Could be. Or something in this awesome chicken parm. Or maybe I'm just tired and grateful to have someone as wonderful as you waiting for me at the end of a very long day." He took her hand and smiled into her eyes. "And my, dear . . . you've been so good. You've earned it."

Maggie laughed. "I have been good. I'll try to live up to

your trust," she said in a half-joking, half-solemn tone. Though she wasn't really sure she could.

Maggie was amazed and secretly proud that she had managed to keep her promise to Charles on Sunday, while spending the afternoon with Lucy, Matt, and Matt's daughter, Dara, at Crane Beach in Ipswich.

The beach was crowded with families and Lucy was often engaged with Dara, watching over her in the water, or playing with a big bag of sand toys. The three of them managed to fashion a life-size mermaid out of wet sand and took many pictures for Facebook—and posterity—before the day ended and the incoming tide nibbled on the mermaid's long tail and tendrils of hair.

Maggie was actually relieved that there had been no time to chat one-on-one, or take a long walk to the deserted end of the shoreline, though she hoped to return soon with Charles and do both of those things; it was one of the most beautiful stretches of coastline in New England and definitely her favorite. After their beach day, it was lobster rolls and fried clams at Woodman's in Essex, where they sat at the picnic tables in back.

It was late in the day and a cool breeze from the open grassland and inlets was very refreshing. Everyone was too worn-out from the sun and surf to talk much anyway.

"How is Charles holding up? Working hard, I bet," Lucy said on the ride back to Maggie's house.

"Yes, he is. Hard to say how long this will last, too," Maggie added. "So how was school this year, Dara? Happy to be on vacation?" She turned to the little girl who sat beside her in the backseat of Lucy's Jeep.

Dara was happy about that and even happier to chat about the end-of-the-term events, including a pool party at her best

186 / Anne Canadeo

friend's house and field day, which her class won. Maggie listened closely, asking a lot of questions, until her house came in sight.

A narrow escape, but she was proud of her willpower. Maybe she could manage this. Just until Quentin Kestler was found, and all the information came out?

But when Maggie spotted Edie, waiting on the porch of her shop on Monday morning, looking as anxious as ever and "practically doing a tap dance"—Edie's favorite expression to describe such a state—Maggie knew her heart was going to overrule her head and her promises to Charles, as well. The information he'd imparted could very well put Edie out of her misery and she so wanted to help her friend.

"So what do you think of this Quentin Kestler character? Have you heard anything? Do the police have any idea where he is?" Edie asked in a wheezy rush.

Maggie unlocked the shop and Edie followed her in. "You'd think with all the gadgets and gizmos they've got, they could track down a measly little deli clerk. The cops on TV do it in two minutes," Edie added.

"The police are doing the best they can, Edie. But this is reality. Not a half-hour crime drama."

"I know, I know . . . but did you see that guy's picture? He's no Einstein."

Maggie agreed on that assessment. If one could judge from appearances. Then again, had Edie ever really looked closely at a picture of Einstein?

"I haven't heard anything from Charles about the search," Maggie said honestly. "But Charles did tell me a few things that should put your mind at ease about Nora," she added quietly.

"He did? What did he say?" Edie stood watching Maggie make coffee. Her mouth—lipstick already smeared—hung open a bit.

Maggie quickly related all Charles had told her—about the connections between Jimmy Hubbard, Cassandra Waters, and Quentin Kestler. "Charles reminded me it's all circumstantial evidence and might turn out to be a dead end. But it's more than they've been able to pull together so far on either of these cases."

Edie released a huge sigh and leaned back. She briefly closed her eyes and touched her chest. Maggie hoped she wasn't feeling heart palpitations again . . . and then hoped Edie didn't ask for a cup of coffee.

"That is good news," Edie said finally. "I just hope they catch him. He could be in Canada by now. Or Mexico. Or anywhere."

"True. But let's hope that's not the case. You don't want any coffee, do you?" Maggie asked.

Edie shook her head. "Just some cold water if you got it."

"I do." Maggie quickly grabbed a bottle from the fridge. "Let's sit a minute," she said, leading Edie out to the shop again.

The air-conditioning was kicking in, as well as the overhead fans, and a breeze greeted them as they sat at the oak worktable.

"I have a few minutes, I guess." Edie glanced at her watch, then took a sip of water from the bottle.

"What happened to your watch, Edie? The gold one," Maggie asked. She'd noticed, not for the first time, that Edie was wearing an inexpensive digital watch, bright pink, made of molded plastic. Not her style at all.

Edie's expression puckered and she shrugged. "Just having the battery changed and the insides cleaned out. That time-piece is on its last legs. I shouldn't wear it at the diner. All the gunk in the air gets inside, messes up the works." She looked back at Maggie. "It's a Swiss watch, you know. Patek Philippe." Edie had mispronounced the brand, but Maggie knew what she meant. "My father's. He passed it on to me, along with the diner."

"I know. You've told me." Maggie sipped her coffee. "It's been at the jeweler's awhile now. Where did you bring it? Here in town?"

Edie shrugged again. "Yeah, sure . . . up the street, near the harbor. The Jewel Box or something? I think they called me to pick it up. Just haven't had time."

Maggie waited a moment, watching her. "Is your watch at the jewelry store, Edie? Or did you give it to Cassandra Waters?"

Edie sat back, looking as stunned as if Maggie had slapped her. She pressed her hand to her chest again and Maggie nearly jumped out of her seat to call 911.

"I'm all right, I'm all right. . . ." Edie raised her hand flat, as if she were a crossing guard in an intersection, directing the traffic to stop. "You just surprised me." She sat back again and took a deep breath.

"I'm so sorry," Maggie said sincerely. "But tell me the truth, is that what happened to it? You don't need to be embarrassed, Edie. She had a long history of tricking people into handing over their most precious possessions. You are hardly her first victim."

Edie sighed. "Hopefully, I was her last."

"So you gave it to her?" Maggie persisted. Edie nodded sadly. "When was this?"

"Let's see. . . ." Edie squinted, trying to remember. "I saw her one night, right before you and your friends had the session here. I know this sounds crazy but . . . I went again. To her house. For another session."

That did sound crazy to Maggie, after everything Edie had said about Cassandra. "To help Nora?"

"No, not really. Oh . . . it's a long story, Maggie," Edie said. She sighed, looking suddenly tired and her full age, or more.

"I'd like to hear it, if you want to tell me."

Edie looked down at the table a moment, twisting the pink watchband around her wrist. "I've been such a damn fool. But she sure suckered me in. I still don't know how she did it," she added with an angry edge.

"Did what, Edie? I'm sorry, I still don't understand."

Edie looked up at her again. Maggie could sense the words forming behind her furrowed brow. But for a moment, she wondered if Edie would simply jump up from the table and go. The ceiling fan gently whirred overhead; the air-conditioning hummed. Edie sighed, staring down at the table again.

What had Cassandra done? How had the psychic been able to pry loose Edie's prized possession—her father's gold watch?

Maggie sat silent, barely breathing, waiting to hear the story. But if Edie didn't say something soon, Maggie thought she might bust.

Chapter Ten

Finally, Edie said, "I got into trouble when I was a teenager. First time I ever messed around with a boy. I was so innocent. It was laughable." She shook her head. "I gave the baby up for adoption. That's what you did in those days."

"How hard for you," Maggie replied with deep sympathy. She'd known Edie all these years and had never once expected that, though she had always sensed some distant, deep sadness in Edie's character; some deeper reason her impatient, prickly side rose to the surface so easily.

"How old were you?" Maggie asked.

"Not even eighteen. Just about finished with high school, luckily. The boy was out of the picture. He was a jerk anyway. I still don't know why I went off with him. Feeling my oats, I guess. He didn't want to have anything to do with the situation, even as much as admit the baby was his. I had to tell my mother. I didn't know what else to do."

"I understand." In those days, women didn't have the options they did now. Unplanned pregnancy was much more complicated . . . and ending a pregnancy was dangerous. That was for sure.

"She was pretty good about it, once she calmed down," Edie continued. "We decided not to tell my father. He was so strict, and had such a temper. My mother was afraid of him. I was, too. You remember my dad, don't you?"

Edie's father, Ed Steiber, had run the Schooner his whole life and been a well-known personality around town, a notorious curmudgeon who did not take kindly to customer complaints or suggestions, and didn't care one whit if he offended anyone with his sour disposition. Reflecting back now, it was amazing the diner had stayed in business, but the food had always been good.

"Of course I remember him," was all Maggie said. "So, your mother helped you?"

"She managed to ship me out to a cousin in Arizona before I was really showing. I was always a big girl, so it wasn't that hard to hide my condition. This cousin was sickly and needed a housekeeper," she continued. "I stayed with her, helping out for my room and board. It wasn't so bad. The cousin was nice to me. A lonely woman, no husband or family," she recalled. "When my time came, my mother came out west and brought me to a hospital to have the baby. A little girl. The nurse only let me hold her in my arms one time." Maggie could still hear the pain and regret in Edie's voice and her own heart clutched. "My mother had already arranged things with an adoption agency. I signed the papers. No one forced me. A closed case. Different rules back then."

Maggie nodded, taking in Edie's sad secret. "And you were never able to get in touch with your daughter, or find out what happened to her?"

Edie shook her head. "I tried a few times. I made out some forms, put it in the file that I'd like to hear from her if she ever wanted to reach out. But I never heard anything back."

"Cassandra knew about this somehow? Is that what happened when you saw her for a session?"

"Oh, she knew things all right. The hair is standing up on the back of my neck, right now, just telling you about it. She knew the date, time, and location. Even the name of the hospital and the name I wrote on the birth certificate for the baby. I don't even remember now why I named her. Didn't make sense, all things considered. But I did and Cassandra knew it." Edie paused, taking a deep breath. The story was leaving Maggie a bit breathless, too.

"She didn't tell me all at once," Edie continued. "Sort of made me tease it out of her. Or gave an initial, or some little clue, and after I said a few things, suddenly the information would come to her. Through the spirit voices," she added with a sneer.

"Yes, that's how she worked," Maggie said. "What did you name your daughter?"

"Sara. That was always my favorite for a girl. Then I couldn't use it when my other daughters were born, Cecilia and Amy," she added. "Though I bet the adoptive parents probably changed her name. But Cassandra came out with so much of this stuff, it was just too much not to believe her. I was a naïve dope," she added emphatically, "but how did she know?"

Maggie was full of sympathy and outrage. Poor Edie, what she'd been through.

"She had her ways, believe me. She'd been living in Arizona before she came here. Maybe she read some files somewhere about the adoption. Lucy uncovered a lot of information about Cassandra. She showed it to us the other night. I think temporary office work and medical billing were on the list of her few and far between legitimate gigs. Or maybe she even paid someone to dig up that sort of private information, which could be valuable to her."

Edie looked relieved to hear that. Then nervous again.

"What if that witch looked me up and found out I was worth something and came here on purpose to lure me in? That is one scary thought."

"Yes, it is . . . but very possible. Lucy found a news story about how Cassandra had pulled the same hoax on a minister's wife, back in Scottsdale, Arizona. That client had also given up a child for adoption when she was young. But how does your father's watch fit in?" she asked. "How did she persuade you to give it to her?"

Edie blinked a bit. Maggie could tell this part of the story was hard to disclose, too. "Well, she told me that my daughter had passed on and her spirit was very sad and unhappy. She'd had a difficult life and blamed me for abandoning her."

"Oh dear . . ." Maggie had a feeling she knew where this was going.

"She also told me that my father, being in the great beyond now himself and knowing everything, knew the truth about what I'd done and was plenty mad at me, too. So the only way to get these angry spirits off my back was to cleanse all that bad energy they were sending down. And make them both rest in peace. Amen," she added with mock sincerity.

"She said the bad vibes were in the watch, didn't she?"

"She did. She told me she'd pray over it and leave it on a special altar in her house and give it back to me when it was 'cleared.' That's how she liked to say it," she added. "She even showed me the spot in her house—a little corner with incense and candles going night and day. Or so she claimed. That sounded dangerous to me: keeping candles lit while you were sleeping or weren't even home?"

"What about your daughter? What did Cassandra ask you to give her to cleanse that connection?" Maggie was already fairly certain of the answer to this question but thought she ought to clarify it.

"Money," Edie admitted. "Not to her directly. She said I had a grandchild I didn't know about. My lost daughter had raised one child, a girl. And Sara's spirit really wanted me to help her daughter and I should send this girl money."

Maggie sat back. That was pushing it. But she already knew Cassandra had no shame and absolutely no boundaries.

"Did you?" she asked quietly.

"No, thank goodness. We never got to that part," Edie said meekly, giving Maggie good reason to believe she'd been about to go through with it when Cassandra's life was abruptly ended.

"Thank goodness, indeed," Maggie agreed. "I guess someone is looking over you, Edie. And with only good energy," she quickly added. "Did you tell the police any of this?"

Edie shook her head. "I felt too embarrassed. I know that's not a reason, but they didn't pay any attention to me. Some little policeman came into the diner to take my statement. He looked about fifteen. I answered a few questions and that was that. Do you really think it matters to them at all?"

"I don't know. Probably not," she conceded. "But you might get your watch back. If Cassandra didn't sell it."

"Yes, I might," Edie said, looking thoughtful again. "I would like that watch back. I do believe that if my father is looking down and knows now what happened with the baby and all, he forgives me. I think when you pass on you see the big picture. The really big picture," she added. "And you understand that you've been a damned fool about a lot of things, and maybe treated people too harshly while you were walking around on this side."

Maggie smiled at that perspective. "I agree with you, Edie. I think that's the way it goes up there, too."

Edie rose and gathered up her purse and knitting bag, which for once she hadn't opened. "Thanks for hearing me out. I feel about a hundred pounds lighter, getting that doozy off my chest."

"I'm glad." Maggie followed her to the door.

"And you know the upside of telling the police? I'm a regular person of interest now. I also had a reason to bash that woman's head in. If they start asking me a lot of questions, I'll lead them on a merry chase, believe me. It will take a little heat off Nora."

"Oh, Edie. Don't even joke about that," Maggie scolded her.

Edie shrugged. "I'm old. I've lived my life, for better or worse. No regrets, like that French song, from the fifties?" Maggie knew the one she meant. But Edie, a fan of Edith Piaf? This was a morning of revelations. "I'd rather it was me than Nora, any day of the week, and jail doesn't look so bad. Didn't you ever see that show *Orange Is Black*?"

"I think the title is *Orange Is the New Black*. And no, I haven't caught it yet," Maggie added. "The police are not going to suspect you. But you might get your watch back. I do believe they will lose interest in Nora very soon."

"As soon as this Quentin character is reeled in," Edie said.

Maggie agreed with that and knew from Edie's tone that she was counting on it.

For the next two days, the news barely mentioned Quentin Kestler, just a line or two restating that the police were still looking for him and soliciting the public's help. But on Tuesday night, right before Maggie was about to go up to bed, the eleven o'clock report opened with a big local story.

"Essex County police announced that they have apprehended Quentin Kestler, wanted for questioning in the investigation of the death of a Plum Harbor businessman, Jimmy Hubbard."

Maggie was tempted to snicker now at the characterization of Jimmy Hubbard as an upstanding businessman, knowing what she did of his—albeit alleged—drug dealing. But she guessed the television station could not take that much liberty, opening themselves to a possible suit for slander. It was still unproven in a court of law.

A strong-jawed anchorman with a serious expression spoke as if he'd personally taken part in the arrest. "Kestler was found just a few hours ago in Lowell, Massachusetts, at the home of a sister, Rita O'Connor. He was brought back to Essex County and charged with obstructing a police investigation. A spokesman for the police department states Kestler is a person of interest wanted for questioning in the investigation of Hubbard's murder."

Maggie wondered if Edie had heard this breaking news, but thought it was too late to call her. She closed the diner early on Monday and Tuesday nights, and was probably already home and in bed by now.

If she hadn't heard yet, Edie would sleep well *tomorrow*

night, Maggie thought, as she turned in. When even more would be known about Quentin Kestler.

When Maggie arrived at the shop the next morning, the first thing she did was tap out a text to Dana:

> Has Jack heard anything about Quentin K?
>
> Are police holding him?

Dana answered with a phone call. Maggie quickly picked up.

"I was just on my way for coffee and some yarn. Jack did hear a lot about Kestler."

"Good. I'm here . . . and so is Lucy," she added, just noticing her long-legged pal headed up the path with her dogs. As Lucy walked in, she said, "Dana is coming down. She knows what's going on with Kestler."

"I was wondering. Did you fall off the no-snooping wagon? I thought you weren't supposed to be so interested in police?"

"I'm not. It's just about this guy, this sandwich shop kid. It would take a load off Edie's mind . . . and her ailing arteries . . . if the police can tie him to both crimes."

"It would take a load off a lot of minds. Including one overworked but much-admired detective we know," Lucy reminded her.

"I meant Charles, too, of course," Maggie added hurriedly, though she wasn't even thinking of Charles at that moment. If I were, she reflected, I actually might not be getting so involved again. But she had already dialed the Schooner and Edie picked up on the first ring.

"They found the guy in Lowell," Edie said. "Did you see the news?"

"I did. Dana is on her way. Her husband heard about Quentin Kestler's questioning."

"I'll be there in a flash. Don't let her say a word without me," Edie answered.

Maggie could picture her already squeezing out from behind the counter, before she'd even hung up the phone.

Edie and Dana arrived at the same time. Maggie and Lucy watched them walk up the path together, Dana smiling, swinging her purse and knitting tote, and Edie patting her red face and forehead with a wad of tissues.

Edie sighed and dropped into the wing-back chair, which seemed to quietly sag and groan under her weight.

"So, what do they have on the kid? Can they pin anything on him? I'm hoping for the psychic, of course," Edie stated bluntly.

Dana sat down near her, her knitting tote balanced on her knees. "I just called Jack. To hear if he's heard more. He just happened to be at the station. The police are about to charge Kestler but all they have on him so far is obstructing an investigation and possession of narcotics. They searched his house and car but didn't find any evidence relating to either victim."

"Well . . . it's a start. Maybe they just have to look harder. What did the kid say about the psychic? Why was he going there? Did he have any reason to want her dead?"

Dana shook her head. "It doesn't seem so. He did visit Cassandra three or four times. He was very open about that. He said he went to talk to his mother, who died last year. He said he believed in Cassandra's powers and was very disappointed to hear she was gone."

"Oh dear . . . I hope his mother's spirit told him to go straight and stop dealing drugs," Maggie cut in.

"I can't say," Dana replied. "But he claimed to be very angry at whoever did Cassandra in."

"Anyone can say that," Edie replied with a snort.

"They checked the story with his sister, in Lowell. Their mother did pass about a year ago, and Quentin had even encouraged his sister to visit Cassandra with him. But more significantly, he has an airtight alibi. He was working late at the sub shop and he's on a security camera, cleaning up at the time of Cassandra's death."

Edie sighed. "How about Jimmy Hubbard? Does he have an airtight story for that night, too? Charles told Maggie that this Quentin kid and Jimmy had a big blowout on Sunday, the very day Jimmy was killed."

"He did?" Lucy glanced at Maggie. She nodded, not wanting to interrupt Dana.

"Quentin admitted that they argued but said it was no big deal. Jimmy supplied him with drugs to sell and he said he had no reason to cut off his pipeline. But Jimmy had brought another dealer into Quentin's territory and Quentin didn't like that. Quentin claims they cut a deal and smoothed it over. Everything was settled by Sunday afternoon. He told the police to check some text messages he and Jimmy had exchanged that prove there was no ill will."

"Anyone can send pleasant messages by day and still plan to kill you come nightfall," Maggie said. "In fact, it's a classic tactic."

"He has an alibi for that night, too. He was with a girl-friend," Dana added. "Though it's not as airtight as the other. Even though there's possible motive for Jimmy, the police can't find any physical evidence to tie him to that crime."

"Are they still holding him?" Lucy asked.

"He's scheduled to go before a judge for sentencing on the

drug charges this morning, and should be out on bail by this afternoon."

"So, even though Quentin Kestler had lots of contact with both victims, and seemed to connect the dots, he wasn't their killer," Lucy said.

"That seems to be the bottom line. I don't think the police will dig any deeper here," Dana replied. She opened her coffee and took a sip.

"So they're pretty much back where they started from," Maggie added.

"Right back to Nora, you might as well say." Edie's tone was gruff, tempered by anger and fear. She sat low in her seat, looking like a deflated balloon.

"Don't say that, Edie. They have other leads," Dana assured her. "Leads we don't know about."

"Oh sure . . . but this one's a no-brainer. I'm sure that part appeals to them. Nora was the last name on Cassandra's appointment list, the last to see her alive . . . except for her killer. She doesn't have any sort of alibi and now the cat's out of the bag about how she was duped by the sicko psychic and her own husband. The police have every good reason to think Nora figured it out before Richard came clean, and maybe confronted that witch at their session and got crazy."

Maggie didn't know what to say. Edie had laid out a good case against her own dear niece and it was hard to poke holes in it. She glanced at Dana, who had already tried to downplay Nora's place in the investigation. Lucy sat quietly, too.

"We all know Nora could have never done such a thing," Lucy said finally. "The police will see that, too. They have to."

"You'd think so. But I wouldn't take a bet on it." Edie

suddenly stood up and grabbed her purse. "I'll see you later, ladies. Got to run."

She quickly headed for the door, her big shoes making a squeaking sound. Maggie jumped up and followed her.

But she didn't know what to say. The words "Don't worry" came to mind, of course. But for some reason, she couldn't offer that ever-ready bromide anymore.

"Take care, Edie. I'll stop by later. And I'll call if I hear anything," she added. Edie just nodded and marched on.

Maggie returned to Lucy and Dana. "Edie's so upset. Do you really think the police are going to focus on Nora now? There must be an entire list of people who had been taken in and felt stung by Cassandra."

"Especially when you look at her past history, all the dirt I dug up on her," Lucy replied.

"I think so, too. But these leads aren't coming up with any blackmail threats. Or anything more than people feeling foolish and chagrined by their own gullibility. And it's happened in secret, just between them and Cassandra, now dead," Dana explained.

"Humiliation might inspire some homicidal fantasies. But usually, when it's been a public situation, or some romantic bond is involved, people don't like to admit what's actually happened."

"So you're saying, most people are likely to take their lumps and slink away, not wanting anyone to find out they'd been made a fool." Maggie stood behind the counter, trying to get ready to open, but unable to really focus.

"That's right. Which is why so few of her clients ever complained to the police, and even fewer pressed charges," Dana said. "It's a lot like someone getting cheated by a prostitute or a drug dealer. Even though a psychic's services are not technically illegal. Not unless they steal from you."

"Yes, that's true," Lucy said. "I just wish some wildcard would pop up. Something we can't see, or have never considered."

"That reminds me . . . we never told Maggie about Daphne Mullens. Unless you did, Lucy," Dana said.

"No . . . I forgot."

"You saw who?" Maggie looked up from the register, where she'd been counting out change. She met Lucy's glance, wondering who they were talking about.

"Daphne Mullens. Cassandra's daughter who lives in Sedona," Lucy reminded her.

"Oh, right. I forgot about her," Maggie said. "You saw her here in town?"

Dana glanced at Lucy and answered first. "We think it was her. We were riding past Cassandra's house on Saturday and we saw two police officers go inside with a young woman, twenty-something, I'd guess. She looked a lot like Cassandra, even from a distance."

"There was just something about her," Lucy agreed. "I don't think we both imagined the resemblance. If it's not her daughter, I'd bet it was some relative."

"Interesting. So she did have some relationship with her mother after all," Maggie mused. "Did you ask Jack about her?"

"I guess it slipped my mind. But I will." Dana stood up and grabbed her bag.

"She must be here to claim her mother's remains," Maggie said.

"And her property," Dana added. "If the police can ever sort that out."

The story about Edie's heirloom watch came to mind, then

floated on the tip of Maggie's tongue. She decided it was not her story to relay, even to Lucy and Dana. Edie had trusted her with that precious confidence.

"I hope if anyone fell prey to that bad-energy scam, their valuables will be returned to them," Maggie said finally.

"That will take a while," Dana said. "Even longer than finding Cassandra's killer."

Lucy's turn had come to hold the knitting meeting at her house, but Maggie called Wednesday night and asked if they could hold it at her shop instead.

"I stopped by the diner just before I headed home," Maggie explained. "Edie's in a state and Nora was there, too. I asked if they wanted to knit with us. I hope you all don't mind, but I didn't know what else to do for them. They'd both like to come, but Edie can't leave the Schooner for too long. It would only work out if we meet in the store."

"That's fine with me." Lucy felt relieved. "I just turned in a project. The only thing I did so far for the meeting was make a long list of everything I have to do tomorrow."

"That works out well then." Maggie sounded pleased, even though the change would make more work for her.

"I'll make dinner and bring it," Lucy said. "You don't have to get stuck with that job again. Dana is going to bring dessert."

"Dana? She barely knows the meaning of the word."

Lucy had to agree. "I can pop a pan of brownies in the oven, just in case her choice is too strange. But I don't want to make her feel bad."

"Edie wants to bring something from the diner. That should work. Dana won't even know it's a backup."

"Perfect solution . . . and I love that Schooner Strawberry-Raspberry pie. Edie only serves it in the summer."

"It is a rare treat. Even Dana won't be insulted by seeing that item added to the menu. I'll ask Edie to bring one," Maggie said decisively.

Having worked out a new plan, Lucy sent a group text to alert the rest of their friends. She was glad to get a pass on entertaining and also interested to hear what Edie and Nora would have to say tomorrow night.

So far, the police had not called Nora in for more questioning. All remained quiet on that front and Lucy wondered if Edie had been worrying for nothing.

Maybe a new victim of Cassandra's unscrupulous talents had been identified, and there had been a blackmail scheme, or an even worse motive for murder. Cassandra had clearly been capable of darker and more twisted hoaxes than she'd perpetrated on Nora. And she had betrayed many other trusting souls in her path.

Lucy was also eager to finish her tote project. If she didn't have to clean and fuss with the house for the meeting, she could definitely get it done by tomorrow. Motivated by Maggie's promise to display it in the shop window, like a carrot—maybe even a brownie—dangled from a stick. Lucy felt a bit childish about that. But smiled to herself as she picked up her needles and stitched on.

"*Look, I finished* the tote." Lucy held up the piece, trying to show how it would look once it was sewn together.

Maggie looked up from her knitting, genuinely impressed. "I love it. Definitely window-display quality."

"It's great, Lucy. So stylish. You can bring it to our beach weekend," Dana said.

"I still need to put it together and felt it. But it should be done by then."

Lucy hadn't felted many projects. Maggie would coach her on that part, she was sure, wanting the piece to look perfect for her display.

"That will give you a deadline." Suzanne gave Lucy a look, one that made Lucy suspect that her well-intentioned friend might bring up Matt again. Suzanne had never followed up their last deadline conversation, had she?

Lucy had decided that she was not going to initiate any heavy talks with Matt about their future, marriage, engagement rings—or any related topics. Not right now. Maybe not ever. It was her decision to make and no one else's. If she had to lock horns with well-meaning Suzanne, so be it.

A knock interrupted the conversation and Lucy's rambling thoughts. "That must be Edie and Nora," Maggie said. "Come in, door's open," she called out and everyone turned to greet them.

Edie handed Maggie a white pastry box, which Lucy knew held the pie. A good thing Edie had remembered it, Lucy thought, since Dana's dessert was some sort of slimy-looking, chia seed pudding. Lucy hadn't found the courage yet to ask what was in it.

Maggie set the box on the sideboard while Edie and her niece found seats at the table and Lucy poured them each a glass of wine.

"This is so nice. Just what we needed, right Nora?" Edie sat back in her chair and caught her breath. She looked tired and vexed, Lucy thought, but determined to put on a happy face for the evening.

"Hey, before I forget, I want to invite you all to my place on Saturday night," Edie said, "my annual Fourth of July blow-out barbecue. It should be perfect weather for the fireworks. I hope you all can come."

"How gracious of you, Edie." Maggie handed her a glass of wine and gave one to Nora, too.

"Not at all. The more the merrier. And Phoebe, too, of course. Don't be shy now, half the town will be there."

Lucy had been invited before to Edie's annual party and knew that was true. The party was always held in the spacious backyard of the big old house where Edie had grown up and had lived, ever since her parents had passed on.

The looming Victorian was set at the end of a row of houses perched on a cliff that overlooked the water, a perfect spot for Edie's old-fashioned Fourth of July gathering and for viewing the fireworks show, set off each year over the harbor soon after sunset.

Lucy did think, with all the troubles plaguing Nora and Richard, that Edie might skip her party this year. But the Steibers were the sort of clan that doubled down and circled the wagons whenever there was trouble. With Edie's many children and grandchildren, and other relatives and friends assembled and having fun, perhaps the hickory-smoked revelry would be the perfect distraction for everyone's worries. Talk about smoking out the bad vibes. This was one way to do it, Lucy realized.

Suzanne was the first to respond. "Thank you, Edie. We wouldn't miss it."

"Count us in, too," Dana said. "Your barbecue is the best."

"Charles mentioned watching the fireworks from his boat," Maggie said, "but I'd be crazy to miss your delicious ribs. They've spoiled me for any others."

"Stop now, you'll give me a swelled head. I do have the racks marinating already in the secret rub. Must be half—no, probably a whole—cow in that cold box," Edie confided with a quiet chuckle.

"She won't even tell me the recipe," Nora said.

"I'll leave it to you in my will, honey." Edie winked at her.

"It is a lot of work for you, Edie. I hope you have some helpers." Maggie sounded concerned. Lucy knew she was thinking of Edie's heart condition. Edie herself did tend to ignore it.

"Yes, I have helpers, no worries. And I'm stronger than I look. Although that old lady act does come in handy," she added.

Nora smiled for a moment, then seemed distracted.

She didn't look nearly as carefree and animated as she had that Sunday morning in the diner, when Lucy and her friends had seen her with Cassandra. But she didn't look as depressed and vacant as she had at some points in the past two years. After Kyle died, for instance. Her state of mind seemed somewhere in between, Lucy gauged. Nora was dressed neatly, her hair pulled back in a clip, and she had put on a dab of makeup and some lipstick. Her eyes looked a bit glassy. The effect of some tranquilizer or mood stabilizer? Lucy thought she might ask Dana about that later.

"So, what are we knitting tonight? Any new stitches up your sleeve, Maggie?"

"Lucy was just showing us the tote she made. She still has

to felt it and add handles. We've mainly been working on that project lately," Maggie explained, pushing the knitted swath to the center of the table.

"That's lovely." Nora smoothed her hand over the piece, first smiling a bit, then looking thoughtful, Lucy noticed. Did the colors and even the mohair strands remind her of Cassandra's flowing blue garments and shawl? Lucy would not have been surprised about that.

"So many textures and tones. Was that in the pattern?" Nora asked.

"I just wanted to use up some of my stash," Lucy replied. "I didn't make a dent."

"Nice work," Edie said, fingering the stitches. "Looks fast and easy. Maybe I can do something like that in yellow yarn . . . for a cute diaper bag."

Leave it to Edie to translate every project into a baby gift, Lucy thought.

"It's possible, I suppose." Maggie glanced at Lucy, looking amused, too, obviously thinking the same thing.

"I could fill this room with tote bags and I wouldn't make a dent in my stash. I've started hiding boxes of yarn in the attic, so Jack won't get annoyed that I keep buying more," Dana confessed.

"Breaking news . . . Dana Haeger confesses to secret vice." Suzanne looked genuinely pleased at Dana's admission.

"Come on, you already knew that." Dana smiled and waved at her. "It's not exactly a secret."

"No, it isn't. And definitely not a vice," Maggie clarified. "Though it does annoy our significant others. That's a perk of living alone. I store my stash in the best closet in the house. I don't have to hide it from anyone," Maggie boasted. "Which reminds me, I did find a project that might also look interesting with different weights and textures of yarn mixed together. A summer shawl, open work. Not very difficult and should be very fast knitting. You can use a large needle and thicker yarn, if you choose."

Maggie looked straight at Lucy, the Queen of No. 50 Needles. At least I'm the queen of something, Lucy thought, suddenly recalling the card Cassandra had assigned to her, the Queen of Cups.

She glanced at the pattern and picture Maggie had passed around, then heard the timer go off in the stockroom kitchen and went back to check on dinner. The pasta dish she'd brought over seemed warm enough. In the midst of a taste test, she heard a knock at the front door.

Phoebe, coming in late. It was her day off and she'd gone to the beach with the guy she liked, the potter. But it was odd that she'd knock and not just walk in. Or use her own key.

Then Lucy heard unfamiliar voices and heavy steps on the shop's wooden floor. She dropped the oven mitt and trotted out to see what was going on.

Detective Marisol Ruiz walked up to the table where the knitters were seated. A uniformed police officer followed.

"Mrs. Gordon, some new information has come to our attention in the investigation of the death of Cassandra Waters. It's important that we talk to you. At the station. Can you come with us now, please?"

Nora looked terrified, her mouth hanging open as if she was about to scream, but no sound came out.

Edie stood up and blocked her niece from view with her big body. Like a female polar bear, protecting a cub.

"Are you arresting her? On what grounds? Do you have a warrant? You can't just walk in here and drag her off. That's not how it works. This is still a free country!" she shouted.

Detective Ruiz didn't look the least bit fazed by Edie's outburst. She stood perfectly straight and still, as if waiting for a huge wave to crash on the shoreline and then slide back into the sea.

"We're not arresting you, Mrs. Gordon. But you are a person of interest in this investigation. It's in your best interest to cooperate and come with me to the station for an interview. Otherwise, we may have to arrest you. For obstruction."

A person of interest? Uh-oh, Lucy thought. The phrase was chilling and would set Edie off on another tirade.

Nora looked up at her aunt, her face like a little girl's. She was twisting her hands nervously, uncontrollably. Lucy saw that her fingers were red and chapped.

"I'd better go with them, Aunt Edie. I don't want to make a scene. I didn't do anything. I loved Cassandra. I have nothing to hide." Her chin trembled, her voice close to tears.

"She has to have a lawyer with her. You can't talk to her without a lawyer there," Edie insisted.

"That's Mrs. Gordon's right and her choice," Detective Ruiz replied evenly.

Nora had come to her feet, her head bowed. She grabbed her purse and knitting bag and Edie walked alongside her as she approached the police officer and detective.

"Don't worry, hon. I'm calling the lawyer right now," Edie said. "Can I come?" she asked the detective.

"You can follow and stay in the waiting room. You won't be admitted inside," Detective Ruiz replied.

"It's all right. It won't help by waiting there all night, Auntie," Nora murmured to Edie. "Call Richard. He'll know what to do."

Nora walked toward the door with the police officer on one side and Detective Ruiz on the other. Edie staggered behind. "Don't you make a peep until the lawyer gets there, Nora," she called after her. "And for God's sake, don't sign anything."

Nora tried to turn around, but the police officers kept her at a steady pace. Finally, the trio walked out, into the quiet night.

Edie stood in the middle of the empty shop, staring at the door. No one spoke. Or even breathed, it seemed to Lucy.

When Edie finally turned, tears streamed down her face, tracing lines in the pressed powder on her saggy cheeks.

"Dear Lord, I knew this was coming. My sweet Nora. Who's going to help her now? The police will get her in one of those rooms and start pummeling her with questions . . . who knows what she's liable to say?"

Chapter Eleven

On Friday morning, Lucy rode her bike straight to the knitting shop. A short distance down Main Street, she saw police vehicles parked around the Gilded Age; yellow tape and orange traffic cones were blocking the sidewalk.

Police officers walked in and out of the building, some in uniform, some in plain clothes, a few wearing hazmat suits.

One cruiser pulled away as Lucy stood there. She wondered if the search team had been there all night and was already finishing up their assignment.

As she balanced her bike against the building, she saw Maggie's Subaru coming down the street, but instead of parking in front of her store, as she usually did, Maggie pulled up in front of the Schooner. She quickly got out of the car and walked into the diner before Lucy could catch her attention.

Of course, Maggie wanted to see Edie right away and hear how Nora was faring. Lucy ran across the street to join her.

She found Maggie sitting at the counter on a swivel stool.

Edie was not in her usual spot behind the register, but Lucy saw her at the back of the café, pouring coffee for a customer.

Lucy took the empty seat next to Maggie. "I saw you come in. I was already at the shop."

"You were? I didn't even see you, sorry," Maggie said. "Too distracted by that swarm of police at the antique store. They're all over that place."

"I wonder if they found anything," Lucy asked quietly.

Everyone in town was probably talking about Nora Gordon this morning, but it seemed insensitive to gossip about her situation in earshot of Edie.

Maggie sighed; she seemed to be thinking the same thing. "Here comes Edie . . . I guess we can ask her."

Lucy turned also to see Edie's impressive, apron-covered form squeeze in behind the counter and head their way. Edie was a brave soul to carry on, business as usual. Despite her ailing heart and all her professed ills, she had a pioneer woman's constitution, Lucy thought. Or maybe just a thick skin and strong will.

"I guess you saw the news this morning: the police still have Nora and they're searching her house, the shop, and everything. I don't know what they think they're going to find."

"They haven't found anything significant, tying her to the crime scene, have they?" Maggie asked.

Edie shook her head and dried a thick white soup bowl with urgent force. "Not a crumb. Her lawyer says they can't hold her any longer unless they do, and he's getting her out in an hour or two."

"That's a relief," Lucy said.

"I knew this was a big bluff. But they had to pick on somebody, to make it look like they're not just sitting on their big donut-stuffed duffs. Nora's the unfortunate victim of circumstances . . . again," she said with a sigh.

"I'm just afraid of what she might have said to them. Even with that lawyer sitting there." Edie set the bowl down and began working on a spot on the counter. "Putting words in her mouth, I'll bet. My poor niece, she's confused enough as it is. All the drugs she takes just to get up out of bed every day and have a life. She ought to get a doctor's note or something. She's not fit to be questioned this way. I've asked the lawyer about that," she added. "I hope he works on that angle."

Nora had looked a bit dazed and drugged the other night, Lucy recalled. But who could blame her?

"Don't the police take that into account? Her physical condition? Why, she doesn't look strong enough to have attacked anyone," Maggie pointed out.

"You don't have to tell me that. You're preaching to the choir. Weak as a kitten," Edie asserted. "But she's had . . . episodes, I guess you'd have to say. It's all on record. Richard once had to call the police to help him."

"Episodes . . . what do you mean?" Lucy didn't understand, though she guessed it had something to do with Nora's emotional instability.

Edie set her wiping cloth aside and leaned closer, her voice barely audible. "I guess you'd call them fits. She'd get sad and wild and angry. Angry at the world, no one in particular," she quickly clarified. "There was this one time she took a kitchen knife out and threatened to kill herself. Then threatened to hurt Richard when he tried to take it away from her. She was half out of her mind with grief, over Kyle. . . . She doesn't even remember it. Now they're using that against her, too."

"Oh . . . I see," Maggie said quietly.

"That's not fair," Lucy added.

"Of course it's not. Go tell the cops, though they don't care what they say once they get you in one of those little rooms. They can say anything they like, too. I heard that once on a true-crime show I watch."

Lucy knew that was true as well. "I don't think they would be allowed to talk about that incident in court, though, Edie."

Edie looked suddenly alarmed. "Heaven forbid. I'd confess myself before I see it get that far. If they're so gung ho to blame Nora they obviously don't care who they put on trial. Everybody knows she didn't do it. She wasn't physically capable of it, and had zero motivation. At that time," she added.

"What do the police think was her motive?" Lucy asked.

"They're saying that somehow, Nora found out that Cassandra had been deceiving her all this time, making up all those messages from Kyle's spirit. They think she must have gone back to the cottage, confronted that evil creature, and flew into a rage."

Unfortunately, Lucy got a vivid picture of this actually happening. But only owing to the heartless scheming of Cassandra, which could definitely elicit that reaction from most anyone . . . not because of Nora, she reminded herself. Even with Nora's history of emotional episodes, Lucy still didn't believe she was capable of this gruesome act.

"Nora denies that, of course," Maggie said.

"Absolutely. But they keep going at her, trying to break down her story, trying to confuse her about when she heard this or that. Or knew what Richard did or didn't do. Those tricky suckers even ask her if she hears voices in her head, telling her to do things. Bad things . . ." Edie looked up at them, her expression somewhere between murderous rage and more tears. "Can you believe that? Baiting a poor, confused, grief-stricken person that way? Why, it shouldn't be legal, I tell you."

Unfortunately, Lucy knew all that Edie said was true. And that it was legal. Once the police focused on a suspect, they used every trick in the book to break down a story and get their confessions. She saw Edie sigh and shake her head, using both hands to brace herself on the ledge of the chrome cooler.

"How is Richard doing?" Lucy asked. "He must be awfully upset."

Despite the hoax he'd been involved in, Lucy couldn't help feeling sorry for him, too. She did believe he loved Nora.

"He's been up all night. Sounds like a zombie on the phone, but I guess he won't rest until she's out. He keeps calling me with updates. He's trying to take care of her, as always. Even though things between them are rough. You can just imagine."

Lucy nodded, feeling a warm rush of color in her cheeks. She felt so guilty, remembering how she'd confronted Richard in his shop, just because she'd seen him at Cassandra's house. She'd forced his hand, making him tell the police why he was really there. And causing Nora to find out, as well. If only I'd kept my mouth shut, she scolded herself. The police would have no reason to suspect Nora.

But Edie was still talking and Lucy focused again.

"The police have put a bug in Nora's head with all these questions. Telling her that maybe Richard and Cassandra were having an affair. Nothing he says can convince her otherwise. Even if the police leave her alone and find the person who really did it, their marriage is still one big train wreck. A smoking, steaming, twisted pile of metal," Edie told them. "If it

218 / Anne Canadeo

wasn't for Dale, I doubt they'd stick together at all," she added in a hushed tone.

Lucy and Maggie shared a quick glance. There was nothing Lucy could think of to say. Neither could Maggie, it seemed.

She heard a cell phone ring and Edie whipped hers from a pocket. "It's Richard," she said, glancing at the caller's name.

She greeted him and listened intently. Lucy watched her grim expression suddenly brighten. She held the phone away from her ear for a moment. "They're letting her go. She'll be home in an hour," she reported.

Maggie released a breath. "Good news."

"Very good," Lucy agreed. She had also been holding her breath without even realizing it.

Edie concluded the call and looked back at them. "The lawyer made them release her. They couldn't charge her with a thing. All they found was a fingernail. On the floor of the shop or something. They say it was one of Cassandra's tips. You know, those long, blue stick-on nails she always wore?"

Lucy remembered them well. They looked like extraterrestrial claws, Lucy thought.

Maggie shrugged. "That could have fallen off when Cassandra was in the shop. Or it could have even gotten caught on a piece of Nora's clothes, anytime that Nora was with Cassandra. It doesn't prove a thing."

Edie shrugged. "Exactly. Richard says they were badgering her, trying to make her remember when Cassandra was in the shop. How is Nora supposed to know where, when, and how the woman lost a nail tip? Give me a break."

Lucy agreed. But she didn't want to distract Edie and send her spinning off on another diatribe about the police department.

"Was there anything else?" Maggie asked.

Edie shook her head. "That's all Richard said. They were also badgering Richard, about a car mat missing from Nora's Prius. Richard said he got some paint on it and it wouldn't come off, so he threw it out. He was planning on ordering a new one but never got around to it."

"A car mat? On what side of the car, did he say?"

Edie thought a moment. "Passenger, I think." She shrugged. "What's the difference. It doesn't add up to an empty cup of nothing."

Lucy admired Edie's poetic use of the double negative.

"If that's all the police can come up with against my niece . . . well, that says it all," she concluded. "Can you imagine, some DA tells a jury, well . . . she was missing a car mat and we found this fake fingernail." She laughed, sounding a bit tired and almost hysterical, Lucy thought. But at least her spirits had lifted. "That ain't happening anytime soon," Edie concluded.

"Not very likely," Lucy said. She felt relieved to hear this news. For more reasons than one.

"On that happy note, I'd better go." Maggie slipped off her stool and Lucy did the same.

"I'm glad it worked out, Edie. Let's hope this is the end of it," Lucy said.

"I'll drink to that." Edie nodded deeply, her double chin multiplying exponentially. "That reminds me, the barbecue is officially on again for tomorrow. We'll be stoking the grills at six. Drop by any time."

Lucy had wondered, but it had not seemed the right time to ask about a party. Maggie seemed surprised, too. "Are you sure, Edie? I'm sure everyone would understand if you wanted to postpone it."

Edie paused a moment before she answered, lining up the salt shakers, ketchup bottle, and napkin dispenser, which to Lucy already looked to be in perfect order. "I'd rather have a double root canal than have this barbecue," she said bluntly. "But all things considered, I think it would be worse not to have it. Like admitting the family has something to hide and we don't think this is the last of it. Or that we take these bumbling police idiots seriously."

Lucy saw Maggie wince a bit at that last phrase, on Charles's account most likely. He was anything but a bumbling idiot. But Maggie didn't debate, just smiled gently.

"In that case, what can I bring? How does guacamole sound?" Maggie asked, answering her own question.

"Sounds perfect. My favorite. That's one thing I don't serve here, so it will come in handy."

"I'll make a big batch and bring chips," Maggie said, smiling. "The Steibers come from hardy stock. I have to say that for you."

"That we are. Don't let anybody forget it, either."

Lucy crossed the street with Maggie and walked toward the knitting shop to pick up her bike. It was time for her to head home, too.

"I was so relieved to hear that the police are releasing Nora. While Edie was talking, I kept thinking it was partly my fault she was there in the first place."

Maggie stopped and turned to her. "Your fault? Why do you say that?"

"If I hadn't made such a big deal about seeing Richard at Cassandra's house that night, and then told the police, the investigators wouldn't have been able to come up with any motive for Nora. Maybe I should have let that go. They would have seen Nora for what she is—another innocent victim of Cassandra's wiles. And they would have moved on to the next possibility."

"Which they will do now," Maggie said with certainty. "But I don't think you can blame yourself for this. You did what you thought was right. Holding back information in a police interview would have been a form of perjury. You had to tell the truth."

Lucy nodded. "I know. I'm just glad it all worked out . . . except for the Gordons' marriage."

Edie's train wreck metaphor quickly came to mind.

Maggie sighed. "Maybe they'll be able to patch it up. They've been through so much together. That must count for something. And they have Dale to think about."

Lucy thought that was true. She wondered how Dale was holding up through this crisis. She hadn't seen him at the diner this morning. Understandably. He must have been either helping Richard or at home waiting to see what would happen to his mother.

But Nora would be home soon. Maybe she was even on her way already. The Gordons needed time to put this dark episode behind them. Lots of time. But maybe they could work things out.

Especially if the police started searching in some fresh direction and found the person who actually did bash Cassandra's head in with one of the psychic's own giant crystals.

As Maggie disappeared into her shop, Lucy pulled the helmet off her bike and prepared to ride away. But a small green compact driving slowly down Main Street and then parking in front of the diner snagged her attention.

She had only caught a glimpse of the driver as the car

passed by, but instantly recognized Daphne Mullens, Cassandra's daughter.

Lucy stood fiddling with her helmet, trying not to be too obvious. She watched Daphne get out, slip a few coins into the parking meter, and then walk toward the Schooner and go inside.

Lucy stood staring at the diner, wondering what the young woman was up to.

Eating food maybe? a little voice chided. Very suspicious, Lucy . . .

Yes, she could have been going in the diner to grab breakfast. Definitely a possibility. Still, Lucy didn't trust that obvious reason. Mainly because Daphne shared Cassandra's genetic material. And perhaps, her mother's scruples, too. Or lack of them.

And if Edie found out the young woman's identity, there was no telling what could happen. Edie might jump the counter in her orthopedic shoes and strangle Daphne Mullens with a dishcloth. Not to mention all the sharp kitchen utensils that were handy. Lucy set the bike and helmet aside and walked straight back to the diner.

She opened the heavy glass door and looked around for Daphne. The dark-haired beauty sat at the counter, twirling a straw in a tall iced coffee, her gaze fixed on a book.

Lucy looked around for Edie. No longer stationed behind the counter, thank goodness. And not sitting behind the register, either. In the kitchen maybe? Lucy took a few steps inside and peered through the swinging doors as a waitress walked out with an order.

"Lucy . . . what are you doing here? Forget something?"

Lucy spun around to find herself facing Edie. She

blinked, not knowing what to say. "Um . . . yeah. I can't find my phone. Did I leave it here? On the counter maybe?" she improvised.

Edie frowned and shook her head. "I didn't see it. Gee, that's annoying. Did it fall out of your pocket somewhere?"

"I don't think so," Lucy said.

Edie pulled her purse out from behind the counter and took out her car keys. "Why don't you call the number and see if you hear any ringing? That's what I do when I lose mine. Maybe the busboys found it and stuck it somewhere," she suggested. "I'm just on my way over to Nora's. She's exhausted. But Richard said it was all right if I stopped by. I will feel better just seeing her. I just want to make sure she's okay."

"Of course you do," Lucy said sincerely. She patted Edie's arm. "Don't worry about my phone. I'm sure it will turn up."

"All right then. See you," Edie said.

She headed outside and Lucy was smacked by a blast of warm air. She turned to see that Daphne Mullens had been watching them. Listening in on their conversation?

Lucy met her blue-eyed gaze—large, luminous eyes, just like her mother's.

Daphne turned away first, placed a few bills on the counter, and slipped off the stool. She brushed by Lucy as she headed outside without sparing her a glance.

Was she following Edie? Lucy wasn't sure what to do. She ran outside just in time to see Daphne's car pull away and head down Main Street, in the direction it had come. She thought of following on her bike. And how ridiculous is that? Especially considering your bike, she had to stop and ask herself.

As she pedaled back to the cottage, her mind wandered, wondering about Daphne. Yes, the Schooner was a popular place to eat. Anyone in town would have recommended it to a visitor looking for a quick bite.

But Daphne had not been eating anything. And had barely dented her iced coffee, Lucy had noticed, before she'd run out.

Right behind Edie. As if she'd gone there to see Edie. Or maybe talk to her? But hadn't gotten the chance.

Was that it, Lucy wondered. But what would the young woman want to talk to Edie about? Her mother and what she'd been up to in Plum Harbor? That seemed the most logical answer.

If Daphne had privileged information about her mother's schemes, she should be telling the police. Not Edie. What did Edie have to do with anything? Except for her connection to Nora. The prime suspect. At least, until this morning.

But the time Lucy rode into the driveway and rolled her bike to the back of the cottage, her head was spinning.

There were so many moving parts to this story, it was hard to keep it all straight. Even the pieces that fit. Or seemed to.

Maybe Daphne was perfectly innocent. Just looking for a cold drink on a hot summer morning.

What had Freud said? Sometimes a cigar is just a cigar.

Very true. Though in this case, Lucy didn't feel that was so. This cigar was probably the trick kind, which looked innocent enough, but would end up exploding in someone's face.

Lucy was still bothered by the question that night, though Dara's company at dinner made the table far more lively and fun. The perfect distraction from thoughts about Cassandra Waters's murder and the troubled Gordons.

After Dara left to watch her latest, favorite movie, *Tangled*,

Lucy had some quiet time with Matt outside on the patio. Crickets chirped in the warm humid night air and fireflies danced over the lawn.

"So the big barbecue at Edie's is on for tomorrow night after all," Matt said.

"That's right. Edie is determined that the Steibers show a good face to the world. Especially now that the police could find no evidence to hold Nora."

"That was good news," Matt said. "I really don't think she did it. Do you?"

Lucy shook her head. "No, I just can't see it." She looked up at Matt. "I had a strange experience today. I was just about to head home from town and I saw Cassandra's daughter, Daphne, go into the Schooner."

"Cassandra had a daughter? How do you know that?"

Lucy briefly considered telling him about her research skills, which were getting sharper each time she and her friends grew curious about ongoing police investigations.

But this was sometimes a point of contention for them. Matt was just concerned that she'd get involved over her head and put herself in danger. Which had never really happened. Well, almost never. A few months ago, when a movie production cast and crew came to town, she and Suzanne had caught a killer trying to sneak out of town. But they brought the culprit down, single-handed, and held on until the police finally arrived.

"It's a long story," Lucy said, fudging it. "But we know. My friends and I," she added.

He nodded. "I see. Go on. So you saw this woman, Cassandra's daughter, go into the Schooner. Then what?"

"I don't know. It just felt . . . odd." Lucy shrugged, feeling an eerie chill again. "I had the feeling she was up to something.

226 / Anne Canadeo

Maybe that's just because of her mother. I'll admit it. But I followed her into the diner and watched her a few minutes. She was just sitting at the counter, drinking iced coffee. Well, not actually drinking it, just twirling the straw around," Lucy clarified. "And reading a book. Or pretending to."

Matt leaned very close and squinted his eyes. "Very suspicious. Did you call the police?"

Lucy made a face and batted him away. "Stop. I'm serious. The thing is, Edie came over and talked to me a minute and I could tell that Cassandra's daughter was listening. Edie left to go to see Nora and the minute she walked out the door, Cassandra's daughter just about jumped up, put some money on the counter, and left. I ran out too and watched her pull away in her car. I really got the feeling she was following Edie."

"And you didn't chase her, on your bike?" he asked, still in teasing mode. "Lucy, you slacker. What will your friends say?"

"They'll be much more interested and serious when I tell them the story, I'll tell you that. Honestly, I don't even know why I told you."

She rarely pouted but decided this was the perfect moment.

Sitting back in her chair, with her arms crossed over her chest, she stared straight ahead, putting on her best mad face.

"Hey . . . you know I'm only teasing." He sighed and tried to hold her hand but she kept tucking it into her folded arm. Matt tried to pry it out, but she softly batted him away.

"Stop. You're tickling."

"Oh . . . sorry," he said contritely. He sighed and watched her. He still looked amused, which she didn't appreciate when she was irritated with him.

"I just have one question."

"Yes?" she asked curtly.

"Are you always going to run around on these . . . capers? I'd just like to know," he added in a matter-of-fact tone. "For future reference."

The word "future" did not fail to catch her attention.

"Future reference? As in . . . our future?" she asked in a pointed tone that surprised both of them.

Matt sat back, looking caught in his own snare. "Um . . . yes, our future. Who else would I be talking about?" he said lightly.

"That's interesting. Because lately, I haven't been completely sure that we have one. I mean, beyond all the sticky notes on the calendar inside."

Oh dear, she had not meant to get into this tonight. And not at all in this way . . . or this tone. If this conversation blew up in her face, she'd blame Suzanne.

"Sticky notes? What do you mean? I'm not exactly sure."

Matt didn't seem upset. But the lightness of his tone was gone, replaced by a nervous edge.

"I mean our future, Matt. Me and you. How do you see our relationship . . . evolving? Where do you see us going? Making a more serious commitment? . . . Getting married?"

He sighed and looked suddenly serious. "Married . . . well. That's a big jump from sticky notes. Give me a minute here to catch my breath."

He smiled at her, his charming, wonderful smile that had hooked her from the start. But she felt her heart deflate like a leaky balloon. This was neither the attitude nor the reply of a man dying to declare his eternal, abiding love.

"Take all the time you like," she said tartly. "Though I don't think that after living together for two years, it's a really difficult question."

She didn't mean to sound hurt. And disappointed. But she was.

"Lucy . . . hey, I'm sorry. You just blindsided me here a little." His nervous laugh dimmed her hopes further. "One minute we're talking about this dead woman's mysterious daughter and the next . . . it's well . . . a pretty heavy conversation."

"Yeah, well. That's how it goes sometimes, you know?"

Lucy didn't know what else to say. She sighed and looked away.

Matt reached for her hand; this time she let him hold it. "I do want to talk about this, if you do. But it's sort of complicated."

Lucy looked back at him. She was not encouraged. In her experience, it was never a good sign when anyone said "it's complicated. " Especially when a man said it.

"Daddy? Something's wrong with the movie. The disk is stuck. Can you fix it?"

They both turned to see Dara in the doorway, her cute face pressed against the screen, a dog on either side, awaiting Matt's reply.

"In a minute, honey. I'll be right there." He glanced at Dara, then turned back to Lucy.

"Okay," Dara said patiently. She sighed and stood there, waiting.

Lucy had to smile. "You'd better fix it for her. It's okay. We can talk later . . . or some other time," she said in a tone that was much lighter than she actually felt.

Matt sighed. He met her gaze with a serious look. "All right. But we will talk about this. Soon. I promise."

He looked as if he wanted to kiss her cheek, but Lucy turned away. She stayed alone, in the dark. She couldn't help feeling off balance. He was taking the question seriously. But she had a feeling that when they finally did talk it out, she wasn't going to hear the answer she wanted. Or had expected.

Edie's Independence Day soirée was in full swing when Lucy arrived with Matt and Dara. The day had passed, busy with their usual weekend activities, a visit to the beach, lawn work, playing with Dara. But a subtle tension lingered between her and Matt.

Lucy was eager to get past it. They would talk again at some point. She had never wanted to force the issue but despite herself had done just that. She wasn't going to do that ever again, she decided. Even if she lived with Matt for the next fifty years without a ring of any kind exchanged between them.

They had to park Matt's truck nearly a quarter mile down the road, well out of sight of the house . . . but not beyond the sound of lively music blasting over the neighborhood and the smoky scent of Edie's famous ribs and other grilled treats luring them forward.

It was already half past six, but the sun was still high on the horizon and it promised to be a perfect summer evening. A perfect night for an outdoor party and fireworks display.

When they finally found their way into the yard, the sight was a bit intimidating. Edie had said half the town would be there. Lucy didn't realize she'd meant that literally.

Dara clung to her hand, looking a little awed by the crowd and noise. Lucy smiled and leaned down to talk to her. "I see some kids here that you know. Over by that climbing thing."

Lucy pointed to a huge wooden play structure, with tunnels, tubes, several slides, and monkey bars. It was covered with children of various ages. Many were kids Dara knew from school.

Dara watched the action from a safe distance, definitely interested. "Want me to walk you over there?" Matt said.

"I can go by myself . . . can I?" she added, remembering to ask permission.

Matt and Lucy laughed. "Absolutely," her father said. He stood next to Lucy as Dara ran off.

He crossed his arms over his chest, watching Dara instantly jump into the mix. "I can't believe how big she got. She's not a baby anymore."

"No, she's not," Lucy agreed wistfully.

But if you want a baby, I'd be happy to help out, she nearly said aloud. Biting down her lower lip, she turned and smiled back at him.

"Should I grab some beers?" she said instead.

"I'll go." He touched her arm. "Be right back."

Matt headed off to the nearest keg to pump out two plastic cups of beer. There were several keg stations around, Lucy noticed.

Under a tent near the house were long tables covered with the traditional red and white checked cloths, bent beneath the weight of every imaginable type of barbecue and picnic food— bowls of chips and dips, a hundred varieties of salads and slaws, baked beans, and an impressive array of pickles. Trays of buns and rolls were arranged in artful pyramids and there was a separate table entirely for toppings and condiments. When Edie put out a barbecue, she covered all bases.

Bunches of red, white, and blue balloons were tied to chairs and poles. Patriotic-looking bunting and crepe paper was draped everywhere as well.

If Edie and her family were trying to show the world that they hadn't the least worry or doubt about Nora's innocence, they were doing a very convincing job.

"Edie knows how to throw a party, doesn't she?" Suzanne stood beside her, balancing a plate piled with grilled delights. "These ribs are awesome. You'd better grab some before they disappear. Edie should bottle this sauce. She'd make a million."

The ribs did look good. Lucy was suddenly feeling hungry.

"I think I will get something to eat. When Matt gets back," she added.

She glanced around and spotted the Gordons, standing near the buffet—Nora, Richard, and Dale, talking to Edie's daughter Amy.

"The Gordons are here. I want to say hello to them later."

"I'm surprised. I wasn't sure they'd show up," Suzanne said quietly. "Good for them. But I guess they sort of had to. All things considered."

"What do you mean?" Lucy asked.

Suzanne shrugged, a plastic fork loaded with baked beans hovering above her plate. "I think Edie wants to keep up appearances. Show everyone it's business as usual for the Steibers. She wasn't going to cancel this party, unless Nora was actually behind bars. Which, thank goodness, did not happen," she quickly added in a hushed tone.

"Sorry that took so long, you must be dying of thirst." Matt appeared, balancing two plastic cups of beer. He handed Lucy one and sipped foam off the other.

"Hey, Suzanne. Where's Kevin?" Matt scanned the crowd for Suzanne's husband.

"He disappeared a while ago on a beer mission, too. He must be waiting at a different keg."

"There are plenty of them," Matt said, taking another gulp.

"Go get your food. I'll save this spot for us," Suzanne offered, setting her plate on a small table nearby.

Lucy and Matt headed to the buffet and found themselves in line behind the Gordons.

Lucy greeted Nora first. "Good to see you, Nora," she said quickly. "I can't believe this party. Your aunt sure goes all out, doesn't she?"

When in doubt, talk about the menu; she'd often found the ploy worked well to smooth over awkward social moments.

Nora smiled, happy to take Lucy's cue, as if to say "Let's both pretend that you never saw me dragged off by the police."

"Aunt Edie's always been that way, since I was a little girl. My mom used to say, 'Overboard is Edie's middle name.'"

Lucy laughed. Nora seemed glad to make "happy talk." She even looked more animated and upbeat, her skin brighter, her hair freshly washed, bouncing in loose waves around her thin face. She wore a pink cotton sundress with white stripes, and a white sweater slung over her shoulders.

Richard looked better, too. His yellow polo shirt and khaki shorts looked crisp and neat. His clean shave and smoothly combed hair said visit to the barbershop. Far different from the rumpled, exhausted man who had bared his soul to her among the rows of dark wooden antiques.

Perhaps the worst was past and they really were celebrating tonight. Lucy hoped so.

Dale was the only one who didn't look at ease, Lucy noticed, standing behind his father, hands dug into the front pockets of his jeans. He wore a plain white shirt, sleeves rolled to his elbows, and looked as if he'd made a special effort to "clean up" for the party, with a fresh shave and his hair combed neatly. Still, he didn't look at all happy to be there. Perhaps encouraged—ordered?—by his parents, who knew the family would be the focus of much attention.

Maybe that's what had put him out of sorts, a dour, distracted expression on his face as he stared down at the lawn, looking as if he was wishing very hard that aliens would airlift him up to their spacecraft immediately.

Lucy noticed a pack of cigarettes in his shirt pocket. Maybe he just wanted a smoke and felt awkward about excusing himself.

As if reading her mind, he leaned toward his father. "I'm going for a smoke. See you later."

"Sure, son . . . go find some friends. I'm sure there's someone here you know. You don't have to stay with the old people all night," Richard joked. He glanced at Lucy as Dale stalked away toward the back of the property.

"Adolescent angst. Par for the course." He shrugged. "You can't take their moods at that age too seriously."

"I guess not." What did she know? She didn't have any children. Yet. She did remember being moody at that age, though.

Richard did seem to be making light of all his son had gone through lately—watching his mother be the focus of a murder investigation. And all he had gone through the last two years, for that matter, in the wake of his brother Kyle's death. Dale Gordon's moods were definitely not the usual teenage blues, that was for sure.

Armed with full plates and more beer, Lucy and Matt made their way back to the little table Suzanne had staked out. She was no longer there, but they did find Maggie, Charles, Dana, and Jack. Matt and Lucy took two empty seats as greetings were exchanged.

"Quite the scene, isn't it?" Maggie said after a while.

"Even bigger than I remembered from last time," Lucy said.

Her dish was so full, the food was falling off as she tried to slice a bite of grilled chicken with a plastic knife.

Some of the selections on her plate were meant for Dara. She'd picked up an extra dish and moved Dara's dinner over.

"I'm just going to get Dara. She must be hungry by now," she told Matt.

He nodded, looking grateful, his mouth too full to speak.

It was starting to get dark; not dark enough for the fireworks, but hazy enough to make it hard to spot Dara on the play structure. As Lucy made her way across the lawn, huge spotlights flashed on, startling her. She bumped into someone and nearly spilled her beer.

She looked up to find Richard, staring at her.

"Oh . . . sorry. The way the lights just went on . . . it surprised me. Someone must have pulled the main switch."

He laughed, a flash of annoyance in his eyes quickly melting. "It's a timer. I set it up for Aunt Edie. We have them all over the house. Don't you?"

Lucy shook her head. Though she aspired to being a do-it-yourself type and sometimes painted rooms, or rewired a lamp, that was about the extent of her repertoire. Matt was pathetically unmechanical and happy to hire professionals.

"You should get some. Scares away the burglars if you're out," he added.

"We have dogs. That's their job," she said.

He shrugged. "Oh sure. Dogs work, too."

Lucy thanked him for the tip and ambled off, more mindful of her cup, which was now practically empty. She took one last sip and tossed it in a trash bin. At the play structure, the party was going strong. The children had not slowed down one bit since their arrival. If anything, nightfall had heightened the excitement of racing around the tunnels and tubes. They were probably excited about the fireworks show, too, Lucy thought.

She soon spotted Dara, who made Lucy chase her a while. When Lucy finally caught her—after pretending for at least five minutes that Dara was too fast—Dara squealed and begged to play a few more minutes.

"You're not thirsty and hungry and tired yet? We got you a burger and chips for dinner," Lucy said temptingly. "And a sour pickle," she added, sure that one of Dara's favorites would do the trick.

Dara cocked her head, making an adorable face. "Five minutes?" she held up her fingers.

"All right. I'll wait."

Lucy stepped back to wait out beyond the fray. She quickly realized she was not alone and turned to see Dale Gordon sitting on a tree stump. He was sipping from a cup of beer and Lucy had a feeling it wasn't his first or even his second.

She knew he was only sixteen. Not legal drinking age in Massachusetts, that was for sure. But she did suspect a lot of teenagers here were enjoying the free-flowing brew. No one seemed to be watching that.

"Hey, Dale. How are you? Try the food yet? It's really good."

Just sayin' . . . if you don't want to fall down flat on your face when you stand up, Lucy added silently.

"I can wait till the line dies down. There's plenty."

She nodded and smiled. "Right. There's definitely plenty of everything."

She sighed and watched the children, not sure what else to say. "These kids never run out of energy do they?"

"Nope. Just play, play, play. I'd give anything to be that age again."

Lucy felt knocked back with surprise at his tone, so sad and sincere. So young to be wishing he could turn back the years. Wasn't this the age that kids ached to be older, and start out on their own?

Not longing to be children again.

But he wasn't the typical teenage boy, from the typical family. He had his reasons for these wishes.

"I'm sorry about your brother. I don't think I ever told you that," she said quietly. She glanced at him. "I'm sure it's been very hard for you. For everyone in your family."

He stared at her, his eyes hard as stones for a moment. Then he laughed, a short, sharp sound, while he stared at the ground. "Oh yeah, it's been rough. My freaking brother Kyle screwed us all up. Because he was screwed up. It's like a game of dominoes or something. One tips over and the rest fall. They can't help it. Just gravity. You can't help gravity. You know? It just . . . pulls you down."

He shook his head. He was drunk. He didn't know what he was saying, she realized. Just rambling. She worried he might get sick.

She walked over to him and touched his arm. "Are you okay? You look like you feel sick."

"I'm fine, man. Just leave me alone." He shrugged her touch away. "Stop with these questions, okay? I'm totally . . . fine."

He closed his eyes, his head swaying from side to side. She thought he might throw up, and quickly stepped back.

"You don't get it. Do you? Miss Lucy-goosey-question-asker?"

Dale mumbled with his eyes closed, head hanging down on his chest. "Kyle did that to himself. He did it. Stupid, junked-up idiot. I told him to stop. I told him . . ." He opened his eyes a moment and stared at her, his expression bleak. Desperate. Then he covered his face with his hands, his shoulders heaving. Lucy knew he was crying. A terrible, heart-wrenching sound. She didn't know what to do.

She looked around frantically and spotted Matt, on the other side of the play set. He must have been wondering what had happened to them. She waved and he quickly walked over.

"Dale is sick. He drank too much. Will you stay with him a minute? I'll find his father."

"Sure." Matt leaned over and touched Dale's shoulder. "Hey, man. What's going on? Want to go up to the house and crash somewhere?"

For a moment, Dale looked like he was going to shake Matt off, too, but finally he sat up and forced himself to focus. He nodded and allowed Matt to help him stand.

Lucy was still there, watching.

"Please don't tell my father," he said, finding her gaze again. "Please?"

Lucy nodded. "Okay."

As long he went inside and lay down a while, she thought it would be all right not to tell on him. His parents would find him soon enough and figure out what had happened.

She was tired of getting involved in other people's business. Especially the Gordon family's.

The fireworks show viewed from the cliff behind Edie's house was stunning. The party crowd oohed and aahed with each burst of light and the children jumped up and down with excitement.

Lucy could never recall being so close to the display or feeling the explosions just overhead.

Dara fell asleep soon after, her cheek pressed to Matt's shoulder as he carried her to the truck.

As Lucy fell asleep that night herself, it wasn't the vision of fireworks that lingered in her head. It was the sight of Dale Gordon, drunk and mumbling about his brother. Not just the sight, but his words. Words that suggested to her Kyle did not die of a brain hemorrhage. At least, not one without cause.

It sounded as if Kyle had died of a drug overdose. And his younger brother, Dale, was left alone with their parents, to pick up the pieces of their shattered family.

The day after Edie's party, Charles invited Lucy and Matt for an afternoon on his sailboat, *Indigo*, even though Maggie warned that the waters were more crowded on July Fourth weekend than the Massachusetts Turnpike.

"We'll go out fairly late, after two or three o'clock," Maggie said. "The tide should be up. We can sail an hour or two, then drop anchor and have a bite of dinner and watch the sunset. You can swim if you feel restless," she added, knowing how quickly Lucy felt cramped in small spaces.

"My, my . . . you're a regular old salt, now, aren't you?" Lucy laughed at the way Maggie was slinging around the sailing slang.

"I'm salty . . . but you can skip the other adjective," she teased back.

The sailing trip turned out to be a good idea. It was a hot day, too hot to stay on the beach for very long. She and Matt took Dara for a few hours in the morning and then drove her to a friend's house where she'd been invited for a sleepover.

Out on the water a few hours later, the air was much cooler. Lucy felt relaxed, lying on a cushion with a cold drink in hand as the canvas snapped in the breeze and the long wooden boat skimmed along the blue and white waves.

Maggie was surprisingly adept at pulling in ropes and letting them out, explaining she needed to "trim the sails" or "pull in the sheets," and shouting things like "Coming about!"

She hopped around the deck barefoot, like a seabird, balancing on the edge of the boat as she followed Charles's instructions to the letter.

Once the boat was under way, they both returned to the small cushioned area in the stern and Charles rested one hand on the wheel to keep their progress steady.

"Maggie's a natural-born sailor," he announced.

"Clearly," Lucy said in agreement. "It's the only time I've ever seen her take orders from anyone, Charles. You've revealed another hidden part of her personality there, too."

Maggie made a face at her but patted Charles's broad shoulders for a moment as she reached around him to grab her knitting bag. "Don't listen to her, dear. I don't think of it as taking orders . . . just doing my part."

"We work together. We're a team," he said, with the cautious smile of a man who hoped he sounded politically correct and nonsexist.

"This is a beautiful boat, Charles. How long have you owned it?" Matt had bought a small, rather rickety Sunfish at a garage sale the previous summer. She knew he had ambitions to step up to a real sailboat at some point. Then again, there was the "unhandy" problem, and she did think you needed to be a bit better with tools and such to keep a boat. If you didn't want to sink.

"Not very long," Charles replied. "I was lucky to find her. I got a nice deal. Indigo is a real classic. All wood. Come on, I'll show you around," he said, quickly warming to the topic.

Maggie was left in charge of steering. "See, I don't just take orders. I'm given important responsibilities."

"Quickly promoted, too," Lucy remarked. "Who knows what's next."

Maggie gave her a look. She may have been in charge of steering but that didn't prevent her from knitting. "How did you like Edie's party? Quite a bash. I felt happy for the Gordons. They look as if they've come out from under a cloud."

"I thought so, too," Lucy said. "Nora and Richard, at least. I'm not so sure about Dale."

Maggie looked up at her. "Why do you say that?"

"I found him sitting alone behind the play set. Just as it had gotten dark. He was very drunk. He could barely stand up."

"Oh, dear . . ." Maggie shook her head. "High school boys and random beer kegs. He probably doesn't know how to pace himself yet. Everyone knows teenagers experiment with alcohol. Not that I think it's a great idea," she added. "But it is a fact."

"I know. But it wasn't just that. He started talking about his brother, Kyle. And about his family. And crying at one point."

Maggie stopped knitting and looked over at her. "That does sound bad. What did he say?"

Lucy took a breath. This was the hard part. "It was incoherent at first. Just saying Kyle was a screwup. An idiot."

"He said that?" Maggie seemed shocked that Dale would say such things about his older brother who had passed away. Lucy had felt the same. At first.

"Then he said something like 'My freaking brother Kyle

screwed us all up. Because he was screwed up. It's like a game of dominoes or something. One tips over and the rest fall.'" Lucy repeated from memory. "I guess he was talking about his family. Saying his family is falling apart."

Maggie nodded. "Yes, I think so. But that does seem true. He's been through a lot. Even beyond his brother's death. Which was such a terrible shock."

"He said Kyle didn't die of a brain hemorrhage, Maggie. Like the family told everyone. It seemed to me he was trying to say that Kyle was taking drugs and had an overdose."

Maggie stared at her, her face going as pale as the canvas sails. "Are you sure?"

Lucy nodded. "He called him a 'junked-up idiot' and said 'he did that to himself.' And a lot of other things I can't remember now." Lucy took a breath. "I know you may not believe me. Especially since he was drunk and not even speaking clearly. But I know what I heard," she said sadly. "I don't think I've made a mistake interpreting."

"I believe you," Maggie said. "Can you imagine carrying that secret? The pressure for him? For all of them. I don't even think Edie knows this."

"I don't think so, either. Kyle may have had hemorrhaged during an overdose and the physical complication was noted as his cause of death. So that's how the family was able to cover it up."

"Yes, perhaps it happened that way." She glanced back at Lucy. "I wonder if Nora talked about this in her sessions with Cassandra. Believing that she was speaking to Kyle."

"I wondered that also. Then I was thinking about Jimmy. How he may have sold Kyle the drugs. Didn't Edie say Kyle worked at the theater at one time?"

Maggie blinked, thinking back. "I think she did say that, you're right. It's very likely. And if so, it gives both Richard and Nora a logical reason to have killed Jimmy Hubbard."

Charles and Matt had toured the lower cabin, opening and closing all the cabinets, and peering into all the nooks and crannies, which were many.

They had then climbed up and gone out to the pointy front part of the boat, which Maggie called the bow, and stood out there talking for quite a while. But they were suddenly coming back.

Lucy met Maggie's glance. "Here they come. I don't think we should talk about this now."

"I don't think so, either," Maggie said. She picked up her knitting and tugged the yarn up and over a needle, quickly stitching.

Lucy gazed out at the water. The sun was low on the horizon and a flock of gulls circled, diving for their dinner in blue-green waves that were touched now with golden light.

There was certainly more to say about the connection between Jimmy Hubbard and the Gordons. But not now.

Chapter Twelve

"I'll see you tomorrow morning, at the shop," Lucy said to Maggie as the two couples parted at the marina. "You're going to show me how to finish the tote bag . . . *remember?*"

Maggie looked confused at first, then quickly nodded. "Oh, right. Come anytime. I'll be there."

Of course Maggie knew Lucy wanted to talk more about Dale Gordon and Jimmy Hubbard's murder.

The next morning, Lucy pedaled steadily toward the village, flying down the last big hill. She barely noticed the incline, or the hollow in the pit of her stomach as her bike picked up speed. She steered into the driveway in a spray of gravel and jumped off, then headed straight for the porch, where Maggie was waiting for her.

"I was expecting you. Where's your knitting bag? Don't they sell one for cyclists?"

Lucy scoffed as she pulled off her helmet and loosened her hair. "You know I only said that because Charles was there."

"I know. And I hate being sneaky around him."

"All you have to do is listen. Is that all right?"

Maggie shrugged. "I guess so. In for a penny, in for a pound. And I have been thinking about what you said last night. About Jimmy."

"I've been thinking about that, too. I have a good guess about what happened." Lucy was not happy about her conclusions. But the pieces had come together for her. And the picture they created felt true.

"Well, go on," Maggie prompted. She was knitting and listening. Lucy knew she did some of her best thinking in that pose.

"Richard and Nora both had good reason to kill Jimmy, if they had discovered he supplied the drugs that killed their son. But only Richard had the strength and easy access, late at night, in this neighborhood. Edie is always saying how he helps her close up and is in that alley, putting out trash and locking up. Then he goes back to his shop and keeps working on his rush orders."

"That does make sense."

"Jimmy knew Richard. He would have opened the door, not knowing that Richard realized the connection. Especially if Richard acted pleasant and neighborly. He's definitely good at that. Maybe he claimed that he'd just come by to warn Jimmy that the light at the back door was out."

"The light he'd broken," Maggie added.

"That's right. He's a very handy fellow. He thinks of these things. So he gets inside the theater, stabs Jimmy, and makes it look like a robbery. Then he locks the door behind him and goes back to his shop."

"And cleans himself up. There must have been some blood."

"Or he wore something to protect his clothing and threw that away," Lucy suggested.

"But what about his alibi? He said he was working in the shop and the tenants nearby, in the apartments above the stores, confirmed that," Maggie recalled.

"I was thinking about that, too. But I learned something last night. There are gadgets you can buy to make lights go on at a certain time. Or off. Timers. In fact, Richard explained that to me. He'd set some up for Edie, in her backyard."

"There's an ironic touch," Maggie noted. "But go on. Sorry to interrupt."

"Maybe he left the lights on in the shop and had some power tools attached to timers? So it only sounded as if someone was working. They only had to run on and off a little while. Half an hour, maybe even less. Before he could sneak back."

"That's brilliant, Lucy. You could be right." Maggie sat up and put her knitting aside, her dark eyes bright.

"What about Cassandra?" she asked after a moment. "How does her murder fit in? Or was that entirely unrelated, do you think?"

Lucy shrugged. "It could be unrelated. But what if Nora suspected, or even knew, that Richard had avenged their son? What if she talked about that in a session with Cassandra? Believing she was talking to Kyle's spirit?"

Maggie sat back again, her expression somber. "I see. Yes, it could have happened like that. Cassandra must have thought she'd hit the jackpot. She would blackmail the Gordons, don't you think?"

"Oh, I think so. But she wouldn't have said anything to Nora. Nora still believed in her powers. Cassandra would have threatened Richard. Now she really had a sword to hold over his head."

"Oh dear . . . I think you're right. But wait." Maggie shook her head, her brown curls shaking. "Richard had an alibi for that night, too. Didn't he?"

"In his shop again. According to Edie," Lucy recalled. "But maybe the lights were on, and the murderer was not home?"

"But he was. He really was working. Someone in an apartment came down and knocked on his door and saw him. They were complaining about the noise. He told the police that and it all checked out. Dana told us. Don't you remember?"

"Oh . . ." Lucy sat back. "I guess I forgot. I'm not sure then. Maybe the two crimes are not connected."

Maggie didn't answer. She got up and poured a cup of coffee. "Want some?"

"I'm fine, thanks." Lucy didn't mean to act deflated but she did feel that way.

"Hey, what's up? Looks like a serious conversation going on here." Dana was coming up the path and they both turned to look at her.

"We are having a serious conversation," Maggie replied. "About the Gordons."

Lucy wanted to ask Dana about Richard's alibi for the night of Cassandra's murder, wondering if Maggie had remembered it incorrectly. But Dana spoke before she could.

"Did you hear *already*? I just ran down to tell you."

"Tell us what?" Lucy turned to look at her, blocking the sun with her hand.

"The police found the missing mat from Nora's car. In the recycling center. It wasn't stained with paint. They used an infrared light and found traces of blood. The blood type matches Cassandra Waters's. They don't know about the DNA yet, of course. But they've arrested Nora and charged her with Cassandra's murder. They went to her house early this morning and took her down to the police station again."

Maggie stood up from her seat. "I still don't believe she did it."

"I don't, either," Dana said. "But if not her, who? Richard?"

"We were trying to work that out, but he has a good alibi, with a witness for that night. That's what you heard from Jack anyway," Lucy said.

Dana thought a moment. "Yes, I do remember now. Richard said he was working in his shop all night. Then he packed up his van and went to pick up Dale at a party, around one a.m. A tenant in one of the apartments nearby came down and talked to him about the machinery sometime before that. The noise and complaint were all within the time frame of Cassandra's murder, so the police eliminated him early."

Lucy sighed. "That's what Maggie recalled. More or less. I was hoping there was some wiggle room in there. But sounds airtight."

Dana glanced at her curiously. "Seems so. Do you really think he killed Cassandra?"

"I'm not sure. Something doesn't fit. I do think Richard killed Jimmy, but I'm not sure now about Cassandra. And I don't think Nora did it, either," Lucy added, feeling very sure of that conclusion.

Maggie turned the sign on her shop door to closed and locked the door. "I've already made too many speculations. I'm going over to the Schooner, to see if Edie's there."

"Good idea. I'll come with you," Dana said. Lucy was glad

Dana was going, too. Edie would surely be in emotional melt-down mode. Dana could help calm her.

Lucy walked down to the sidewalk with them, then turned toward her bike. "I have to get going. I have to call a client soon. I'll talk to you later, Maggie, and check in."

"Yes, do that," she called back over her shoulder. "Maybe Edie will know something more about Nora."

Lucy rolled her bike out of the driveway as her friends crossed the street and headed to the diner. But instead of ped-aling up the hill toward home, she headed toward the harbor, deciding it would be nice to get a little extra exercise before starting the workday. Plus sitting by the harbor a minute or two might clear her head of all these distressing questions.

As much as she wanted now to figure out this Rubik's Cube of betrayal, blackmail, and murder, her head was spin-ning and she had to give it all a rest.

And leave it to the police. Who might actually know what they're doing? Most of the time, she silently amended. Not this morning, when they had arrested Nora.

Nora did not kill Cassandra. Nora Gordon did not kill anybody. As Lucy pedaled past the lovely Gilded Age antique shop, she felt a pang of sympathy for the poor, misjudged woman. Down the alley beside the store, she saw Richard's workshop. Both buildings looked deserted.

Surely Richard would be at his wife's side right now? Not at her side exactly, if the police had her in custody. But certainly at the station, waiting to see her, dealing with her lawyer. Nora would be charged and booked and held a while, before she could come before a judge. But she could soon be out on bail. Very soon, Lucy hoped. Her mental state was frail. Surely a good lawyer could use her condition to some advantage?

Lucy wasn't sure why, but she suddenly steered the bike in a big U-turn, swooping by the antique store again from the opposite direction. Then, on impulse, she crossed the street and turned down the alley.

She hopped off the bike and balanced it against the trash bins near the wood shop. Then she peered in the small, grimy windows, shaded from inside with a film of sawdust. She couldn't see a thing and hardly knew what she was looking for. She tried the doorknob and the door opened with a soft creak.

Surprised at that, she stuck her head in and called out. "Hello? Is anyone here?"

No one answered. The space was dimly lit, slants of thin sunlight, filled with dust motes working their way through the shadows. Long beams of wood were tilted at angles against the walls like giant chopsticks.

Other piles of wood—sheets of plywood, two-by-fours, strips of carved molding, and types she didn't recognize—were balanced on sagging metal shelving that extended up to the peaked ceiling.

A countertop ran along the walls, where an array of professional power tools sat ready for use—jigsaws and drills and many she didn't know by name. Most looked sharp, jagged, and dangerous, especially to someone who didn't know how to handle them.

What was she looking for? Lucy wasn't sure. She searched for electric sockets, following a twisting network of extension cords. One led to a nearby wall and she knelt down under the counter. At the hub of a tangle of wires, she saw a small white box that covered the outlet, the plug stuck in the box, like a surge protector.

Only it wasn't a surge protector. It had a timer dial. It was the gadget Richard had described to her. And I'll bet my new bike that this one is not attached to an outdoor spotlight, to scare off burglars, Lucy thought as she followed the length of wire to its source. As she suspected, it led to a large tabletop saw. One that could buzz all night long, with no one at the controls.

"You shouldn't wander around in here, Lucy. You could get hurt."

She saw the shoes first. Heavy brown work boots stained with varnish. Then the paint-splattered jeans and flannel shirt. It was Richard. No longer the neat suburban husband she had chatted with at the barbecue, but bleary-eyed, unshaven, and haggard-looking again.

Possibly a little crazy, too. The glint in his eyes nearly set off an automatic scream for help. But she didn't dare.

"What are you doing in here? Lost something?"

"I'm sorry . . . I just wanted to ask about Nora," she fibbed. "Why aren't you with her?" she challenged him. "She must be scared."

"I was on my way home for a change of clothes. I saw your bike out there. How did you get in?"

"The door was open. Honestly."

"What's in your hand? Are you stealing from me?"

"No . . . of course not." She quickly dropped the timer on the counter.

"You're a very clever woman. For a blonde," he said snidely.

Lucy bristled at the dumb joke. She stood up straight and stared at him. "Very funny. Listen, sorry to hear about Nora. But I'd better get going."

"Not so fast, Blondie." He stepped closer, blocking her only path to the door. "You could have an accident in here very easily. This metal shelf, for instance? Way too much weight on there. Say you bumped into it? You could be buried alive. It would be very painful."

He grabbed a thin metal strip supporting the shelves and shook it. Hard. Showers of dust and splinters and even some bugs rained down on them.

Lucy squealed and covered her head with her hands.

She heard Richard laugh.

"You'd better stop . . . it's going to fall on both of us," she warned.

"But I don't care. That's the difference between us." He shook the shelf again, laughing even louder at her reaction.

"Stop, Dad. That's enough!"

Lucy looked all around but couldn't tell where the voice had come from. Then she saw Dale in the back of the shop, making his way up a narrow space between the machinery and shelves of wood.

Richard turned to face him. And Lucy began to slowly back up, desperately seeking another escape route. Or at the very least, a safer spot. The door was totally blocked. No way out there, she realized with a sinking heart.

"I told you to stay home, Dale. Go on. I'll deal with this!" Richard shouted.

"It's over, Dad. I can't do this anymore. What I did was wrong . . . and what you did was wrong, too. I'm going to the police. I'm going to tell them everything."

Richard's eyes widened with anger. He pounded the countertop with his fist. Drill bits, tools, stray nails, and screws flew in all directions.

"No you're not. We already talked about this. Just do as you're told." Richard's voice was loud and angry, then suddenly, soft and pleading. "Please, son . . . please. I know what to do. Just listen to me, okay?"

"What about Mom? Don't you care about her at all?"

"Your mother will be fine. She'll never go to trial. I told you that. She'll never have to know."

"But I know. I know everything."

Richard sighed and met his son's gaze, holding it. "It's going to be all right, Dale. If you just go home now. Why can't you just believe me and do as I say?"

Lucy knew from the look in his eye that if Richard won this debate it would be anything but all right for her. Her slow backward creeping had created a little gap, but led her to a dead end. She turned to find her back pressed against the edge of another countertop.

Richard's gaze slipped down to the workbench, and he selected a long, heavy piece of wood. It looked like a table leg or a piece of fencing. He tested the weight against a callused palm. Then he moved toward Lucy again, who skimmed along one side of the shop, like a small animal, trapped between a hunter and the proverbial hard place.

"Get help, Dale! Please . . . hurry!" she shouted.

Dale paused a moment, then turned. He looked about to go, to exit the shop from wherever he'd entered—a back door or window maybe?

But Richard was already marching toward her, the wooden weapon swung back over his head. Lucy wondered if she could dodge his blows long enough for help to come.

Suddenly Dale spun around and ran at his father. He jumped on Richard's back and grabbed for the wood. Richard gasped and fell, his son's arm squeezed around his throat.

Though the two were nearly the same height and Dale had

an athletic build, Richard had at least thirty pounds on the boy. It was hardly an even match, but both fought fiercely.

Lucy screamed and narrowly squeezed clear of their tumbling, flailing bodies, nearly pulled down to the ground on top of them.

Gravity. The force of gravity, it just pulls you down, Dale had said to her.

They rolled and grunted and fought each other in the narrow, dusty space. Lucy scrambled for some way to help Dale but couldn't think of anything. And she couldn't seem to step around or over them. Their twisting, grunting bodies entirely blocked her path to the door and her fate was the prize of whoever won this battle. A frightening thought.

"Police! Break it up! Put your hands up, where I can see them!"

Charles ran in, holding out his badge. Lucy saw a gun hanging from a holster under his jacket but he didn't reach for it.

Two uniformed police officers rushed in behind him. They grabbed Richard and Dale and pulled them up from the floor. "Hands above your heads," they repeated.

Father and son raised their grimy hands, panting and gasping for air—their faces, clothing, even their hair covered in sawdust and sweat.

The uniformed officers quickly handcuffed the Gordons and led them out of the shop.

Charles made his way to Lucy, who had collapsed from sheer relief against a counter. He briefly touched her arm. "Are you all right?"

She nodded, still too shaken to speak. "What made you come back here?"

"You can take the cop off the beat, but you can't take the beat out of the cop." He shrugged and offered a small smile. "Just an instinct. I drove by Maggie's shop and saw it was empty, then noticed the CLOSED sign on the door. That got my radar going."

Maggie never closed, even if she was sick, or there was a hurricane blowing. Well, maybe a hurricane. But she stayed open until the last possible minute. He knew that about their mutual friend by now.

"So I drove by again, very slowly. I passed this place, too. Slow enough to notice a bike back here. And Richard's van. I thought that was suspicious, him being here. He should have been at the station with his wife. Or at home."

"That's what I figured," she said.

"What were you doing here?" His tone was a bit more stern now, she noticed.

"I have to confess, I was snooping. Looking for this." She picked up one of the timers and showed it to him. "It was connected to the table saw. I think that's how Richard killed Jimmy Hubbard and appeared to be working at the same time, so he had a solid alibi."

Charles nodded, taking the timer from her. She could see he got it. "Good one . . . but what motive would Richard have to kill Jimmy?"

This part was harder to say. "Kyle didn't die of a brain hemorrhage. It was an overdose. Or maybe a hemorrhage brought on by one. He worked at the theater for a while, before he died. Jimmy must have supplied him with the drugs that killed him. Richard found that out somehow and took revenge for his son's death."

Charles let out a breath, his eyes narrowed. "Who told you the kid died from drugs?"

"Dale did. More or less. At the barbecue. He was drunk and babbling. I would have told you but it took me a while to put it together."

Charles looked a bit cross now and folded his arms over his chest. "We can check that easily. Anything else you would have told me? Richard had an alibi for the night the psychic was murdered. An eyewitness saw him here. You don't think he did that, too, do you?"

"No, he didn't play that card again," she said. "Though I think he despised Cassandra enough to do it."

"It was Nora," Charles replied. "She told everyone she was taking a sleeping pill, but she left their house, killed Cassandra, and went back home. Except she got blood in her car. And when she saw it, she threw out the mat. Her husband and son didn't get home until at least one thirty. They found her sleeping in bed. Dale had been at a party and Richard picked him up, after working here. That was well after Cassandra's time of death."

Lucy shook her head. "I don't think it was Nora, either." She knew Charles wouldn't believe her, but she felt sure of it now. "I think Dale killed Cassandra. I'm not exactly sure why. But there's a good chance Cassandra knew that Richard had killed Jimmy and was blackmailing the Gordons. Or threatened to. I think Dale found out and was trying to protect his parents. Maybe he was tired of seeing Cassandra exploit them."

Charles didn't look like he was buying it so easily. But he was at least entertaining the idea. "So you think he went to the psychic's house, after his mother's session, and confronted her. And maybe she tried to brush him off, or they argued, and he flew into a rage?"

"Something like that. Dale was under tremendous pressure keeping the secret of his brother's death and knowing how his father had avenged that death by killing Jimmy. Cassandra was dragging out his family's agony. And torturing his parents even more," Lucy said.

Charles considered this theory but didn't look as if he believed it quite yet. "So you think the night Cassandra died, Dale left the party, killed the psychic, and went back to the party. His father picked him up and took him home. None the wiser."

"Yes . . . Richard picked him up, for some reason using Nora's car instead of his van. Richard was delivering a table and set of chairs early the next day. Maybe he'd already loaded the van and there wasn't any room for a passenger. I heard the bloodstain was on the passenger side of the car. Not the driver's."

"Right, a bloodstain—Cassandra's blood, we believe—is on a mat from the passenger's side of Nora's car. But you think it's because Dale sat in that spot, with Richard driving," Charles clarified.

"Yes, I do. And one of them must have found it later and tried to get rid of the evidence."

"Richard was the one who told us he threw it away and ordered a new mat," Charles said.

"He must have realized what Dale had done. But of course, he would do anything to protect his son. His only child now," Lucy reminded him.

"Very true. There's a partial footprint in the stain. Just a scrap. But we might be able to get a match to one of Dale's shoes," he mused aloud.

Charles seemed to believe her theory now. But Lucy was

not pleased to have to figure out this puzzle, as bleak and heartbreaking as any Greek tragedy.

The night of the barbecue, Dale had been rambling about dominoes, falling one on top of the other, once the first was tipped over. The image fit so well for the demise of his family.

"One more thing," Charles asked. "Does Maggie know you came here?"

Lucy shook her head. "She went to see Edie and she thought I went home."

"And she doesn't know anything about this? About your theory?"

"Well . . . we talked about it a little. I talked, mostly. She just listened."

He smiled a moment but didn't ask any more questions. He touched her shoulder and led her out to the light.

Police officers flanked both of the Gordons and helped them into the rear seats of two separate cruisers.

Charles took hold of the bike and rolled it along. "I'll give you a lift home. You can come to the station later and sign a statement."

That plan suited Lucy just fine.

She longed to be back in her quiet, snug cottage. To stand under a long hot shower and scrub the sawdust from her skin and hair. And wash away the deep sadness she felt for the Gordons, if that was ever possible.

Maybe in a few hours, or even tomorrow, she'd catch up with Maggie and the rest of her friends. At that moment, Lucy felt too drained to tell anyone this story.

All of Lucy's friends called and sent text messages after her ordeal with Richard, to see how she was doing. But all agreed that she'd wait until they were together to tell them the whole story. They did agree to skip the Thursday night meeting, since they were spending the weekend together. Even though their plans had been changed a bit.

Suzanne reported in a group e-mail on Tuesday night that the beach house would not be free and clear until Saturday around noon.

I know, bummer. But we can stay through Monday morning. It's only ten minutes from town. We get up early and zip back to the village to return to reality, by 9 a.m. (Phoebe, you can wear your PJs on the trip home. No problem.)

Lucy didn't mind the slight delay at all. She felt drained after her adventure and took it easy around the cottage and her office. Dara was staying with them all week, before she left for camp and Lucy was grateful for the little girl's cheerful, energetic company. She was happy to let Dara plan their days —going to the beach, washing the dogs, and making cookies— while Matt was at his office.

Matt had been very caring and solicitous all week, not even scolding Lucy for the risky behavior that had nearly gotten her killed. Lucy still sensed a subtle tension between them, though Dara's company was a good excuse to act as if everything was just peachy.

Still, Lucy wondered what Matt was really thinking and when he'd broach the sensitive topic she'd raised again. Would she have to remind him? That would be so discouraging. She didn't think that she even could.

Dara was leaving for camp Saturday morning and Lucy

was relieved to be leaving with her friends at just about the same time. She was in the bedroom, packing her beach clothes and knitting after breakfast when Matt called up to her.

"Lucy? We're leaving. Dara wants to say goodbye."

Lucy left her clothes in a heap and trotted downstairs. "And I want to say goodbye to Dara," she said.

She had to be the cutest camper ever, Lucy thought. She wore a Camp Blue Lake T-shirt, polka dot shorts, and brand-new pink sneakers. A huge duffel bag and brand-new sleeping bag sat at her feet. A large green backpack with a frog face—a good-luck gift from Lucy—was slung over one shoulder. Her ponytail, which Lucy had spent considerable energy fastening just minutes before, was already hanging loose. Her smile, excited but nervous.

Lucy felt a little teary but forced a huge smile as she gave Dara a big hug. "You look awesome. Ready for action. Don't forget to write me and tell me everything. The postcards are all addressed and stamped, in your duffel."

"I will," Dara said. She put her arm around Lucy's neck and hugged back. "Bye."

"Bye," Lucy echoed. She stepped back and waved. She hoped that she didn't cry.

Dara was already hugging and kissing the dogs and didn't notice. Which was a good thing, Lucy thought.

Matt looked a little glassy-eyed, too, but he put on his gruff, cheerful face. "Come on, squirt. Time to get on the road. You go out to the truck. I'll be right there," he said as Dara walked out the door.

He turned to Lucy and met her glance. "You have a great time. Should I call?"

Lucy shrugged. "Sure. But the cell service is not very good out there," she added. Plum Island was barely fifteen miles from the cottage, but the service there was spotty.

"I'll try," he promised. "I'm going to stay over with Will and Jen. But I'll be back tomorrow."

"Good plan. Tell them I said hello."

"I will." He paused. Matt picked up Dara's duffel and sleeping bag with one arm and his small pack with the other. Lucy felt a heaviness in her heart. They were speaking to each other so . . . formally. What was going on here?

Matt felt it, too. She could tell. Finally he said, "Listen, I know things have been a little off with us since we had that talk. The night before Edie's barbecue? At least it feels that way to me."

"Me, too," Lucy admitted.

"Well . . . I don't want you to worry. We'll sort this out." He shrugged. As if they had disagreed about who should empty the dishwasher. "I'm sorry to make you wait but . . . it's complicated."

Lucy felt sucker-punched but tried to hide her reaction. "Must be. That's what you said before." She didn't mean to sound snide, but her words had come out that way. He looked about to reply, then seemed to think better of answering her. Maybe that was just as well, she thought. This was hardly the time for some big, emotional showdown.

She guessed Matt had initiated this little chat to reassure her. But she felt anything but reassured.

"Hey . . . it's all right." She shook her head. "We'll figure it out. Whatever . . ."

She also hated when people said "whatever." Maybe even more than "it's complicated." But she found herself scrambling for emotional cover in the face of an unexpected meteor hurtling down upon her.

It sounded like Matt did not want to make a commitment. Lucy was not only surprised but deeply hurt. It was all she could do to keep a stoic expression as he leaned over to kiss her goodbye. She'd expected a real kiss. Wrong again. An awkward quick peck landed on her cheek as he wobbled from side to side, unbalanced by the weight of the duffel and pack.

He grinned self-consciously. "Don't forget the sunblock."

"I won't."

She stepped out on the porch and watched him toss the bags in the back of the truck, then slip behind the wheel.

Dara was already wearing headphones but waved to Lucy as the truck pulled out of the driveway. They seemed to be sharing a joke, which Lucy couldn't hear, of course, and laughing wildly. Matt tapped the horn as they sped off.

For some strange reason, she did think he looked relieved—and maybe even happy—to be getting away from her.

Suzanne was late. Over an hour. Lucy hovered around the house, looking for little jobs to occupy her time. She felt too restless to read and didn't want to walk the dogs in the midday heat and start the trip feeling hot and sticky.

It was hard to distract herself from disturbing thoughts about Matt and what he might say when—and if—they returned to the touchy subject she had raised. Did couples often break up over this issue? She knew that was true. If one partner laid down an ultimatum.

But I'm a long way from that stage. Unless Matt has a panic attack and plans the old "I can't give you what you need" exit strategy.

262 / Anne Canadeo

Just stop. You're driving yourself crazy. This weekend is supposed to be a relaxing, fun-filled time with your stitching and bitching soul sisters. You look like you're on the way to a funeral, Lucy told herself, glancing in the mirror.

At least there would be plenty of time this weekend to ask for their advice. And get their encouragement, which went without saying. She'd return home with a strategy of her own. The plan made her feel a little better. Good enough to smile at the sight of Suzanne racing into the driveway and waving from her window.

"We're here! Are you ready?" She was clearly ready, dressed in a hot pink tank top and huge black Wayfarers.

"Totally," Lucy called from the door. With her bags slung over her arm—one for clothes and one for her knitting—she quickly locked the door. Tink and Wally had jumped on the couch, staring out with serious concern. A neighbor was coming in a few times a day to take care of them. She knew they'd be fine, but also knew she'd miss them a little.

Next time—me, dogs, beach house. That combination might end up a necessity.

Lucy was the last on Suzanne's route. Dana slid over to make room for her in the backseat and she tossed her bags in the trunk and slammed the door.

"Tuck it in or lose it, ladies," Suzanne announced, backing the bus-size vehicle out of the small driveway.

"Did Dara get off to camp all right?" Maggie asked from the front seat.

"Without a hitch . . . or a tear. She seemed a little worried but also excited."

"As it should be. It's a big step, first summer at sleepaway camp," Maggie replied.

"Then they get to the stage when they don't want to come back," Dana added.

"We're having our own sleepaway camp this weekend, sort of," Phoebe mused. "Fresh air, exercise, crafts?"

"Gourmet food and wine," Suzanne noted. "That cooler in the back is seriously stocked. Including . . ." She stopped herself and met Lucy's curious gaze in the rearview mirror. "Well, lots of good stuff."

Lucy met her gaze in the mirror. She could tell by now when Suzanne was hiding something. Or trying to. She was awful at keeping a secret.

"I hope you didn't bring a birthday cake or anything silly like that. I just want this getaway to be about hanging out, all of us. Definitely not about my birthday, okay?"

Now Suzanne and Dana and even Maggie looked a little uneasy.

But Maggie's tone was decisive. "There is absolutely no birthday cake, or anything like that, in this vehicle. That's the God's honest truth."

"All right . . . if you say so." Lucy still had a funny feeling they were planning something. Maybe a cupcake with a sparkler in it?

She finally had to smile. Her friends were the perfect tonic for her anxious mood and she already felt better.

"This trip is about relaxing, totally," Suzanne chimed in. "I estimate we will be on the beach, knitting within the hour. The great thing about Plum Island is that it's so close. But when you get there, you feel really far away."

Lucy loved the spot, for that reason and others. She and Matt went there often in the summer when they wanted a change from their local beach. And just as Suzanne had predicted, they were soon crossing the land bridge that connected the island to the mainland. It was sometimes washed out by a big storm, or even submerged under a particularly high tide. But today they drove across quickly and soon found themselves on the island's main road.

"Wow. That was fast," Dana said, checking the time on her phone. She leaned over the seat and spoke directly to Suzanne. "We're here already. It's not even two."

"Yes, I know. I can see that." Suzanne sounded annoyed at Dana's announcement for some odd reason. Lucy wondered why. She'd hoped to get here even earlier. But it was still early. She was just stressed. I'll be in a better mood later, Lucy thought.

Suzanne slowed down and pulled her phone out of a cup holder. "Somebody read this thing, okay? I can't google and drive at the same time."

"I'll try." Maggie took the phone and slipped on her reading glasses. "There's a little red pulsing dot. Is that the house?"

"No, that's the car," Suzanne corrected.

"Oh . . . let's see. What am I looking for?"

"A blue dot," Phoebe snapped. She was squirming with impatience. The way adults feel watching a child try to feed herself for the first time, Lucy thought.

"Oh, okay . . . Oh my goodness. I touched something wrong. The whole darn map disappeared."

Maggie looked back at them, baffled. Phoebe snatched the phone from her. "What's the address?"

Suzanne told her and Phoebe quickly tapped a few times. "Got it. Looks like we're going entirely the wrong way; you have to turn around."

Suzanne made a face. "Oh, all right. I should probably know better but I don't have many listings out here."

It took Suzanne a while to find a good place to turn the SUV. The road was very narrow, with sandy trenches on either side.

Finally, they were pointed in the right direction. Lucy hoped.

"Okay, let's try this again," Suzanne said more cheerfully.

But the island was a maze of twisting lanes and sandy dead-end streets. Lucy started to wonder if they'd get to the beach house before sunset.

Maggie sighed as they needed to double back once again. "My goodness, so close and yet so far."

"I'll say. How long have we been driving around?"

Dana checked her phone again. "About half an hour. Oh well, there's plenty of daylight left. I like the beach best in the later afternoon anyway, when the sun isn't so strong."

That was Lucy's favorite time at the shore, too. She didn't mind going to the beach late. But she was feeling a bit carsick. She hoped they'd get to the house soon.

They finally found the street and searched for the house number. The atmosphere on the island was funky, another reason Lucy loved it, with lopsided cottages that weren't winterized, set next to more modern homes. But all jumbled together on small plots, the decks and balconies shimmering with wind chimes and colorful flags. And lots of wet beach towels.

"There it is. Finally." Suzanne sighed with relief as she pulled into the driveway in front of a reasonably sized cottage, freshly painted pale yellow and decorated with buoys.

"It's adorable. So . . . Plum Island," Dana said with appreciation.

"It's perfect," Suzanne agreed. "Let's check it out and pick bedrooms before we bring all our stuff inside."

They emptied out of the SUV and followed Suzanne up the path. Lucy was right behind, with Dana dawdling as she fumbled with sunglasses and Maggie moving even slower behind her. Phoebe was last to get out of the car and trotted to keep up.

"Let's see . . . which is the front door key?" Suzanne had a key ring in her hand, with a fat rubber shark dangling from one end.

She finally opened the door and stepped inside. "Hey, this is nice. Even better than the photos. Take a look at that view, everybody."

Suzanne beckoned from an entryway, smiling with delight, and Lucy quickly followed. She stepped into the foyer and looked into the house . . . and saw a crowd of people facing her.

"Surprise! Happy birthday, Lucy!"

Lucy screamed and covered her face with her hands. "Oh my God! What is this?"

She couldn't believe it. Matt broke free from the group and ran up to her. "Happy birthday, honey. Gee, you were really surprised, weren't you?"

Lucy blinked, not knowing whether to laugh or cry. "I was . . . I still am. Totally."

"We fooled you, Lucy," a small voice said gleefully. Lucy looked down and found Dara, standing next to Matt.

"You totally fooled me. Why aren't you at camp, miss? Was that all a big trick?" Of course she knew it had been, but she enjoyed watching Dara relish the moment.

"Uh-huh." Dara nodded vigorously.

"She's actually leaving tomorrow. Her mother is going to take her," Matt explained. "Dara didn't want to miss your party."

"I'm so glad you didn't," she said to Dara, then looked up at Matt again. "You did a stellar job of tricking me, too."

"I tried. I could barely hold it together at the end," he admitted. "Your buddies helped."

"We were only bit players," Suzanne cut in. "Though it did get tricky. He didn't want you here before three. And I nearly told you that the cooler is full of party food—and raspberry mojitos."

Lucy laughed at that confession. "You're usually an ace with directions. I almost got suspicious. But I was too carsick."

Suzanne shrugged. "Blame Matt. He planned it all. He even found the house."

"Wow . . . pretty good." It was all Lucy could say as Matt's glance met hers and held it. He planted a big wet kiss on her cheek and slung his arm around her shoulder as they walked farther into the big living room to greet her many guests.

This has to count for something good, Lucy decided. He wouldn't go to all this trouble if he didn't care about me. Would he?

Well . . . don't get your hopes up yet. This birthday bash could be a consolation prize, another voice warned. A bid to get into your good graces before he delivers the "complicated" bad news?

Lucy glanced at him. She wasn't sure. But she suddenly didn't care. Be here now. At your party. Worrying won't make any difference.

As she moved into a sea of friends and family, all trying to hug, kiss, and wish her well, she didn't want to change a thing.

In addition to her closest pals and their significant others—Charles, Jack Haeger, and Kevin Cavanaugh—Lucy also spotted Phoebe at the edge of the scene, talking with a tall, thin, cute guy with a big brown beard. The potter with soulful hands, she guessed. That seemed promising. There were many friends she knew from town, other couples she and Matt socialized with, along with friends from her book group and even a few old friends from Boston.

Her sister Ellen and her family were there, of course. Ellen hugged her excitedly. "You should have seen your face. I took pictures! They're already on Facebook," she announced, happily waving her phone.

"Thanks!" Lucy gave her a hug, vowing she'd never go on Facebook again.

Lucy guessed the photos made her look like the star of a slasher movie. Ellen was not known for her photographic skills.

What could you do? Family was . . . family.

"What a great party. If only Mom was here," Ellen said wistfully.

Lucy's spirits dipped like a kite. "Yeah . . . too bad. But she's stuck in Africa a few more weeks. No help for that."

"Not quite," another voice cut in. Lucy spun around to find her mother, beaming at her. She couldn't imagine where she'd kept out of view all this time, but glancing at Matt, Lucy could see this second surprise had been carefully crafted as well.

"For goodness' sakes, look who's here. Isabel, all the way from another hemisphere," Matt remarked with mock astonishment.

Lucy's mother did carry a certain foreign air, wearing a toast-colored linen shift and a bright shawl, fashioned from a swath of fabric she'd surely found in some far-off, native marketplace. Her jewelry, handmade as well; bright beads on a dark strand of hemp and several woven bracelets. Her hair, fair like Lucy's but streaked with silvery white, was wound in a loose bun at the back of her head. Her round face was lightly tanned and bright eyes peered out from behind large-framed, professorial-looking glasses.

"Mom . . . you made it. Wow . . . thank you so much."

Lucy hugged her mother tight and Isabel hugged her back, then looked up smiling.

"I'd definitely planned to be here. But I did want to surprise you. It took a bit of maneuvering. But it was more than worth it to see the expression on your beautiful face."

Her mother patted Lucy's cheek, as if she were a little girl again. "Where has the time gone? It seems like you and Ellen were just . . . well, Dara's age. I don't feel any older at all," she said with a laugh.

"You don't seem any older, Mom. Keep up the good work. A good sign for me and Ellen," Lucy added, glancing at her sister.

Her mother had waited to have children. "Until I was ready to be a good mother. Not because somebody said I had to," she always told Lucy. She'd been even older than Lucy when Ellen was born. It was uncommon in her era, but not at all now. If Lucy could remain as curious, active, and inspired as her mother was still, she knew she would be a happy woman.

The guests had filtered out to the deck and the beach, where there appeared to be enough food and drink to last all weekend.

There was music and dancing and the guests just did as they pleased. It was just the kind of party Lucy would have planned, given the chance. Matt knew her so well in that way.

It was after midnight when the last guests said their

goodbyes and drifted home. There had been some help cleaning up, but she and Matt agreed to just leave the rest for the morning. The beach house was theirs for the weekend— a gift from her friends. Maggie and Charles had brought Dara to her mother's house earlier, leaving Lucy and Matt all alone.

They collapsed side by side on the couch, their feet up on a hassock, and stared out at the perfect view. The moon, almost full, hung against the inky black sky, right above the water. A shimmery silver beam of moonlight rested on the waves, stretching from the shore to the horizon, like a path to a far-off dreamland.

"What a great night," Lucy said, then sighed. "This was the best birthday gift anyone ever gave me," she said sincerely.

Matt met her gaze, his eyes sparkling. "But this isn't your birthday gift, Lucy. Not the whole thing anyway," he added.

"There's more?" Lucy watched him curiously but couldn't tell what he was up to now.

"Absolutely. Come out on the deck." He jumped up from the couch and pulled her hand. "Close your eyes."

"Um . . . okay." Lucy made her way outside with Matt gently leading her. She felt the warm wood of the deck under her bare feet.

"Can I look now?"

"Just a second." He left her for a moment and she heard some rustling sounds. "Okay, you can look now."

She dropped her hands and saw a sleek, ultra-expensive bicycle with all the extra accessories one could ever hope for. She knew that she should be bursting with joy at the sight, from the high-tech toe clips to the shiny handlebars that had been custom-fit to her reach and height.

Still, she secretly wished the extra gift had come in a small velvet jeweler's box. But she quickly rallied and showed her delight.

"You got the bike after all? You didn't have to do that," she insisted.

"Not had to. Wanted to. I promised you, didn't I?"

"Yes, but . . . well, the party was more than enough of a birthday present."

"Oh, Lucy . . . just go ahead and try it. Stop arguing with me." He laughed.

Lucy had already walked over to the bike and ran her hand over the smooth black seat, eyeing the many fine touches in the mechanism and gears. "Dana is going to be so jealous. She may never cycle with me again."

"I got this gadget to clip on your helmet, with a little rearview mirror . . . oh, and here's the bottle I was telling you about. The latest technology." He pulled a slim chrome water bottle from the holder just below the handlebars.

"It has a filter so you never have to worry about refilling it."

Lucy took the bottle in her hand. "Nice."

"Open it, let's see how it works," he said eagerly.

She glanced at him. He did get excited about these little interesting inventions. Lucy unscrewed the top and the much-lauded filter, all fifty pieces of it, came apart in her hand.

"For goodness' sakes . . . I hope I can get this back together. Did it come with instructions?" She glanced up at him.

"I'm not sure. Open your hand, let's see what fell out."

Lucy opened her palm. Matt was good at puzzles. She was about to hand him the entire mess when he suddenly pulled one piece out.

"Interesting . . . what have we here?"

He held up a gold ring, with a bright round ruby displayed in a vintage setting.

Lucy gasped. She suddenly couldn't breathe. She finally shrieked with shock and heard Matt laughing softly.

"You . . . you . . . You got me a ring!?"

"Uh-huh. Like it?"

Lucy's face crumpled; she felt she was about to cry. "It's perfect," she nearly wailed. "Just . . . just . . . what I wanted."

"Oh . . . great. I wasn't exactly sure," he admitted. He sighed and let out a long, slow breath. "But I am sure—completely and utterly positive—that you are the wisest, funniest, sweetest, most lovable person I have ever known and I could not imagine my life, my future, without you. I love you completely, with all my heart and soul, and would be the happiest, luckiest guy in the world if you would spend the rest of your life with me. Will you, Lucy? Will you marry me?"

Lucy couldn't speak. She met Matt's gaze. "I love you absolutely and totally, too . . . and I would love to marry you."

He sighed and slipped the ring on her finger, then pulled her close and lifted her off her feet. After they shared a deep, long kiss, he looked down at her and laughed.

"See, I told you not to worry. And that we'd talk and work it out."

Lucy laughed. "Yes, you did. And you said 'it was complicated.' Maybe you meant that water bottle?"

"True . . . but the rest is easy. Just like riding a bike."

He kissed her again and Lucy couldn't remember what she'd been worrying about.

Chapter Thirteen

On Monday afternoon, after returning home and coming back to reality as much as she was able, Lucy sent a group text to her friends, thanking them again for helping with the party and for the wonderful present of the beach house.

> We really do have to go out there together some weekend before the summer is over. It's perfect. If anyone is around tomorrow a.m., would love to meet up at the shop.

She not only wanted to take her bike for a test spin but was dying to tell everyone the big news. And show off her ring, if she was absolutely truthful.

Her friends responded almost instantly, confirming they'd be there. Lucy set out early, expecting to be the first to arrive, except for Maggie. But as she glided up to the shop, she found all her friends waiting on the porch. They clapped as she swooped into the driveway.

"Way to go!" Suzanne called out. "Woo-hoo."

"What a set of wheels, Lucy," Dana shouted.

Lucy very gently rested the new bike against the fence and pulled off her helmet. She grabbed her water bottle and carried it up to the porch.

"It's not only pretty, it's a supersmooth ride. What a difference. I feel like I'm pedaling on a cloud," she said, thankful to step into the shade.

"I'll have to pad that fence," Maggie noted. "I don't want your bike getting scratched. Maybe a sheath of velvet?" she mused in a serious tone.

"Just the thing. I'd appreciate it."

"So . . . great party, great gift," Suzanne said with a shrug.

Lucy knew what she was really thinking and could see how hard she was trying to hold back.

"Yes, the best birthday I've ever had," Lucy agreed. "Not to mention all the trimmings. Like these spiffy new gloves." Lucy waved a hand, showing off her riding gloves.

"Yes, totally spiffy. You're all . . . spiffed up," Suzanne said drily.

Lucy held her hand up and slowly tugged off her left glove. "They really protect my hands. I don't know how I got along without them."

She held out her bare hand, practically pushing it into Suzanne's face.

Finally Suzanne saw the ring. Her jaw dropped open and her mouth formed a small, silent O.

"Oh my God! Look at this!" she grabbed Lucy's hand and was practically slinging her around the porch. "Lucy got a ring! They're engaged!"

She turned and stared at Lucy. "You are . . . aren't you?"

Her tone was suddenly fretful, wondering if she'd made some mistake.

"We're engaged," Lucy echoed, nodding.

The rest of her friends jumped with gleeful squeals and surrounded her in a group hug that nearly knocked her off her feet.

"I'm so happy for you," Dana said sincerely.

"I knew Matt would come through. He's a good guy," Phoebe offered.

"I had a feeling something like this was going to happen," Maggie added. "Tell us all the details now. We want to hear everything."

Lucy had a feeling they'd ask her that. She carefully described how Matt had waited until they were alone and brought her outside to see the new bike, then hid the ring in that silly water bottle.

"Aw. That is so cute." Suzanne was practically gushing. "Just like a chick flick," she reminded Lucy.

"Yeah . . . just like it. Except that for a few days, it was more like one of those indie movies where the girl gets dumped. At least from my point of view. I did have a serious conversation with Matt about our relationship. I never got to tell you," she added. "And it wasn't exactly reassuring. In fact, I wasn't sure if we were still going to be together for my real birthday," she added, which was coming up on Thursday.

"But he pulled up his boots and came through for you," Suzanne said.

"Actually, he told me that he had been planning to propose on my birthday for a while and wanted it to be a surprise. When I asked for the bike, he thought it was the perfect cover

276 / Anne Canadeo

for his real gift. So, no, the 'Big Talk' had nothing to do with it. But he didn't want to spoil the surprise, so he put me off. Very effectively, I must add."

"I think it's very romantic that he went to all the trouble to surprise you. Even if it did make you a little nervous." Maggie smiled down at her knitting, looking very pleased by the news.

"It was romantic. I feel like we were away for a month. Instead of a weekend."

"Also, as it should be," Dana said with a soft smile.

"You do have a certain glow, Queenie," Suzanne noted. "Not just from the sun."

Lucy felt herself blush. Now she was really glowing, she'd bet, but before Suzanne could tease her more, she quickly changed the subject.

"What's going on around here? Any news about the Gordons?" she asked as she took a seat.

"You probably heard last week on the news, both Dale and Richard have entered pleas of 'not guilty,'" Dana replied.

"Yes, I did hear that. Though I wasn't really following as closely as I have the last few weeks."

A bit burned-out from her own adventure with Richard, she knew.

Suzanne picked up a huge cup of some sort of icy coffee drink and stirred it briskly with her straw. Lucy could only imagine what it was called—a "Mocha-Mumbo-Jumbo with Extra Cream"?

"Why do you think they did that? I mean, it seems like there's solid evidence stacked up against both of them," she said.

"And I heard that Dale, at least, gave a full confession," Maggie added.

"I think Richard did, too, finally," Dana said. "The thing is, if they simply enter a plea of guilty, there will be no trial. Richard will get life imprisonment. Possibly, death. Dale is a minor. It's different for him. He's been sent to a juvenile detention facility in Worcester, where he'll undergo a month of psychiatric observation. His attorneys hope some diagnosis helps his case. I think both are hoping for a better chance at a lighter sentence with a jury who might have compassion for the family's story."

"I feel terrible for both of them," Lucy said, "but especially for Dale. He is so young."

Maggie sighed and put her work aside. "The Gordons' story is definitely one worthy of compassion, for all, if ever I heard one."

"How is Nora holding up?" Lucy asked. "How is she managing without Richard . . . and with everything that's happened."

"She's staying with her sister, who lives near Worcester. So she can visit Dale," Maggie said. "Edie and her daughters are helping her, too. Edie says Nora never wants to come back to Plum Harbor. She's closed the shop permanently and Edie is trying to find a buyer for her."

"That makes sense. Of course she'd want to get away from here. All the attention right now, for one thing," Phoebe said. "It must be just awful and she's not that tightly wound."

"One way of putting it," Maggie murmured.

"I hate to gossip but . . . how does she feel about Richard now? Did Edie say, Maggie?" Lucy asked. "Does Nora visit him at all?"

"That's a good question. I don't know. Perhaps she has some empathy for his impulse to seek vengeance on the man who more or less took their son's life. Even if she's repulsed by the actual act. I've sometimes wondered if Nora was surprised to learn what Richard did. It does seem now that he had a split personality . . . or at least, a very dark side he didn't show to the world at large. But maybe she was well aware of that side of him?"

"I've wondered that, too." Dana suddenly turned to Lucy. "With all this happy news, you never told us about your encounter with Richard at the wood shop. The day the Gordons got arrested."

"You mean the day Lucy nabbed Richard Gordon, almost single-handed?" Phoebe corrected.

"Not quite," Lucy said with a harsh laugh. "More like the day I narrowly escaped becoming his next victim . . . "

Lucy finally told her friends the whole story about her visit to the wood shop the morning of Nora's arrest and about facing down Richard there. And then how Dale arrived and the two men battled fiercely, her fate hanging in the balance.

"It's impossible to say now; everything happened so quickly. But it seemed like Richard was winning. I don't know what would have happened if Charles hadn't felt some tingle of police officer intuition when he spotted my bike and Richard's van in the alley."

"He's got a real knack for that." Maggie's tone was quiet but proud.

"Yes, he does," Lucy said. "He was also more open to hearing out my theories than I expected. I did make sure he knew that you didn't have anything to do with my snooping, Maggie," Lucy added.

"Thanks, but Charles and I have come to terms about all that. He more or less admitted to me that you helped him sort out this massive tangle. And he gave me a little credit, too. Totally undeserved," she quickly added. "I don't think he'll ever encourage my snooping. But it does look like he's decided to live with it."

"It comes with the package and he definitely likes the rest of that," Suzanne said tartly.

Maggie just laughed. "I suppose you could put it that way."

"And we definitely welcome you back to the fold." Dana had been knitting steadily, working on a new project that Lucy didn't recognize.

"Making something new?" Lucy asked. "I didn't know you finished your tote."

"I did . . . I'm just waiting for Maggie to help me felt it." She glanced in Maggie's direction.

Lucy sighed. "I didn't sew mine up yet. My life has been so exciting lately."

"Well, get a move on. We'll felt them all together. In the shop," Maggie suggested.

"Will you still put mine in the window?" Lucy asked.

"I've saved the spot. But it can't stay empty forever," Maggie reminded her.

"I'll finish this week, by Thursday night."

"All right. Why don't you all aim for that; we'll have a combination happy birthday and felting party then, I guess." Maggie shrugged.

As much as Lucy had loved her big surprise party, she was still looking forward to the more intimate celebration with her very best friends.

"Good deadline, Maggie. I like it. Right, Lucy?" Suzanne said pointedly.

"Sounds perfect. And my mom will be here visiting by

then. She's with Ellen now in Lexington but she's coming to Plum Harbor for a week. So she'll be at this party, too."

"The more the merrier. I like your mom, Lucy. She's really cool," Phoebe said.

"Another party? I thought you girls just had one." Edie had come halfway up the walk without anyone noticing her, which was a bit remarkable, Lucy realized.

"It's Lucy's real birthday on Thursday and we're going to have some cake and champagne . . . and felt our totes," Maggie explained.

"Would you like to come, Edie?" Lucy said. "We'd love it if you could join us."

Edie looked surprised by the invitation, and touched. "I'd love to, dear. I'm sorry I didn't make it to your big surprise party on the beach. I heard it was epic."

Lucy was surprised to hear the bit of slang from Edie. Outdated as it was.

"More than epic. I'd say a milestone." Suzanne waxed poetic. "Lucy and Matt are engaged. He proposed right after the guests all left."

Edie stared at Lucy in happy surprise. "He did? Way to go, girl!" She hugged Lucy to her ample chest and Lucy thought she might be smothered in a cloud of flowery perfume. "I'm tickled pink," Edie said, finally releasing her.

"Thanks, Edie," Lucy said laughing, smoothing herself out.

"Finally, some good news." Edie sighed as she dropped down in a wicker chair.

Maggie nodded. "Yes, it is a bright spot."

"And nice to end our chat on a high note," Dana said. "I have to get to the office. See you all soon."

Suzanne was also ready to go and Lucy decided she ought to head home, too.

They wished Maggie and Edie goodbye and Dana walked Lucy down to the drive to see her bike.

"It's a beauty, Lucy. Light as a feather, too," she said with a note of envy as she tested the weight. "Now we have to plan a long trek."

Lucy already had her helmet on and swung herself up on the seat. "That will be great; maybe the Cape?"

"Perfect. But you'll be the one leaving me in the dust," Dana noted with a grin.

Lucy answered with a shocked look as she began to pedal away. "Never, Dana. Sheep always stick together. Even on bicycles."

Dana just laughed and waved. "Enjoy your new ride."

"I am already!" Lucy shouted back. Her new cycle couldn't have been nicer, with all the extras she could ever want, including a gorgeous ruby ring that seemed to wink at her as she tugged on her riding glove and headed home.

𝖬aggie was content to sit with Edie without talking, after all the excited conversation this morning. She and Edie watched from the porch as Lucy pedaled up Main Street, heading back to the Marshes. Lucy waved and Maggie waved back.

"It is nice to see Lucy so happy. She said the new bike is like floating on a cloud. But I think she'd be floating even without it right now."

Edie sighed and laughed. She fanned herself with a knitting magazine she'd found on the side table. "She just about sparkles. I nearly had to put my sunglasses on just to chat with her."

"Hmm." Maggie nodded. "And you're sparkling a bit, too, this morning, I noticed." She met Edie's glance. "Your father's watch is back?" she asked quietly.

Edie looked down at her wrist and the heavy gold watch. "Yup, back safe and sound. Talk about out of the blue. Never thought I'd see this again. Unless I scoured every pawnshop in the country and even then, the chances would have been doubtful."

"Did the police return it to you?" Maggie did wonder how the police were going to sort out any property they'd found in Cassandra's possession. She'd expected that would take a long time.

Edie shook her head. "Nope. The cops had nothing to do with it. You'll be surprised to hear who did." She leaned back and pulled a folded piece of paper from the pocket of her dress. "Here . . . read this. It came in the package. With the watch."

Maggie was curious now. She put her knitting aside, adjusted her glasses, and unfolded the sheet. It was a letter, handwritten in cursive script. But neat and legible.

"Dear Mrs. Steiber," she began aloud.

"It's all right. I've read it. A few times. Read it to yourself." Edie sounded impatient.

Maggie saw that the letter was from Daphne Mullens, Cassandra's daughter, and quickly scanned the lines:

I believe this gold watch belongs to you and I want to return it. My mother sent it to me and asked that I keep it in a safe place. It is doubtlessly, very valuable. I'd guess, even more precious to you for sentimental reasons. My mother didn't tell me much, but I can imagine how she persuaded you to give it to her. She did ask me to pretend to be the long-lost granddaughter of an older woman that she was working with in your town. I assume it must have been you. I didn't want to participate in that ruse. For better or worse, her relationship with you never progressed to that point.

I did want to speak to you face-to-face, Mrs. Steiber, and return this while I was in Plum Harbor. I came into your diner several times, and even found out where you lived. But I could never work up the nerve. I didn't give it to the police to return, because I was afraid it would lead to too many questions asked of me and get lost in their bureaucratic system. Also because I know that many of my mother's clients would have been too embarrassed to report their loss. Even something so valuable.

I can understand that. I'm deeply ashamed of my mother's behavior. I know that this small gesture means nothing compared to the unhappiness she brought to so many, including your family. I know you have your own opinion of my mother and there's little I can say or do that would ever change that.

I do want you to know that my mother's claims weren't entirely bogus. She was gifted with incredible intuitive and psychic powers. She just chose, most of the time, not to use them for good.

I've learned that this is a choice we all make, wherever our life path, and our unique gifts, lead us.

"Yours truly, Daphne Mullens," Maggie murmured when she came to the bottom of the page.

She put the letter down and stared at Edie. "This is surprising. You were lucky, Edie. Lucky that she's an honest, thoughtful person. Or at least, chose to be in this situation."

Maggie didn't know much about the law. But she was aware that receiving and holding stolen goods was illegal and did make a person an accessory to a crime. But then again, Edie had willingly given the watch to Cassandra—to have it cleansed of bad energy. So perhaps mother and daughter both believed themselves to be in the clear in that regard.

"I guess I was lucky about that much," Edie said in a measured way. She adjusted the watch a bit on her wrist. "But she's lucky she never gathered up her moxie and introduced herself to me. Especially once Nora was in the hot seat with the police. I don't know what I would have done. You would have been talking to me through a pane of bulletproof glass right now."

Maggie didn't reply. She knew Edie just needed to vent but also knew that wouldn't have been a pretty scene.

"I don't care what she says about her mother," Edie added. "That Cassandra was no good in my book and never will be. I will say, just between us for now, that one good thing came out of this. For me, at least. Getting this watch back is the least of it."

Something better than the lost heirloom? What could that be? But Maggie didn't have to ask.

Edie leaned closer. "Remember when I told you about my Sara?" Maggie nodded. Of course she remembered the story about the baby Edie had given up for adoption.

"Well, I said to myself, What kind of an idiot are you? You're asking some phony-baloney fortune-teller about your own child—where she is, what's she doing. Why don't you just hire somebody to find out if she's dead or alive? Because, I tell you, Maggie, deep in my heart, I knew Sara wasn't dead. Call it intuition, a sixth sense, mother love . . . or just wishful thinking. But I suddenly had to find out."

"Really? What'd you do?"

"I hired a private detective. Duh?" Edie mocked the teen-age expression. "Out in Arizona. A few weeks ago now."

"You did? Good for you," Maggie said sincerely. "Have you heard anything? I suppose it's too soon, though. . . ."

"Heck, no. He found her right away. Just like that." Edie snapped her fingers. "On the Internet or something. She's not dead, like Cassandra said," she added with an angry edge. "Sara is alive and kicking. In her mid-fifties already, with two grown children. I've lost so much time," she said sadly. "But I do have another granddaughter and a grandson. Both in top-notch colleges. Very smart. I think the girl's on a music scholarship."

Maggie's smile grew even wider. She patted Edie's freckled hand. "That's wonderful news. I think I might cry."

"Thanks, Maggie. You're a pal."

Maggie smiled. "Any plans yet to meet?"

"I'm going to Arizona in a month or so, when it cools down out there. Sara is dying to meet me. I am, too, to meet her. It's going to take some getting used to. I haven't even told Amy and Cecilia yet," she confided, mentioning her other daughters. "I'm not sure how they're going to take it."

She sounded nervous. With good reason, Maggie thought. These announcements were often very jarring to a family's status quo.

A real game changer.

"You're doing the right thing, Edie. It will all work out," she said finally.

"One way or the other." Edie sounded resigned. "The funny thing is, if it wasn't for that witch Cassandra, I may have never gone looking for Sara and found out what had happened to her. Though I've worried about her every day of my life, since I gave her up. I have to be thankful for that."

"And you discovered that you have two more grandchildren in the bargain." And are already bragging about them, Maggie added with a secret smile. "At least some good has come from all the damage and pain Cassandra brought to your family."

Edie nodded with a serious expression. "Very true. I don't think many people who got suckered by Cassandra Waters can say that." She sighed and sat back, fanning herself slower now. "I'm just grateful now for my kids and grandkids. How they're all stepping up to help Nora, and even Richard and Dale, through the rest of this mess. And for friends like you, Maggie. And the rest of your pals. I've always been the independent type, you know me. But it's nice to know you girls have got my back."

Maggie looked up from her work and smiled. "Anytime, Edie. The Black Sheep knitters are always happy to ride to the rescue."

Notes from the Black Sheep Knitting Shop
Bulletin Board

Dear Friends,

Even I don't think of summer as a big season for knitting, but the shop has been very busy, keeping me on my sandy toes. I held the felted tote class twice and there still seems to be interest. Especially after I put Lucy Binger's finished tote front and center in this new window display.

I will teach that class again in the fall, but until then, if you want to tackle a knitted bag on your own, here's a link to a free pattern for a handy, loosely knit bag you can take to the beach or for grocery shopping. Just think how trendy and ecological-minded you'll look, taking that choice to the market instead of plastic. This is a very flexible pattern and the author encourages creativity. Bravo! I'm sure you will enjoy her website—I Live on a Farm—chock full of quality, free patterns and recipes.

All best wishes,

Maggie

Link to free pattern:
http://www.iliveonafarm.com/lbag.html

From the Black Sheep Bulletin Board

To Whom This May Concern,

Never thought I'd give away this deep, dark family secret, but stranger things have happened to the Steibers this summer, I'll tell you that much. Between the TV news, the local newspaper, and the gossip all over town, I bet everyone reading this note knows exactly what I'm talking about. So I won't even go there. Some dark times, no question. But we'll pull through. We Steibers always do.

It does serve to remind me that I'm definitely not getting any younger. So, I've decided to give in to the pleading and begging I hear every time I serve my finger-licking, lip-smacking, barbeque ribs.

Here it is. Not quite the very last of my secrets, but close to it. Right up here on Maggie's bulletin board—my recipe for Fourth of July Barbeque Ribs. Easy as . . . well . . . pie, I guess.

Just for good measure, here's the recipe for the Schooner's Summertime-Only Strawberry-Raspberry Pie. Perfect follow-up to the ribs. Along with some vanilla ice cream, of course.

You enjoy it. That's an order. Life's too darned short, if you ask me. Heck, have dessert first.

Very truly yours,

Edie Steiber

P.S. I will tell you right up front; one BIG secret to my ribs is that you don't barbeque those suckers much at all. You slow cook 'em, in the oven. So don't wait for the Fourth of July to start.

Edie Steiber's Fourth of July Barbeque Ribs

Before I get into the particulars, people always ask, "Edie, what is the difference between spareribs, also called St. Louis ribs, and baby back?" The long and short of it is—excuse the pun—St. Louis ribs are bigger. They have more meat and more fat, but can be a little chewy. Baby back are leaner and cook to that tender, fall-off-the bone texture you crave. A little more expensive, but worth it.

Regarding barbeque sauce, it's simple to make your own. But if you don't have time, some quality store-bought does the trick. My favorite is Sweet Baby Ray's, which is what I say to use here.

This recipe serves 6 normal people (and about 3 Steibers)

4 pounds of pork ribs

½ cup light brown sugar

1 teaspoon hickory smoke salt (smoke flavor optional)

1 Tablespoon paprika

1 Tablespoon garlic powder

1 to 2 teaspoons cumin

1 to 2 teaspoons chili powder

½ teaspoon ground red pepper (optional) and/or about 10 turns of the black pepper grinder, depending on how spicy you like it

1 teaspoon oregano

2 cups of your favorite barbecue sauce (I like Sweet Baby Ray's)

Preheat oven to 250 degrees F. Line a baking pan with aluminum foil.

Combine all of the dry ingredients in a small bowl. Prepare the meat by removing the membrane from the back of the ribs. It is best to work this skin away from the meat with the back of a spoon, slipping it along underneath.

Sprinkle about half of the dry rub on the bottom of the ribs and rub it in. Set the ribs on the baking pan with the seasoned side down, and sprinkle the remaining rub on the top.

Bake uncovered at 250 degrees F for 2 hours.

After the ribs have cooked for 2 hours, remove them and pour some barbeque sauce on the top. Using a spatula or brush, spread the sauce all over the ribs. Cover the entire pan tightly with aluminum foil and return to the oven, baking for an additional 2 hours. Or test a bit earlier for doneness. If the meat is tender and pulls away from the bone, you're in business.

You can spread a little more sauce on the bony side of the ribs and finish them under the broiler for 1 to 2 minutes.

Or finish on the barbeque grill—cut them into serving size portions, 2 to 3 ribs per serving. Put some sauce on the bony side and lay them on the grill 1 to 2 minutes. Total cooking time: 4 hours.

Schooner's Summertime-Only Strawberry-Raspberry Pie

Ingredients for pie filling:

16 ounces of fresh, ripe strawberries (3 cups), washed, hulled, and sliced in half

6 to 8 ounces of fresh raspberries (about 1 to 1⅓ cups), rinsed and set out in a single layer on a towel until air dried

⅓ cups granulated sugar (add more to your taste)

1 Tablespoon vanilla extract

2 to 3 Tablespoons cornstarch (or white flour)

1 egg yolk, beaten with 1 Tablespoon of water

For pie crust:

One recipe Schooner No-Fail Pie Crust, see below. Or use two sheets of premade pie dough found in the refrigerated section of the supermarket, or one package premade, frozen pie crust, with extra crust for top.

Preheat the oven to 400 degrees F.

If you are making the dough for pie crust, best to work on this first and refrigerate for about one hour so it's cold when you roll it out. Otherwise, read directions on store bought crust and proceed.

To make filling:

In a large bowl, combine all the berries, sugar, and vanilla. Add cornstarch or flour and mix gently until everything is blended. Be careful not to break raspberries.

To assemble pie:

Roll out one ball of pie dough on a flat, smooth surface using a rolling pin and a little extra flour. Roll it in a circle as large as a pie plate or tin. You can measure by placing the tin over dough and making sure there will be some overhang for the crust.

Place the circle of pie dough on the ungreased pie plate or tin. Press to form and fill with berry mixture. (Or fill premade frozen crust with berry mixture.)

Roll out a second pie crust. (Or roll out premade dough or frozen crust for top of pie.)

Cut dough into about 10 strips, ¾ inches wide, with a sharp knife or pizza wheel.

Arrange half across filling horizontally, pinching edges to crust. Arrange the other half vertically, to form a cross-hatch pattern, pinching edges to crust.

Trim ends of strips and fold over. Flute the edge of the crust with fingertips. Brush the beaten egg yolk over the crust and place on the center rack of the oven. (This pie is juicy and will spill over, so best to cover lower rack with a sheet of foil to avoid a tough cleanup.)

Bake 45 to 50 minutes until filling is bubbling and crust is golden. Cool for 2 hours.

Schooner No-Fail Pie Crust

2 ½ cups flour

1 Tablespoon sugar

1 teaspoon salt

1 ½ sticks (¾ cups) unsalted butter, very cold

2 Tablespoons shortening, chilled

⅓ cup ice water

Combine dry ingredients in a large bowl or a food processor. Mix through by hand with a fork or wire whisk (or pulse in a food processor to mix). Add butter and shortening.

Mix by hand with pastry tool, or fork, until butter is in small bits—you should still see pieces about raisin-size (or pulse in a food processor to mix). Do not overmix. This dough is better to be lumpy and undermixed.

Add water and continue to mix until dough just begins to make a ball. Pour out on floured board and shape into 2 balls of equal size. Chill for 1 hour in refrigerator before use.